L.A. MIRAGE

Anne Lambton

To
Paul
for his endless faith and support
with much love and thanks

First published in the UK in 2007 by Timewell Press

All characters and events in this publication, other than those clearly in the public domain, are fictitious and any resemblance to real persons, living or dead, is purely coincidental.

A catalogue record for this title is available from the British Library.

ISBN-13: 978-1-85725-220-0

Typeset by TW Typesetting, Plymouth, Devon

Printed and bound in Great Britain by
William Clowes Ltd, Beccles, Suffolk

Timewell Press Limited
10 Porchester Terrace
London W2 3TL

Contents

Tulsa Time

Though Cranberry was born on the right side of the tracks, you'd never know it. Not from any affectation on her part, but merely because she had failed to grasp the importance of the fact herself.

Her enormously wealthy parents had dropped out in the 1960s, and single-mindedly given no thought to convention in any shape or form since. Thus, in their opinion, giving their precious daughter the gift of leeway, to become precisely who she was. No constricting pigeonhole loomed waiting for her coming of age. 'The world's your oyster,' they often told her.

This lack of rules, far from giving her confidence, as they'd fondly presumed, made her feel abandoned, adrift on an open sea. The choices were too varied. There were no restrictions. And for Cranberry, who was naturally rebellious, this was a problem.

She couldn't, in all honesty, share the thrilling times when her friends were doing harmless, forbidden things, since for her they were not forbidden. And were quite often unpleasant; like drinking till you were sick, or kissing weedy boys you didn't even fancy, or smoking cigarettes, or joints, or even bloody PCP, she imagined. None of it mattered. For her everything appeared permissible. She pretended to be superior and above it all, but in reality she felt left out. She didn't fit in anywhere. By giving her unlimited freedom her parents had made her a misfit.

She decided to sell one of her christening presents, a delicate diamond drop pendant. It felt like a betrayal in some way even though she'd never met the old, now defunct Queen of Romania who'd given it to her. The point was that with the proceeds she'd be able to sally forth into the world and find others like herself.

A week later, after some hard negotiations with a rather fly woman who had a stall in the Portobello Road, Cranberry took a deep breath and, adopting a deliberately disaffected stance while clutching an airline ticket and a wad of travellers' cheques behind her back for secret courage, told her parents she was leaving,

'To be a war correspondent?' her father joked.

'Don't tease her,' her mother snapped, springing to her defence.

Cranberry couldn't believe it. Here she was, just seventeen years old and 'a young seventeen at that' so people said, out of the blue telling her parents that she was leaving home. And they were vying as to which could be the more liberal. Neither had even thought to ask where she was going. Well then. She wouldn't tell them, and they'd never guess, of that she was absolutely certain.

Boarding her plane at Heathrow, destination Tulsa Oklahoma, she started to cry. What had possessed her to buy a ticket to Tulsa? 'Twenty-four Hours from . . .' or 'On Route 66' just didn't seem enough now. Why not Paris, Bangkok or Rajasthan? She cried for the misery of her fate: alone, friendless. No one even knew where she was. Let alone cared. And, to top it all, she was going to Tulsa. She fixated on the open door of the plane, wondering whether to make her escape before it was too late, when her attention was taken by an excessively large woman who had just embarked. She had green hair. Presumably it was supposed to be blond, but it was definitively green. She watched as the woman squeezed inexorably forward. Her body took up the entire width of the aisle but moved with a surprising elegance considering all that excess weight it was carrying. The entire bulk was topped off by a face of beauty and kindness, laced perhaps with a whiff of cunning.

On reaching Cranberry's row she swung her bulk in. 'You're in luck, I always buy two seats, and I only take up one and a half,' she growled in an impossibly low voice. 'You can spread out,' she said, while stashing varying-sized grocery bags in every available empty space.

'Excuse me, I'm thinking of getting off,' Cranberry said, but the woman didn't hear her; she was far too busy tidying her provisions. With one last shove, a bag from which a baguette protruded disappeared under the seat and she straightened up smiling.

'What were you saying, honey?' the woman asked, lifting up the separating arm of her seat before sitting down and attaching a red nylon extension to her safety belt.

'Nothing.' Cranberry half resumed her seat.

'See what I mean,' the woman sucked through her teeth, as she contemplated her body, 'Hell, I don't even fit in those first-class deals. It has to be two tourist.'

When the woman said 'fit', it sounded like an omen to Cranberry. She didn't fit either, albeit in a different way. And here they were, two misfits together, allocated neighbouring seats on a plane to Tulsa, Oklahoma. What were the odds against that? OK, so she'd stay on the plane, go to Tulsa as planned. Anyway with her return ticket and travellers' cheques she was free to run back home at any time.

'What you doing in Tulsa?' the woman enquired.

'Wish I knew,' came the wavering reply.

'Bin cryin' honey?' the woman asked, sucking through her teeth again.

Cranberry found this a fascinating habit and had already started unconsciously imitating it. She didn't answer and they both sat there a moment sucking their teeth. Bleakness hovered in the air.

'Life's a bitch,' the enormous woman said out of the blue.

'Especially when you don't fit,' Cranberry replied.

The stranger patted her hand. That small gesture of solidarity caught Cranberry off guard. The floodgates opened and for the rest of the long flight she told the woman, whose name was Loretta, all her grievances, real and imagined.

Loretta was a Tulsan and the daughter of an oil millionaire who owned the local football team. She listened to perfection, all the while preparing delectable snacks from her selection of bags. These she ate so delicately, with such obvious enjoyment, that Cranberry gave in, and for the rest of the flight, mid-sobs and between sips of very lemony Bloody Marys, she munched on morsels of caviar and dressed crab until they arrived in Chicago, where they had to change planes.

Once they'd disembarked and were inside the O'Hare International Terminal, an English voice announced a two-hour-forty-five-minute delay to their connection.

'Why are they always English, when they've got shit news to give?' Loretta growled.

'Are they?' Cranberry said.

A singsong affirmative came from Loretta's closed mouth. 'Mm-hmm,' she purred, drawing out both syllables to maximum effect.

'Oh,' said Cranberry.

They wandered around sizing up their options: Fat Boy burgers, a perfume counter, Peaches record store, to name a few.

Suddenly Loretta grabbed her arm. 'Let's get us a couple of martinis,' she whooped, 'only sure way to fuck the blues.'

Cranberry hesitated. She'd didn't really drink but Loretta pulled her into the O'Ho Blues Bar regardless, and two hours thirty-five minutes later, the two new best friends staggered to their gate, high as kites. Cranberry was to stay with Loretta in Tulsa. She was going to give Cranberry the old maid's quarters in her five-bedroom house. 'It's got its own separate entrance,' Loretta said, and was situated just off Peoria, wherever that was. Cranberry, no longer friendless and alone, just exhausted and drunk, sank into a deep stupor the moment their second plane left the ground.

Her first impression of Tulsa was from a dismal perspective. Her eyes and mouth were dry, and her head ached more, or so she imagined, than if she'd put it through a windscreen.

'Prairie oysters. They'll set us up,' Loretta announced, 'that's if Hofer ain't finished the eggs.'

'Who's Hofer?' Cranberry asked.

'J. D. Longhofer IV. He lives in the coach house. And eats. Boy, he sure does eat. Was a preacher, now a songwriter. A dead one if he's finished the eggs.'

Cranberry lay back in the taxi and closed her eyes. She'd been brought up on a diet of Robin Hood, William Tell and other adventurous heroes in her very English childhood, so naturally the image of Friar Tuck sprang into her mind, but Friar Tuck armed with a guitar instead of his simple staff was a bit too much for her befuddled brain to take in.

She was woken by the driver emptying the cab under the watchful eye of Loretta. Cranberry's bag was being carried into the house by a cowboy. From the back, which is all Cranberry could see of him, he looked archetypal, over six feet tall and wearing the obligatory Stetson, waistcoat and boots. Even his walk, deliberate, slow and bow-legged, evoked covered waggons and cattle drives. Before she could see his face he disappeared into the house.

Cranberry stumbled out of the car and took a bag from Loretta as she waded up the path laden down with many.

'That's Hof's place,' Loretta pointed to a little cottage on the far side of a grassed-over yard, 'and here's yours.'

Loretta unlocked a side door of the main house. It opened into a lovely little room. The floorboards and walls were made of pitch-pine and gave off a particularly pleasant smell. A brass double bed, already made with white linen and a patchwork quilt, stood across from a rocking chair beside an open fire. A rag rug and marble-topped dresser completed the picture. The glimpse of a cowboy, and now this old-time room were enough to throw Cranberry and her quixotic mind straight back a hundred years into the Wild West. And there she firmly stayed, a pioneer woman, glad that she'd left her cosy English home to stand on the threshold of this idyll, ready and eager to confront her fate.

'That's the bathroom.' Loretta pointed at a door to the left of the bed. 'Settle in, hose yourself down then come on through and eat.' Loretta glided her large frame across the floor and opened an identical door on the right. 'You'll find the rest of the house through this one.'

Electric light spilled into the room and made Loretta glow, as she stood silhouetted in the doorway, a Rubens angel with a luminous halo of green hair. 'Hofer, you git your sorry ass up here right now,' she yelled into the unknown beyond.

Cranberry was shocked. That wasn't how she'd talk to a former priest. But then again, she knew that she didn't talk like Loretta to begin with. Although she did like her style. It was plain and to the point.

After she'd unpacked her bags, and 'hosed herself down' as Loretta put it, Cranberry ventured out of her room and followed the sound of country music playing on a radio somewhere. It led her into a large kitchen dominated by Loretta, who was placing a steaming pot of coffee and a dish of bacon down on a table already weighed down with breakfast vittles – steak, eggs, biscuits and gravy.

'Your timing's right on the nail honey. Here, knock this back, you'll feel better,' she said, handing Cranberry a suspect-looking drink.

Cranberry took a large gulp. Her worst nightmare, repellently slimy and so spicy it blew her head off. 'What was that?' she spluttered.

'Prairie oyster,' trilled Loretta. 'Raw egg, dash of tomato juice and a good shake of Tabasco. Greatest fixer-upper in the world. Food's ready. Hofer, come meet Cranberry.'

The sound of the radio stopped and the large cowboy she had seen earlier emerged from the corner of the room. He was so tall his head remained in the shadows, providing her with an outline the same as before, but this time from the front. Instead of her bag his hand now held a silver guitar that glinted by his side. His face remained a mystery. The boots, she noted, were ostrich. A large gold and silver buckle depicting a bucking bronco caught the light on his belt, and the shirt beneath the vest had a ruffle down the front. This was Friar Tuck?

He lowered his head, and reached for his hat. Now she'd see the face. What would he look like? Gary Cooper, Sam Shepard? It was tantalizing, intense. Her mind, still exploding from the Machiavellian drink, fought to keep a perspective.

'Pleased to make your acquaintance Ma'am,' he drawled in a voice as soft as butter, lifting his hat appropriately.

'Likewise,' gushed Cranberry with anticipation. The hat in his hand went down to his side, his head lifted, and there it was. The face. Cranberry tried not to stare, but it was hard. Poor, poor man, she thought, tears pricking the backs of her eyes. Can he ever have had a girlfriend? Whatever had happened to his face? It was so pockmarked it looked as though it had been sandblasted. He later told her this was very close to the truth. He was a pacifist, and not being able to think of another way to dodge the draft in Vietnam, had resorted to stripping his face with a sander. A ruse that landed him six weeks in the county hospital and a psychiatric dispensation.

'Time to eat,' Loretta announced.

'Was that you playing just now?' Cranberry asked Hofer, as she settled in and busied herself with a napkin.

'Sure was,' he smiled. 'Just something I'm trying to finish. Hope I didn't disturb you.'

'Not at all, it was lovely,' she replied, watching with alarm as Loretta piled her plate high. 'Please, that's more than enough Loretta, thank you,' she said.

Loretta took no notice, and returned to the range. 'It's no damn good without a few hash browns,' she pontificated, spooning some delicious-looking potatoes on to Cranberry's plate.

As they ate Loretta and Hofer kept up a lively banter. Cranberry loved their stories, the way they told them even more. When she'd eaten all she could she stood up to clear the plates.

'Leave 'em,' Loretta insisted, as she bread-sopped the pristine platters clean. 'Mary'll git 'em later. Ask her if you need any washing done.'

Cranberry resumed her seat and listened to Hofer finish a story about taking his nephew Randy skiing in Aspen Colorado.

'The boy's only fourteen and not fully growed into himself,' he was saying, 'he'd not skied that much, but he's a plucky little guy and went down that mountain quicker than shit off Shineola.'

'Good on him,' Loretta said.

'I imagine,' Hof said. 'Trouble was he knocked some ole gal down on the way. So this fella comes up spitting and lays into Randy.'

'I imagine,' Loretta said.

'I hear you,' Hof said back, then continued, 'Randy he apologizes real nice but that ole boy he just keeps on comin'.'

'Did he harm him?' Loretta queried.

'No, but I had to get in between 'em. "Hey buddy," I said, "cut him some slack, he's just trying to get down the hill, same as everybody else. Just coz he's going a little faster, that don't make him a bad person" – and he chilled.'

Cranberry was sure anyone would chill confronted by Hofer.

They finished breakfast, Loretta announced she was 'fit to bust', and Hofer went back into the corner to work on his song. The metal instrument he was playing, he told Cranberry, was a national guitar, sometimes known as a hound-dog. It was a beautiful thing made of steel, and shone like silver with patterns cut into its face that created a resonator and gave it amplifying powers far beyond the normal acoustic variety. Cranberry had never seen one before and delighted in its mournful tone.

'Leon Russell's playing at Seager's tonight,' Hof announced.

Cranberry immediately wanted to go.

'Who's Seager?' she ventured.

'Seager's a bar,' Loretta volunteered. 'Owned by a crazy motherfucker of the same name. Wanna go?'

'I'd love to, but I'm not old enough,' Cranberry admitted.

'Oklahoma's a dry state honey. All ages can get in a bar, but you have to be a member to drink,' Loretta chuckled, eyeing Hofer. 'Right, Hof?'

'I imagine,' he answered, engrossed in a riff he was trying to perfect.

'Come on, I'll show you the lay of the land.' Loretta took some bottles out of the vast fridge and put them in a cool-box. She emptied a bag of ice over them and turned to Hofer. 'Brakes fixed yet?' she asked.

'Yup,' Hofer replied, picking up the cooler and disappearing with it.

Loretta took the keys off the table. 'Catch you later,' she said, swinging open the door that was divided in half horizontally with an upper and lower part. It reminded Cranberry of their house in the north of England, which had stables with doors just like this one. Same hinges even. All her summers growing up had been spent there, most days outdoors riding her pony over the Yorkshire Dales, making camps, pretending to be Davy Crockett, 'king of the wild frontier'. She'd been obsessed by the mountain man and his exploits ever since her father had returned from a trip to America when she was seven years old with a small, furry Davy Crockett hat that fitted her perfectly. It had a raccoon tail that hung down the back and was completely groovy. Every night for the next week her father told her one of the famous tracker's feats as her bedtime story.

Her reverie was interrupted moments later by a honking horn. Cranberry looked out of the window and saw Loretta appear at the front gate in a vintage black Cadillac, all exaggerated tail fins and chrome with conical red and amber spaceship-type lights at the back. Americana at its very best.

She ran out and jumped into the passenger seat that stretched across the front in one long continuous slide of red leather and white piping. Her first bench seat. True, at home you could sit on the middle seat in the front of the Land Rover, but it wasn't comfy, doubled up with your feet on the hot gearbox.

'So as I can spread out,' Loretta said, catching Cranberry's appreciation of the sprung upholstery that lay between them.

Cranberry was impressed. 'It's a fantastic car.'

'Used to belong to Elvis,' Loretta said as she swung the Caddy out into the road. Cranberry wondered whether she was joking – probably not.

Loretta's lay of the land consisted entirely of scenery spied en route to her favourite eateries. They started by driving through a wealthy residential area where wide tree-lined roads wound gently past large elaborate houses built in a mish-mash of styles. 'That used to be JJ Cale's.' Loretta pointed to a faux-dilapidated Spanish hacienda.

Cranberry wondered why, if they had money, anyone would choose to build their mansion so close to another. Even though they were set back from the road with sweeping grass frontages they still had no privacy; it had to be to show off.

Loretta spun the white Bakelite steering wheel to the left and they turned on to a bleak thoroughfare that dramatically left affluence behind. 'Don't be put off by the place,' she said, pointing to a tiny roadside counter, 'they've got the best burgers in town.' Cranberry saw a shack that was as basic as could be, with no walls and beaten-up sheets of corrugated metal for a roof. The front overhang was supported by two wooden poles and provided enough shade for about three customers. It stood perilously close to the traffic and was doing a roaring trade to what looked like real Red Indians.

'Descendants from the Trail of Tears,' Loretta confirmed, telling her of the nineteenth-century Indian Removal Act, when over four thousand Cherokee died while being herded off their lands. 'I'm not counting Choctaw Chickasaw, Creek or Seminole,' she said, 'the five nations considered "civilized" by white society, but they've had the last laugh. The shit land we gave 'em was awash with oil. Now, the more Indian blood you can prove runs in your veins, the more revenue you git from the government.'

Cranberry smiled, pleased that some small positive had eventually trickled down from that shameful episode in American history.

The roads were easy now, straight, laid out on a grid system. They drove past block upon block of indistinguishable small houses in order to peer at a restaurant hidden away in a mall. 'Better veal than in Milan,' Loretta said and wheeled the car around, 'but we're going to get us some ribs.' The radio played Don Williams's new hit, 'Living on Tulsa Time'.

'Hallelujah,' Loretta sang as she made for her favourite barbecue joint, which lay over on the black side of town.

Cranberry was astonished that there was a black side of town; she thought segregation had finished in the 1960s, when Rosa Parks sat in the front of the bus reserved for whites only, screaming faces of hate surrounding her. Cranberry had watched some footage of it a few years ago and those faces often appeared in her dreams. Now everyone she saw out of the Cadillac's windows was black, and the already poor-looking houses took a sharp nose-dive, as did the road surface.

About fifteen minutes later they arrived in the car park of a small establishment – Lucky's Bar-B-Chew. Loretta applied the handbrake; it made a satisfactory ratcheting sound. As soon as they left the car they were surrounded by a gaggle of six small children.

'Got any candy, Loretta?' they clamoured.

'Mmm-hmm, lots in here.' She patted her vast stomach.

'Mmm-mmm,' they screamed and patted their own little bellies.

Loretta grinned and slipped the ringleader a dollar. 'Git yourself some candy and watch the Caddy,' she said.

Inside Loretta and Cranberry were greeted like family by the eponymous Lucky, a large well-built man in his sixties. His skin glistened from the heat of the kitchen, and made his shock of silver hair look all the more stunning.

'Loretta, where've you been?'

'England to visit the Queen, but guess what? She hid.'

'Aw, shucks. All that way for nothing,' Lucky mocked sympathy.

'Un-huh,' Loretta shook her head. 'Not quite. This here's Cranberry: she's English and wants to taste your Bar-B-Chew.' She took her seat at the counter. 'Cranberry meet Lucky and praise the Lord for what you're about to eat.'

Cranberry and Lucky smiled at each other.

'English, huh? You sure are welcome,' Lucky said as Cranberry took a stool next to Loretta. Two old guys were tucking in down one end of the counter, painters judging by their dungarees, while another much younger man in a smart suit with a briefcase sat five stools away at the other end by the wall. Loretta ordered what sounded like a mountain of food: two sides of ribs, mashed potatoes, greens, corn on the cob and cole-slaw on the side, then proceeded to fill Cranberry in on some of Oklahoma's hard-won history. Blues music played from an old transistor radio that hung from a hook in the ceiling just above their heads.

'First thing first,' she said. 'Oklahoma was the last state to join the union. Known as the Sooner State – like in the sooner you got here in your covered waggon, on your horse, or by any other means of transportation the more land you could grab.'

'They had 'em a race,' Lucky added.

'They did,' Loretta affirmed.

'They should have 'em another one, that's what I say,' muttered Lucky, busy with the sizzling bones.

'I hear you,' Loretta agreed and went on to tell Cranberry about how Senator Dewey F. Bartlett had 'gotten up a big old ceremony' and conferred the honorary title of 'Okie' on the young, charismatic John F. Kennedy after he'd been made commander-in-chief.

'Of what?' Cranberry asked.

'Of nothing, honey. It's just another way of saying President of the United States,' Lucky said.

'That's right. Anyways, he reclaimed the word. Okie used to mean lower than shit,' Loretta said. 'He turned it around: O for Oklahoma, K for Key, I for Intelligence and E for Enterprise, and the world, or the Okies at least, believed it. Gave 'em some pride back after the dust bowl and all.'

'That's right,' Lucky mumbled, 'dumb-asses.'

'The niggers should do that . . . reclaim the word,' Loretta boomed, gnawing at the remnants of a rib on the blatantly black side of town.

At this point Cranberry had two revelations: one, that she was woefully uneducated in America's history; and two, Loretta was dangerous to hang out with.

'How much do we owe you?' Cranberry said, trying to cover her awkwardness.

'A five spot'll cover it,' Lucky smiled. 'Don't mind her,' he chuckled, jerking his head at Loretta. 'She's just pig-ignorant.' He wiped his hands on a cloth hanging from his belt. Cranberry opened her wallet and Loretta deftly plucked out a five-dollar bill and slapped it down on the counter.

'Catch you later Lucky. You playing with Tripplehorn next week?'

'Sure thing,' he answered.

'See you then,' she said, pushing out through the screen door.

'Thank you. Goodbye, I hope I see you there too.' Cranberry grasped the ebony-coloured hand Lucky offered and shook it vigorously.

Back at the house Cranberry felt exhausted from keeping up with Loretta. She went and lay on her bed and, like a boa constrictor post-goat, fell into a deep sleep. Nearly two hours later she woke to dusk and her second hangover of the day, which was a first for Cranberry, who'd never even had one before. As she was splashing cold water on her face she dislodged a pewter mug from the shelf above the sink. It crashed down and clattered about on the tiled floor and she had an image of her parents complaining about the noise she was making the morning after a party.

Throughout the day she had done her best to explain to Loretta that she didn't really drink, but after her friend had assured her that the cold beer in the cool box on the back seat of the Caddy was 'domestic shit with almost no alcoholic content' and that it was essential if she wanted to keep from burning up, Cranberry accepted the iced bottles. It had been a searing ninety-eight degrees in the shade and the Cadillac was too old for air-conditioning. As she finished brushing her teeth, she put the toothbrush and paste in the mug that she'd replaced on the shelf and crept through to the kitchen. Loretta had obviously bathed and changed and wore a long brown embroidered skirt with an orange loose-weave poncho over a yellow striped cowboy shirt with pearlized buttons at the cuffs. The whole ensemble looked good against her green hair. And although Cranberry had only drunk a fraction compared to her friend, one look told her that it was she who seemed ten times the worse for wear.

As Cranberry came through the door Loretta took one sideways look at her and went to the fridge. 'Hair of the dog,' she said, pressing a bottle into Cranberry's hand, with a knowing wink.

'Domestic shit?' Cranberry said with a wry smile. Feeling delicate in the extreme there was no option but to take it and drink, which she did while wondering if she would ever grasp the vagaries of a dry state.

Fortified, Loretta and Cranberry set off for Seager's, after picking up Hof from across the yard. Seager's was a small dark dive in the centre of town. A throng of cowboys and yellow-haired girls stood outside the door waiting to check their guns at a counter by the entrance. There was no such amenity for coats.

A small stage stood at one end of the room and a bar at the other. Behind the bar liquor bottles lined the shelves. Strips of white gaffer tape were stuck across their labels with a different name written in on each.

'See them Cranberry? They're members' names, and those there bottles are for their personal use only,' Loretta said, turning to the barman. 'Hit us Jimmy.' He pulled a bottle labelled *P. T. Brand* seemingly at random from off the shelf behind him and poured three little glasses of amber liquid. 'Tequila,' Loretta said, giving Cranberry a glass.

'I'd rather have a coke,' Cranberry said.

'And a coke for Cranberry,' Loretta called back as she went off and sat down at a small round table with a reserved sign on it in front of the stage.

As Cranberry waited for her drink she saw two pool tables in a large recess to the right of the bar. She was extremely good at billiards. At home they'd had a full-size table in what used to be the music room, and she used to play for hours, perfecting trick shots she dreamed up in her sleep. She'd quit only when she became so good it got serious. Now the green baize beckoned, and she felt her fascination with the game returning.

A kerfuffle broke out. There was shooting and blood and then a man in front of Cranberry at the bar was screaming and she saw that his ear was a mangled mess. 'You shot my fucking ear off, motherfucker.'

'Well knock my dick in the dirt if I didn't,' a benign-looking desperado replied. In a flash they were gone, hustled out of the bar by two enormous gorilla-type men who appeared out of nowhere.

'What happened?' quaked Cranberry, sitting down at the table severely shaken.

'Saturday-night specials,' Hof said. 'Cheap gun rentals. Can't shoot straight worth a damn. Don't worry darlin', they always miss.'

Somehow, this didn't comfort Cranberry at all.

'I thought you were meant to check your gun,' she said.

'I hear you,' Hofer agreed.

'But why would anybody shoot anybody in a club where Leon Russell's about to play?' she persisted.

'Maybe he looked at Jake's girl,' Loretta suggested.

'Jake? The man who fired . . . You mean you know him?'

'All forty-seven years he's been on God's earth, and I can guarantee you he's never killed a living thing. Maimed yes . . . Killed, never.' Loretta's assurance, while doing no more than Hof's had done to allay Cranberry's fears, carried such conviction and was spoken in such an authoritative, explanation-enough tone, that Cranberry realized it would be churlish to try and argue the finer points and she meekly sat back down at their table.

A small glass was placed in front of her.

'Tequila,' Hof's voice said. 'It'll settle you.'

Cranberry needed no second urging. She knocked it back in one. The liquid hit her throat and burnt all the way down her chest, taking her breath away. She tried to grasp what was happening to her. Things were spiralling out of control, she thought. She was too young. Frightened and completely at a loss she looked around for Hof. He was standing behind her, taller than ever. She craned her neck back to see him better. Her head spun.

'Don't worry, little darling, I'll look after you,' his voice of velvet floated down and through her as he laid a protective hand on her shoulder.

'I want to play pool,' she said and burst into tears.

Loretta and Hofer roared with laughter.

'And you shall,' Hof said, taking her arm and steering her towards the recess.

Cue in hand, Cranberry felt considerably better. Initially she was wide of the pockets on all her shots, being used to a much larger table in which the angles were all different, but as the game went on her eye gradually came in and she began to draw an appreciative crowd. From Hof's point of view it was easy to see why. She was no bigger than the cue she was wielding so expertly, and cute as a button in those jeans.

Tipsy with the tequila kicking in, Cranberry played up to her audience, trying, and realizing, some of her wilder, self-invented shots of old. Small glasses of tequila from unknown admirers lined up along the table in homage. Each time she won a game, she'd drink one. She was having a great time now, loving it all.

'Where did you learn to play like that, darlin'?' Hof asked.

Cranberry didn't answer.

An amplified voice came from the stage. 'Check 123, Check 123.' The crowd whooped and whistled in anticipation of the evening's entertainment.

Quick as you like, Cranberry sunk the black, drank the remaining shots, acknowledged her newly formed fan club, and told Hof she was running to the loo, leaving him looking puzzled. A toothless old cowboy stopped her, raised his hat and said, 'Pleased to make your acquaintance, Ma'am. You wanna go fuck?'

Cranberry, her newfound liquid confidence firmly in place, replied with perfect social aplomb, 'No thank you, but thank you so much for asking me,' and with not a break in her step, sailed blithely on.

Unfortunately, by the time she managed to reach the lavatories, a lot of women with mayonnaise-coloured hair in shades ranging from home-made to Hellmann's had beaten her to it and she was in a queue. Feeling queasy from the caustic smell of hairspray and the din of the chattering voices, she focused for equilibrium on two gum-chewing girls who were next in line. Heavily made up to look like Barbie dolls, they were dressed in polyester trouser-suits, one mauve the other pink. The jackets cut with a yoke across the shoulders were western-style and each had a matching pastel Stetson hat with a tiara for a hatband. They must be rodeo queens, Cranberry thought, straight from some official function.

'I said to him,' the one in mauve was complaining, 'if you can ride me like you ride that bull out there, honey, I'm yours.'

Cranberry knew about bull riders. A televised rodeo had been one of her main inspirations for choosing Tulsa. She'd been seduced by the romance of the travelling show and rodeos had somehow seemed more plausible than running off to join the circus. She was a fearless rider, having been taught by her father practically before she could walk, and had long harboured a secret ambition to be a barrel rider. She could imagine herself slaloming around the barrels against the clock. But ride a woman like a bull?

Sex, that's what they were talking about. Cranberry was aghast. As the product of two latent hippies from the sixties, English ones to boot, she had only ever conceived of making love gently. Violent, passionate sex, on a par with a bull rider mounting a bull, had never even occurred to her. Cranberry, who had felt green with envy at the vision of the ladies and their pastel outfits, now went green from an overload of alcohol and information. She passed out cold on the rest-room floor.

She came back to the land of the living to find herself safely tucked up in the patchwork bed. She turned over, vowing that if she could get back to sleep and wake feeling better alcohol would never again pass her lips. But she never managed to go under completely and remained in a halfway state of conscious dreams then nightmares. The toothless cowboy appeared, morphing into her father.

'D'you wanna go fuck,' he asked, his patrician face unchanged.

She saw Loretta squelching around, pouring tequila down her own throat. The liquid passed straight though her ample body, which seemed to be made entirely of mayonnaise, and sprayed out of her skin all over Cranberry's face and mouth, forcing her to break her vow of abstinence. Cranberry thrashed about trying to avoid the recycled poison. She saw Hofer's face (how could she ever have thought him hideous) and heard his voice of velvet: 'Don't worry little darlin', I'll look after you.' Cranberry sat up. She was sweating and felt sick. Right, she thought.

Her illuminated clock said 3.10 a.m. She got up and threw her coat over her naked body. The question as to who had undressed her flitted into her mind then straight out again, as she proceeded to pull on her boots and, as if possessed, make her way over to Hof's cottage. She burst through the door without knocking. Hof, who'd been asleep, sprang out of the bed. He had the bedside lamp switched on and her head in an arm lock before she had time to reach the centre of the room. When he saw who it was, his grip relaxed, but his arm remained where it was.

'D'you wanna fuck,' Cranberry heard herself slur. She couldn't believe it. She'd hadn't even kissed many boys before, let alone been to bed with a man. Since sex had never been forbidden, she had chosen not to have it.

'How old did you say you were, honey?' he said softly, stroking her neck with the thumb of his restraining arm. Cranberry didn't reply.

'You're shivering,' he said, lifting her up as easily as he might a baby and putting her with great care into his bed, before he got in beside her. She inched closer to him. They lay there a moment until Cranberry wriggled out of her coat and rolled over on to him. 'Shh,' he crooned, and gently, forcibly moved her aside and laid her head down on his chest, where he held her safe, stroking her back and whispering for her to get some rest. Then she'd feel better.

'I missed Leon, didn't I?' she whimpered.

'Yes honey, but there'll be another time,' he cooed.

Cranberry relaxed and gave herself over to the luxurious effect of Hof's strong hand running repeatedly down the length of her back as she fell into a deep, sensuous sleep on her first night away from home.

In the morning he brought her fresh coffee, and juice with warm crusty bread smothered in butter and honey. Ravenous, she pulled the sheet around her and sat up. She began to eat as Hof sat down on a chair at the foot of the bed and watched. Feeling a little better, she pushed herself as far back into the pillows as was humanly possible and tried to hide behind her coffee mug. Dreading the answer, she plucked up her courage and asked, 'Why didn't you want to make love to me last night?'

'My Momma told me never to take advantage of a girl in a diminished state. And honey, you were.'

'Yes, but I'm not now,' she braved.

'That's right,' he said simply and kept right on sitting there, watching her. He picked up his guitar and started to play a song about catfish, bayous, and hookers. All the while his eyes never left her. Cranberry felt her body begin to tingle. The sensation gathered in intensity, until her muscles started jumping imperceptibly of their own accord and she was unable to meet his gaze. She closed her eyes, and concentrated on trying to keep her breath steady. The guitar stopped playing. She felt him approach, and saw him through her squinting lids as he stood over her for a long moment. She heard him sigh, start to say something, stop. Then he bent down, pushed aside the bedding and started to kiss her, very slowly, and deliberately, from the top of her head to the tip of her toes. On his return journey, Cranberry couldn't wait to kiss him properly on the lips and when they did she wouldn't let him take his mouth off hers, holding him tight to her, engulfed in the moment. His hand slipped between her legs. 'Am I about to break the law, little darling?'

'No. Promise,' she swore, with as much solemnity as she could muster under the circumstances. 'I'm just like Al Pacino lying to Diane Keaton in *The Godfather*,' she thought. Then all thoughts left her mind, and instinct took over, as she made love for the first time.

To make love. Nothing, she thought, had ever been more aptly named. What Cranberry did with Hofer that whole day could not have been described in any other way.

Looking back on that night Hofer realized that he had known almost before he entered her that Cranberry was a virgin, and he'd even suspected she'd lied about her age. But what was he supposed to do about it, demand she produce her passport? She had been so eager, sexy and free. As if her entire body was one vast erogenous zone. He'd never come across anyone like her. Curious too. Like the moment she flung back the bedclothes, examined his cock like a favourite toy, cupped his balls in her hands, chastely kissed the whole package and then put the covers back.

'Do you mind,' she asked earnestly, 'if I learn more about that later? I'm just so loving what we're doing now.'

He laughed, 'You learn what you want, when you want. Or never if you like. Your choice. There's no exam waiting.'

Over the next eighteen months, Cranberry did exactly that – sexually and otherwise. Happy feeling her pioneer-woman dream intact, she moved in with Hofer the next day and learned to cook, clean house and give superlative blow jobs. She wanted to learn those things. She had the objectivity to realize that she had, perhaps, found a way of life of which her parents might finally disapprove: that of a typical, run-of-the-mill housewife in Tulsa, Oklahoma. She didn't care. She was happy.

Hof called her Nadine. She wasn't sure why, but she liked it. If she lost her temper unreasonably, which she was wont to do, he would trap her head in the crook of his arm, rap gently on her skull with his knuckles and say, 'Hello . . . Is there anyone in there?' The sheer powerlessness of her predicament, coupled with the absolute idiocy of his actions, would always snap her out of it.

Loretta hung out with them at first, until she took up with an avocado-dealing, Harley Davidson-riding man called Gary. He was as big if not bigger than Loretta. They called themselves the Big People. As happens when people couple up, Cranberry and Hofer saw a lot less of Loretta. She was always away on some mysterious trip with Gary, riding in a sidecar he'd bought for her. They made an arresting sight: the Big People on their Harley.

'Avocados ain't the only green things he deals in, I reckon,' Hof said.

Cranberry never told Hof her family had money. It didn't seem necessary and she was paranoid it might ruin their relationship. He was so good at being the provider and seemed to enjoy the role so much she didn't want to rock the boat. She also loved the anonymity she had in Tulsa, but finally needed some independence; her traveller's cheques were dwindling. At Cranberry's request Hof helped her find a job, via a friend, one T. G. Bushey, who was the biggest country and western agent in town. Cranberry had to book bands into rodeos for the Bushey Company which, thank God, took care of the money. Cranberry adored her job. It involved checking all the equipment with the sound guy, then ushering 'her band' (she loved saying that) on to the back of a flat-bed truck at the rodeo's half-time. The group would play their music for the fifteen-minute break as they were driven slowly around the ring and afterwards she was free to hang out. She made friends with the tiara-headed, pastel-suited girls who had changed her life in Seager's on that first night. As she'd suspected they did turn out to be rodeo queens: the Misses Muskogee and Arkansas respectively. She interrogated them as to how they'd achieved their lofty titles, and they told her that you had to be crowned a Miss Congeniality of someplace first before qualifying. So that ruled her out, Cranberry thought.

Missing home crept up on Cranberry. She didn't suddenly make up her mind to return, just found herself thinking about it a bit. She had written letters to her mother and father, feeding them qualified information, never providing them with a return address. Now she found herself wondering periodically about them, or about her friends. What were they up to? University, she'd imagine. Who knew? It didn't bother her. She was happy. She just wondered, that's all.

They went to visit Hof's folks in South Carolina for a week. His mother, Lucille, an erstwhile southern belle, cried when she met them at the door.

'Why you crying, Momma?' Hof asked with tender concern.

'Because I know the Lord sent you to me, just as I know he's going to take you away again in one short week,' was her heart-rending reply.

Enveloping her in a bear hug, Hof tried to talk her down.

'We're here seven whole days Momma, don't take on so. What will Cranberry think? Save your tears for the sixth day, when we will be near to leaving, not just arriving.'

She saw the logic in that and managed a smile.

'Come through and greet your Pa,' she said leading the way.

Cranberry was frightened of meeting the father. She'd heard a lot about J. D. Longhofer III. He was a preacher who could talk in tongues. He'd built seven churches in and around Charleston. Hof told her that he was a gentle man, revered in these parts and once she'd met him Cranberry found that to be true. He could not have been less frightening if he tried. The

J. D. stood for Jalbert Doddington. Who'd ever heard of such a name? Certainly not Cranberry.

Cranberry loved talking with Jalbert, he was so easy-going and wise. One day they were sitting together on the porch. It was sundown and he told her how come he was a minister of the Church of our Absolute God. It was no crank faction, he said, but derivative of her own. Cranberry was an atheist but she didn't let on.

'Our church was born,' he said, 'when the first Jalbert, my grandfather, came over in a canvas-covered waggon, a little bitty boy way back when. Crossing America from the east to the west. Ice tea?' he offered. Cranberry nodded and he poured some into a glass that already had a sprig of fresh mint in it.

'Somewhere in the middle of their long journey, right around here, the waggon-train's Bible got damaged – same time the preacher was shot dead by Indians,' he continued, handing her the glass, 'so remembering as best they could, all the families from all the waggons got together and transcribed the missing bits of the good book. They felt kind of wedded to their version,' he said with a smile, 'and they liked where they'd landed up too, so they stayed.' He took a sip of his tea and sat back in his chair. 'Then they thought: new Bible – new place – new name. As there was no one about to ordain the replacement preacher but God, they thought why not put the big fella in the title? And now here we are; it's nineteen seventy-nine and we got thousands in our congregation.'

It was so simple when Jalbert explained things, Cranberry thought.

The following Wednesday they were going on a trip to some lakes, which were far enough away to necessitate an early start and 6 a.m. found Cranberry sitting in the kitchen with Jalbert, waiting on Lucille and Hof.

'You know I'm living with your son,' she said, her brain awake before her manners. 'How can you reconcile that with your religion?'

'Well,' he said, taking the question very seriously, 'it says in the Bible, the sins of the father will be visited on the sons . . . And Lucille, she loves loving . . . And I, I love loving . . . And look at you. It's six-thirty in the morning and you're as purtty as a picture . . . and . . . hell! Let's go sing us a gospel song.'

And that's just what they did. The lake trip was put on hold and Lucille, Hof and Cranberry gathered around the piano, while Jalbert played. For two hours straight they sang gospel with such gusto, and it was so uplifting, that Cranberry thought it was lucky they'd only come for a week or she'd be in danger of becoming a religious zealot. It all made such sense in the company of Jalbert and Lucille. They were such good, happy people, married forty-six years and still completely in love.

Lucille had been right to cry at their arrival as the week passed quickly. All too soon it was Sunday, the day of their departure. Leaving was hard. Lucille tried, with little success, to be brave. Jalbert and Hof did better, masculine gruffness disguising their sorrow. Seeing the old couple, waving them off at their front door, hearts near to breaking, made Cranberry sad and her thoughts turned to her own parents, not because of any similarities between them and the Longhofers, but simply because they too were parents, who'd said goodbye to their only child. It became clear to Cranberry how much she missed them, and she started to pine for home and things familiar.

As they drove back to Tulsa via Memphis to look at Graceland and Elvis's grave, Cranberry told Hof about her life for the first time. He sat back in his big comfy Chevy with the cruise control on and listened intently as they sped down the long straight highway. She saw in his face that her life seemed as rare to him as his had to her to begin with. She told him of the riches she came from and the liberality of her parents' way of life, of the absence of God, or any such moral values and how she felt this lack of structure and boundaries had affected her life. Everything came tumbling out. She laughed as she described it all. She talked for a long time and it gradually occurred to her that all the things that her parents had done to her, which she imagined as monstrous, now seemed funny, touching even, and she ended it all with, 'They were only trying to do their best; I see that now.'

'And for eighteen months your poor momma hasn't known where you're at,' Hof said quietly.

'No,' she said, feeling small for the first time. Seeing her selfishness. 'I'll ring them, shall I?'

'I imagine,' he answered firmly.

The following morning, with great foreboding, she did. Shaking as she sat on the bed in the Heartbreak Motel's honeymoon suite she dialled the operator to ask for the number. Hof stood behind her massaging her shoulders. How would she start? What would she say? Someone picked up.

'Mama,' she said tentatively. And there it was. Her mother's voice.

'It's Berry!' Cranberry heard her mother scream up the stairs and pictured her standing in the hallway next to the scented geranium.

What had she been doing? Was she well? Her mother's questions left no room for answers. Did she realize she'd never given them a way to get in touch? Was she happy? Her mother repeated that question again and again.

'Yes Mama, yes Mama, yes, yes, yes.' Cranberry repeated back laughing.

Her mother continued without taking a breath. 'The dog has had nine puppies,' she said and went on to describe each one's character and markings. Hof, who had waited to make sure she was all right, left.

They talked, her mother on the main phone, her father on the extension in the bedroom, and she on the bed of the Heartbreak Motel, for over an hour. The longest conversation they'd ever had together. It ended with Cranberry promising to come back for the twenty-third of May, her father's fortieth birthday, and stay for the summer.

When Hof returned, Cranberry was curled up on the plastic, red, heart-shaped sofa in the authentically replicated Graceland's boudoir. 'Nadine, honey, what's up?'

'Oh Hof,' she sighed, 'I said I'd go home for the summer.'

'I figured . . . I brought you this,' he said, giving her a small box. She opened it, and there was a diamond ring in the shape of a horseshoe, sized to her engagement finger.

'Hof, is this what I think it is?'

'Only if you want it to be,' he said, lifting her up, and carrying her into the bedroom.

The next few weeks were agony for Cranberry. She was frightened of going back to England. She was happy here. And knew somehow, she wasn't quite sure how, but somehow, that the very act of going home would jeopardize it all. And the ring. She loved it, but keeping it was out of the question. She recognized she was at a fork in the road of her life, unable to swear for ever. She gave it back three days before she left. 'I love it. And you, much, much, more. But I know you meant it as an engagement ring, and I'm sorry. I just can't promise.' Hof said nothing.

They had a farewell dinner. Loretta and Gary came to say goodbye. Loretta pressed a large white pill into the palm of her hand, 'Quaalude,' she said mournfully, 'you can use it to sleep or bend it and stay awake if you like. Either way it'll dull the pain.' For Cranberry, the evening was more like leaving home than when she had actually left two years ago.

The following morning, Hof drove her to the airport. On the way, like a magician, he produced the ring from behind her ear. He'd had it resized for her little finger. Cranberry was moved beyond words. Parting couldn't have been worse. It created a physical ache in Cranberry, like the onset of a nasty flu. The only thing that made it bearable was that Hof had promised to come over in July for a whole month. Once settled in her plane seat Cranberry took Loretta's pill, and escaped into merciful oblivion.

It was good to be home. Cranberry had now to admit to herself that although she'd always thought them worthless because they were so rich, she'd been wrong. They had great worth. Her disapproval had been firmly rooted in inverted snobbery. No necessity to struggle from nine-to-five in her mind had equalled 'no good'. She was shocked by her revelation, as it exposed her as an erstwhile bourgeoise. Well, at least she'd done some growing on her own, she thought, having travelled into a bourgeois identity, through it and come out the other side unaided.

Her parents couldn't wait to meet Hof and were fascinated by her tales of Tulsa. Her father, with his lifelong passion for horses, persisted in imagining Hof as a cowboy who'd never left the range, let alone the saddle of his horse. Try as Cranberry might, she couldn't rid him of this notion, nor did she want to. His misconception amused her. Fantasy ran in the family.

It wasn't all sweetness and light. She wasn't impervious to old triggers. 'The world's your oyster,' her mother said apropos of nothing one evening when the three of them were having dinner. It 'annoyed the shit out of her' as Loretta would have said.

'How?' Cranberry asked.

'What?' her mother.

'How exactly is the world my oyster?'

'In any way you want it to be,' said her mother.

'No Mama,' Cranberry cut her off. 'I said how, exactly, is the *world my oyster*? Don't say I can do anything, I left school at fifteen. I'm uneducated. An ignoramus. And when you say "the world's your oyster" it makes me feel like shit.'

'Don't use that language to your mother,' her father interjected, siding, as usual, with his wife. 'Anyway, why don't you write?'

'Become a war correspondent, I suppose,' Cranberry snapped, surprised to find herself still smarting from a silly, two-year-old snub.

'You're certainly good enough,' was his astonishing reply.

'Don't be stupid, how would you know anyway?' she retorted rudely.

'How could I not, Berry? You've scribbled stories on every available scrap of paper since you were six.'

'And your letters,' her mother joined in, 'put Eric Newby in the shade.'

Cranberry looked blank.

'Famous travel writer,' her father explained. 'Wrote *A Short Walk in the Hindu Kush*. Wonderful book.' A silence fell over the dining table. Her mother always said a silence like that was an angel passing.

That dinner sowed a seed in Cranberry's mind. It was true she had always written. Periodically she'd recorded episodes of her life into a copybook, two versions, one in the form of a diary, and the other as an adventure, from an alter ego's point of view – Nadine, the pioneer woman's, for instance, versus Cranberry's own perspective. The two had different thoughts and feelings about the same event and it was fun to look back on both accounts. Maybe her father was right. Not about being a war correspondent, but about being a writer. She dwelt increasingly on the idea. It would be a wonderful way to live. She enrolled in a three-month writing course in London. It meant delaying her return to Tulsa, but she could always drop out if Hof minded. She wouldn't say anything yet, she thought, who knew? She might hate it. She didn't. Even though she found the whole process incredibly hard. It seemed to her to require the same brain muscles as doing crossword puzzles. She had no problem getting all the right words down on paper; it was just they were in the wrong order. All her stories were like massive word anagrams that had to be deciphered. Gradually, the more she immersed herself in the process the more the brave pioneer woman from the turn of the century began to recede.

Six weeks later she went to meet Hof at Southampton. He was coming to visit for four weeks. Having a phobia about flying he had come over on the *QE2*. She saw him arrive guitar case in hand, in all his finery; new boots and a magnificent new cream Stetson, bought in honour of crossing the water. It had been over two months since they'd seen each other. She watched him amble through immigration, tipping his hat, and exchanging a few words with the officers before leaving them smiling. When he came towards her Cranberry was nervous. Would it be the same?

'Well. Look at you,' he said, lifting her off her feet, in a wonderful Hof-hug, instantly dispelling any doubts she had.

She drove him back to her parents' Holland Park flat in her mother's Volkswagen, lent to Cranberry for the duration of Hof's stay. They were still up in Yorkshire and Cranberry was going to take Hof up to meet them at the weekend. That gave them two whole days alone together to get reacquainted. Cranberry had stocked up on all of Hof's favourite food and they stayed in, hanging out, taking the occasional walk in one of London's great parks, but basically just falling back in love again, which was heaven, considering they'd never fallen out.

England was a riot with Hof. Road workers drew imaginary guns on him in the street. Everyone grinned when they saw him coming, and beamed when he opened his mouth and that honey-voiced drawl came out.

At the end of the week they drove up to Yorkshire to meet her parents. Cranberry was nervous until they arrived and she saw her father and four dogs waiting to greet them. He must have been looking out for them from the library window. All five were instantly captivated by Hof. It was as though he were a wind that had just blown in, bringing with it every canine and Englishman's fantasy of the wild, wide-open spaces of the original cowboy's West.

Her mother fell for his charm as soon as he entered the conservatory on the south side of the house. 'At last,' she exclaimed. 'I've heard so much about you, please come and sit next to me.' She indicated a comfortable-looking wicker chair with floral chintz-covered cushions. 'Now what shall I call you? Hof? *Mr* Longhofer or, what pray tell, is your Christian name?'

'Hell Ma'am, just call me good-looking,' he answered, raising his hat and bowing to her slightly before he sat.

'Right you are.' Cranberry's mother roared with laughter. 'Would you like something to drink, good-looking?'

The whole thing was that easy. Cranberry needn't have been nervous at all. She should have known that Hof's sheer height and size, coupled with the blatant goodness of his spirit, would win over all and sundry – it always did. The weekend went well and they left, their ears ringing with her parents' entreaties for Hof to return whenever he wanted.

On the way back to London Cranberry tried to show Hof the best of England. They travelled via Northumberland, where they made love in a cave, followed by a B&B in the Lake District, then on to North Wales where they did the same on the bank of a stream, culminating with a four-poster bed in their hotel in Stratford-on-Avon where they were having such a good time, they missed the production of *A Midsummer Night's Dream* they'd come down to see. Amazingly, considering it was England, they ate good food wherever they went thanks to Hof and an obscure gastro-pub guide he'd found in Tulsa.

Once in London she took him to St Paul's Cathedral, the Tower of London, and numerous music venues. Dingwalls in Camden Lock was his favourite. He liked being able to go out and sit under the night sky by the canal when it got too hot inside. On his penultimate night she took him to dinner with Kathy, a friend from the writing class.

'Don't you love her stuff?' Kathy asked.

'I've not been given any to read,' he replied, making Cranberry realize that she had excluded Hof from her other immediate passion in life, apart, of course, from him. They walked home arm in arm through the park in silence.

Back at the flat she gave him one of her stories, saying, 'You needn't read it if you don't want to.'

He sat down, read, and when he finished he was very quiet.

'Did you hate it?' she asked, worried.

'No, darlin' . . . you're good.'

Cranberry lay on the carpet in front of the gas log fire while Hof played the guitar. He played for a long time, until finally he set it aside, and came and sat on the floor next to her.

'Nadine honey, I've been thinking, you gotta stay and see this writing through.'

'What d'you mean?' she asked alarmed, because she knew precisely what he meant. She felt an ease with her new world she'd never felt before, she fitted in at last. She'd begun to voice stuff in her writing that she needed to say. She was writing plays again. She hadn't done that since she'd left school. 'Six months' is all she said out loud.

They agreed. The jury was out for six months. They'd review their love then. The last few days were intense. They both understood it was the end. Cranberry knew she'd never live in Tulsa for the rest of her life, as much as she might want to. She'd leave, five, ten, fifteen, twenty years, it didn't matter, at one point she would leave. And the longer she stayed, the worse the parting would be. And there was no way Hofer could live in England. He was much too big; he'd suffocate. They pretended, but she knew it. And Hof, he knew it too.

Their transatlantic calls, initially intense, became less frequent. There was less to talk about. They no longer knew the minutiae of the other's day. Six months came and went. They had a long conversation on the actual day, both studiously avoiding the subject. Finally the calls petered out all together.

Cranberry was too busy to miss him. She submitted one of her plays to the young writers' festival at the Royal Court. They accepted it. Cranberry was over the moon. Harold Pinter had started there, hadn't he? Maybe not. On the eve of the first performance she was terrified. Critics were coming.

In the middle of the night she was woken up by the phone ringing. Who'd call at this time of night? Looking over to the clock she saw an illuminated 3.10 a.m. *Déjà vu*, she thought, reminded of her first night in Tulsa. Same time, same clock. She grabbed the receiver.

'Hello,' she croaked.

'Nadine?' Hof's voice. Not possible, they hadn't talked for nearly two years. 'Nadine. Is that you honey?'

'Hof?' She couldn't believe it. 'Hof?' she repeated.

'I imagine,' he said, sending a pang of longing through her heart. 'I'm just ringing to wish you luck, and tell you that I know it's gonna be great tonight. You're a writer darling, I know it. For eighteen months, you wrote my dreams for me, and I loved your every word.'

'How did you know it was happening?' she asked.

'I hear things,' he replied, then added, 'I'm always looking out for you, darlin', you know that.'

'Oh Hof,' she said. Her voice broke. 'I do wish you were here.'

'Shh, get some rest. You gotta look good tomorrow. Goodbye, my little Nadine.' And with that he was gone. She lay there crying. She wasn't sad. He'd made her happy by ringing. She was just crying, gently, for what might have been.

As Hof had predicted the evening was a success of sorts. She received one review and it had the word promising in it, which was enough to keep Cranberry going.

Thanks to her, Hof said, he got engaged to a girl from the Cherokee nation.

'You helped me get over my prejudices,' he told Cranberry when he called to tell her. 'I'd never gone with a minority till I met you.'

They saw each other one more time a year later in Kentucky. Betsy-Kay, her rodeo-queen friend who'd married a horse breeder, wanted Cranberry to be godmother of her baby, Brandy-Lee. Cranberry accepted, feeling distinctly honoured. This was to be her first godchild and she flew over for the christening.

The timing of Cranberry's American return was ironic. Hof was getting married in two weeks. Cranberry had made up her mind not to ring him. She'd been invited to the wedding but wasn't going. It wasn't that she minded, she just couldn't see the point of risking heartbreak.

Betsy-Kay's farm was utterly picturesque. The house and the barns were all painted red and white and set in the middle of rolling green paddocks. Champion Morgan horses trotting around them very prettily, a high gloss to their coats. Friendly too, they came straight over to nuzzle Cranberry as she leaned on the post-and-rail whitewashed fence that separated them. The christening went well. Brandy-Lee lay peacefully in Cranberry's arms for the entire ceremony except when the priest dipped his hand in holy water and drew the sign of the cross on her forehead – only then did she expel the devil with one small angry cry.

Afterwards they had a barbecue, hybrid Anglo-American style, with square dancing and mint juleps, which they drank under the chestnut trees, followed by champagne with the cake, which was a gaudy affair with storks, rosebuds and lace. It was late when Cranberry eventually returned to her hotel and reeled up to the room that Betsy-Kay had kindly booked and paid for. Flopping on the bed she closed her eyes. The mint juleps must have been strong; she felt sozzled. Water and aspirin was what she needed, she thought, feeling for her bag at the side of the bed. Her hand flailed around without landing on anything, forcing her to roll over and open her eyes.

Letting out a small cry she threw herself back down on her pillow and lay for a moment, her eyes clenched tight shut. Her clock showed 3.10. She rolled back, grabbed the phone by the bed and dialled. She had to.

It rang only once. 'Yup,' Hof said. His voice sounded awake but Cranberry could tell he wasn't. She couldn't speak. 'Who's this? You OK?' he asked. Nothing. He was taking the receiver from his ear when he heard a small voice.

'Hof,' her voice catching in the middle of the word.

'Nadine. Nadine honey is that you?'

She started to laugh. 'Sing it,' she said.

They talked. She asked how the wedding plans were going. 'I'm not arranging the gig darlin' but I reckon it's gathering pace . . . Have you forgotten the time difference honey?' he asked with no recrimination.

'Not . . . sorry . . . worse. I know it's the middle of the night. I'm in Kentucky but I'm leaving the day after tomorrow.'

'Kentucky,' he said. 'I'm coming that way tomorrow.'

'Why?' she asked.

'Business,' he lied. 'You wanna drink tomorrow night?'

'Yes, that would be great.' She gave him the name of her hotel. They rang off and Cranberry rolled over smiling. She had butterflies in her stomach as she fell asleep. At the same time in Tulsa, Hof jumped up and threw a toothbrush, a clean shirt and underpants in a bag and started his drive across two states to see her.

He got there at five the next afternoon and rang her from the lobby. She asked him to come up, said she had a veranda that was pleasant to sit on and that she'd order drinks to be sent up. What did he want?

As he walked up the stairs to the first floor she ordered a mint julep for her and an Amaretto sour for him. She felt very nervous. Why had she rung him, she thought. Stupid. There was a knock on the door and he was there, larger than life. It was awkward at first. They heard each other's news in stilted bursts. She learned that Hof had his songs sung by the best now, all the great women – Emmy Lou, Dolly, Debbie – they all covered them. 'I have a boyfriend,' Cranberry said. Conversation didn't flow, in fact the whole reunion was excruciating until they hugged goodbye.

Any gaucheness disappeared at that moment and, before they knew it, they were in bed together, where they stayed for three days straight. Luckily the room wasn't reserved. They were frantic to connect again and by the end of the three days they'd caught up on everything there was to know about their missing slices of life. Hof knew his fiancée must be worried sick and said he must go. Cranberry didn't have that problem – her boyfriend wasn't serious – but she knew he was right. They were subdued. Cheating didn't suit them.

'Hof, I'm sorry. I shouldn't have rung,' she said.

'I had a hand in it too, honey. It's me who gassed it over,' Hof said and kissed her tenderly. 'You stay well now, my Nadine. I love you. I always will, you know that, don't you, honey?'

'Me too you,' she whispered, reaching up and missing him already, as her fingers traced the contours of his cratered cheeks.

RA

I'm in trouble. It's painfully obvious to me this evening, sitting here having dinner with Jimmy in one of the snug red-leatherette booths at Musso and Frank's, LA's oldest restaurant. My body language conveys extreme interest in his conversation, I'm leaning forward drinking him in, smiling, laughing, captivated apparently, happily waiting for the next pearl to drop from his enchanting lips. Apparently.

In reality I'm worrying where our children should go to school. I always do this, jump way ahead. But this time it's extreme. It's only our second date.

The crotchety old waiter, for whom I've developed a perverse fondness, brings my order of sand dabs and fries. The tender fish turns to sawdust in my mouth as the lightning bolt of self-realization hits. Yanked firmly back into the present, I start to recite – ONE DAY AT A TIME – over and over in my head. The sheer repetition facilitates a partial recovery and allows me to get through the rest of dinner without indulging in any more dangerous fantasies. Dangerous because they have a habit of tumbling straight out of my mouth, unbidden, at the most inopportune moments. I sometimes wonder if I have some mild form of Tourette's syndrome.

Apart from that one slip. REMEMBER THEY CAN ALWAYS SENSE THEM. The evening had gone very well, so much so, that here we were the next morning, lying in my bed fused together with post-coital sweat.

'I'm hungry,' Jimmy said.

'Mmm,' I purred, half asleep. 'What would you like?'

'Got any eggs?' he asked.

'I'm getting them frozen,' I murmur.

'What?' he said.

'What?' I said back, my blood running cold. I'd done it again.

This time it was Oprah's fault. Her show last week had been about female 'baby boomers' – my generation – and how over 75 per cent of us are missing our chance at pregnancy by letting our biological clock run past its sell-by date. The instant I heard this, I had what Oprah calls a 'lightbulb moment' and rang my gynaecologist to make an appointment. I told his secretary that it was an emergency. It was. I needed to know a.s.a.p. about the possibility of having my eggs frozen in case there was a need for artificial insemination at a later date.

'Did you say you had frozen eggs?' Jimmy asked, sounding a little revolted.

'Yes, but they're weird. I've got fresh too, much better. Would scrambled do you?' I blustered, now horribly awake.

'Whatever,' he said kissing me lazily and rolling over, completely oblivious to my cataclysmic faux pas.

I left the bed, grabbed the kanga hanging on the door handle and wrapped myself in it as I fled downstairs. Once in the kitchen I relaxed. Phew, that was a close one, I thought, breaking eggs into a bowl. I must be more careful. Still . . . it was nice cooking for a man. Damn it. ONE DAY AT A TIME. I need to go to a meeting.

That evening, after my gynaecologist's – he told me it was going to be a fearfully expensive process, this egg-freezing business – I went to Robertson Hall. I was late and the testimonials had already begun. Everyone was mawkishly applauding a sobbing woman who'd evidently just finished speaking. I took my place quietly in the seat my best friend had saved next to him. He threw me a grateful little glance as he got to his feet.

'Hi, I'm Kamal,' he said to the assembly. 'And I'm a Romantiholic.'

'Hi, Kamal,' everyone replied as one.

Kamal was of Lebanese descent. He was a designer and every bit as hopeless as me when it came to romance, as were all the people in this hall. Romantiholics Anonymous isn't much help, except that whenever I hear one of my fellow addicts speaking, it's rather like listening to a country and western song. My life feels great in comparison.

'Love me. Love me. Love me . . . NOT,' the group chanted before breaking up into derisory laughter.

Kamal must have been being needy again. I'm not quite sure how. I drifted off. Forgot to listen. Great friend I've turned out to be. But honestly, surely he should know by now how vile RA is about self-pity, even though we all wallow in it. This is one of the many points where I disagree with them and their stupid creed. I mean why shouldn't Kamal feel a little sorry for himself? He's an anomaly: a burly, gay, Middle Eastern bundle of nerves. Eternally optimistic for the happily ever after. *Inshallah*.

I expect Kamal will be wounded by their taunting, so when he sits I give his hand a little squeeze of solidarity and sure enough there's the burning heat of disgrace in his palm.

The mission hall's full; all the usual suspects are here tonight and apart from Kamal, I'm not pleased to see any of them. Lavinia, who's terribly high society, 'Hi-So', had begun speaking. Her problem this week was that her boyfriend of sixty-eight had made out with a girl of nineteen, in front of her twenty-one-year-old daughter. His punishment, she informed us gleefully, was not letting him escort her to the *Vanity Fair*

Oscar bash. Both she and the boyfriend were Hi-So, but Lavinia – much more so – could bring him to heel with really grand invites that he invariably didn't have and coveted.

Lavinia was followed immediately by Jack, a small, amphetamine-propelled wreck of a guy. He couldn't wait for the applause to die down before springing up to vow that he had been on his own for so long that listening to others agonize over their lovers made him feel like Isak Dinesen – '*I once had a farm in Africa.*' We laughed, as no one could think of an encouraging thing to say. No one ever could when Jack got up.

Then it was Connie's go, exquisitely pretty Connie, who swayed when she announced that she always wanted to have much more sex than her lover of the moment. 'I mean, I crave the smell, don't you?' she said to the dumbfounded room.

Patti, the long-distance freak, ran in clutching a Louis Vuitton carryall and interrupted Connie. 'Sorry guys,' she said, 'but it's an emergency. You gotta give me a pep talk.' Patti couldn't love someone unless they were a minimum of three hundred miles away. She continued breathless. 'I'm catching the red-eye to New York . . . business trip,' and scanned our faces for a lifeline. All of us shifted uncomfortably in our chairs. We knew she was lost. She was already so hot under the collar that she was using her boarding pass as a fan.

Paul, the pathologically secretive Jewish psychiatrist, took his turn, and did his usual guff about wanting – no needing – to open up, come clean. The recipients of his passionate lust were invariably married or lesbian and necessitated clandestine behaviour. The trouble with Paul is he can always out-rationalize, or double-speak the lot of us into submission, so we've all basically given up trying with him.

Fear of commitment. Rejection. Self-loathing. Name it and you'll find it in this room.

There is one partial success. Nicole, the beauty of the group, who for the last twenty-five years accepted a jewel from her husband the size of the Koh-i-noor diamond each time he was unfaithful, has finally broken her pattern. Deciding she was rich enough, she left him. So now she's paranoid that every guy is after her money.

I check my watch. The whole thing seems to be going on and on, the same old same old. It really is interminable. There are a couple of new people but they've only got old problems. Why do I bother?

We reach the RA prayer said at the end of every meeting. Finally the last couplet: 'Lord give me the strength to love who's good for me. Shun who's bad. And the wisdom to know who's who. Amen.'

Before everyone opens their eyes I grab Kamal and run. We dodge Lavinia, who spots us and calls, 'Coo-ee. Hang on Caro. Kamal I'm coming.'

It's wicked I know, but on those teetering six-inch heels of hers she hasn't got a hope of catching us if we keep going and we do. I need to talk to Kamal seriously.

Soon we're settled comfortably at a table on the terrace of Pane e Vino, our favourite Italian restaurant on Beverly, where tiny sprays run along the beams of the shade-giving pergola and mist you like a wilting flower on hot LA days like today. We do our order, then I tell Kamal all about Jimmy and the horrors and delights of the last twenty-four hours.

'Heinous' or 'Divine' he says after each of my revelations, then laughs himself silly at the idea of the frozen-egg routine. No empathy there at all. Miffed, I return to the business at hand.

'Now look Kamal,' I say full of stern resolve, 'RA isn't doing us any good at all; we've been going for a year now and here we are having exactly the same conversation.'

'I know, heinous,' Kamal replies.

'I think we should be serious. Get one-on-one, real, proper professional help,' I say.

'Break our patterns?' he ventures.

'That's it,' I agree. 'I've got the number of someone who's meant to be brilliant.' I take my cellphone from my bag, and dial the number printed on a dog-eared card that I've been keeping in my wallet for weeks. As I press the last digit on the keypad I pass the card to Kamal.

'You in?' I say, pressing my hand over what I *think* is the tiny mouthpiece to give us uncertain privacy. He peruses the card, takes a deep breath, and replies resolutely, 'You go girl, I'm ready.'

And I do as instructed: between bites of carpaccio and shaved Parmesan drizzled with a mustard sauce and sips of Pellegrino, I commit us to a six-week intensive course with, Kamal was thrilled to read:

CARMEN SWALLOW
LA's premier psychic
Aura reader & destiny instructor.
(Guaranteed to find your adult without.)

We high five across the table to our rehabilitated futures and continue lunch.

Rhoda Hardhorne

George Truckle came from a fine New England family, a long line of politicized Democrats, who swelled the party's coffers with substantial contributions and campaigned diligently at each and every election to get their man instated. Kennedy, Carter, Clinton and more before owed debts of gratitude to the Truckle family's philanthropy. George, on the other hand, was proud to be a card-carrying Republican, right-wing, confident and happy.

His mother threatened to disinherit him with monotonous regularity for what she saw as his aberration. Whenever she issued this threat it was easy for her to see him as he used to be, a spoilt little boy in the same sailor suit his father had worn before him, stamping his foot and threatening to hold his breath till he turned blue. And, as ever, she'd relent.

He turned out well, he thought, in spite of her and her liberal drivel. And in a way he was right: good-looking with fine sandy-coloured hair that flopped across his unlined brow in an appealing manner and the proud possessor of a remarkably fine physique. In short if he ever had to describe himself for a stranger it would have to have been as the classic all-American jock. As for his temperament, he would have to admit that he was surprisingly intelligent, basically kind, and possessed a piercing sense of humour that could be used to decimate if necessary, and if not, took a much-needed edge off his pomposity, or so said his friends.

He worked for the Republican Party, running the Virginia campaign for the local candidate, a Mr Tom Morrissey who was George's contemporary and, George couldn't help but notice, hardly more qualified to hold office than himself.

It was his job to make Tom shine, which he did to great effect. Everybody liked George and acknowledged his effort.

He, meanwhile, had realized, while introducing Tom to the podium at a small town hall meeting, that he liked public speaking and, if he was honest, being the centre of attention. Enough of being the warm-up guy, he thought, it's time to become the headliner. And it was to that end that he was moving to the West Coast: to pursue further his newfound passion for public recognition.

The party felt they needed a charismatic candidate for congressman and why not George Truckle? He was highly personable and had proved himself a hard-working, loyal party member. Besides, he could claim to be one of California's native sons, even though, aged thirty-six, this was his first visit. Luckily his grandfather on his father's side had been one of the founding fathers. Highways were named after him and the Truckle Museum was known as the finest in the state. So it was generally thought that returning to his ancestral roots was no bad thing, and could in many ways be a plus.

His surname still held such kudos that the whole of Californian society would endorse him simply to be able to say they had a Truckle coming to dinner.

Life was good for George. Made even more so by his recent engagement to Polly. They'd met, years ago at Brown; she was his best friend's kid sister who'd come over for her brother's graduation. Only sixteen years old, she was cute enough, he remembered thinking. Apart from that he hadn't really taken her in, except to note that she was English, the granddaughter of an earl, a bit on the liberal side with a good sense of humour. Now, seven years on, here they were about to be married; strange how life turned out.

Funny he'd settled on her, considering how much she reminded him of his mother. But unlike with his mother, they laughed constantly. Polly found everything funny, especially him. When she disagreed with some of his more outrageous statements or found him what she labelled stuffy, she'd call him a square. He knew he was merely being sensible, but she'd taunt him anyway, even in public, using her two index fingers to draw a small square in the air between them. 'An air-square,' she explained the first time, making him laugh and bringing him right back down to earth.

But perhaps the best thing of all about Polly was that she was Honourable, really Honourable. Her name was the Honourable Polly Tweedmouth. She was related to everyone in England, including the Queen. Unfortunately, he wouldn't get a title when they married. But, hey, who cared about that when they were in love?

Besides, she was going to be a real asset to his burgeoning career with that English accent . . . irresistible.

He didn't believe in sex before marriage. It pissed her off. She'd say, 'Let's just see if it fits.' Though he knew she meant to be funny, he couldn't help but be revolted by her vulgarity.

At last it was 14 August, the day of Polly's arrival. She was coming out for three weeks to help him find a house, which made perfect sense, as eventually she would be living there too.

They hadn't seen each other for nearly six weeks. Polly would know precisely how long it had been down to the minute, George thought with affection as he drove his favourite route through the oilfields to LAX airport. The top of his black Mercedes 500SL was down so that he could fully appreciate the view. It was one of the many anomalies of Los Angeles, he thought as he turned on to La Cienaga and crossed Washington

Boulevard. The home of Hollywood, capital city of illusion, and the first thing visitors saw on their way in from the airport was desert scrub covered in desultory oil pumps working twenty-four seven. They reminded him of giant praying mantises. He loved them, the remorseless dipping of their great ponderous heads and all the wealth that endless metallic rhythm represented.

Still some people, like Polly for instance, might like to see something more to do with the movies as they arrived. The studios had scene painters, for Christ's sake; surely they could knock up any backdrop they pleased? So why not create an enormous *trompe l'oeil* corridor of forests or meadows or, perhaps, a Disneyesque castle, complete with colourful pennants flying from the ramparts and a courtly, mounted retinue winding up the hill towards the already lowered drawbridge. He was still thinking of things to please Polly and hoping she was going to like California when he drew up to the kerb of the Tom Bradley International Terminal.

Right on cue she came running through the automated doors, knocking into people with her cart. Not that it mattered. Polly's face, lit up with the merest hint of a smile, could melt any heart. Too angular of feature to be considered pretty, the combined effect of her dark hair, pale skin and wide-set, laughing eyes had a potency which was impossible to ignore. Aware, as ever, of heads turning all around her, George was overcome by an involuntary surge of pride. Spotting him immediately she laughed and waved. He shook his head smiling and waved back. What was he going to do with her? She was dressed in too many vibrant colours, clashing pinks and greens, with an oriental-style, yellow silk brocade jacket. And wearing flat shoes instead of the high heels he liked. It was lucky she was an Honourable. As much as he loved her, he wasn't sure he could afford to be seen with such a . . . he didn't know what exactly. She'd say she was a free spirit. The nearest he could come was the old adage: 'You can dress her up, but you can't take her out.' With Polly, you could take her out, but you couldn't dress her up.

'Hello darling,' she cried, throwing her bags on to the back seat. Then she jumped over the closed door of the passenger side and smothered him with kisses.

'Careful of the paintwork,' he replied, instantly cursing himself for being such a downer, so lacking in spontaneity. She didn't notice, and continued kissing him. He found it vaguely annoying. She was like an over-enthusiastic labrador.

He took her back to the Four Seasons, where he had moved (in truth been moved by flunkies) for Polly's benefit from a double room to the penthouse suite. She was delighted with their accommodations, if a little wistful at the separate king-size beds in their separate king-size rooms. Still, to have a room each with a large salon in between, and a palatial terrace overlooking the pool, was amazing. But the crowning glory for her was that they both had their own enormous, peach-coloured, marble-clad bathrooms replete with baths long enough for giants to lounge in. Separate shower cubicles, and extra nooks that housed their personal bidets. Inexplicably both had double basins. All the fittings – taps, hinges, bathplugs etc. – were fashioned out of gleaming gold. D-e-c-a-d-e-n-t, she thought, even before she saw the telephones. Two. One for use in the bath; the other made it convenient to chat while sitting on the loo! She loved it.

The next morning over a sumptuous breakfast in his king-size bed – Polly had sneaked in and snuggled up to George the moment her eyes had opened, which due to jet lag had been 5 a.m. – they discussed their quest for a home. It was a perfect sunny day. Polly wanted to drive around spotting things, getting a feeling for the different areas. George, on the other hand, had no interest in exploring. He knew precisely the areas he wanted to live, the best: Bel Air or Beverly Hills, that type of place where their kind lived, and he couldn't see the point of wasting their time looking elsewhere.

So began one of their spats. She accused him of being unadventurous, of not living life to the full. He accused her of . . . nothing. He didn't like discord, especially early in the morning. He didn't want to say something he might later regret. Anyway, he knew he'd have to capitulate in the end because she would never let it go. 'Talk to me,' she'd plead. 'Better out than in,' she'd say. 'Why?!' was all he could think again and again in the face of her diatribes.

As he anticipated, he had to give a bit in the end, and that bit was looking at a 'perfect' house in the hills recommended by an old acquaintance of hers, Wolf, a blues guitarist.

Well, if a blues guitarist called *Wolf* thought it perfect George knew it was going to be a waste of time. But he acquiesced. There was a method to his madness. By giving her that, she in turn agreed to them registering with the top realtor in town, thus cutting down a whole day meandering around slum districts to one single fiasco.

They set off, driving up an avenue lined with palm trees towards Beechwood and the hills with the famous Hollywood sign. There was a forced civility in the air. 'It's a wonder they don't snap,' Polly said about the slender thirty-foot trunks swaying under the weight of their heavy fronds, which rustled far above their heads, audible even through the purring engine.

'Rat condos,' George said. 'The leaves are full of the vermin, I've been told.'

'Right,' she replied. Then after a few moments added, 'You know there's been more suicides off that sign than I've had hot dinners. I've been told they had to fence it off.'

She lay back and closed her eyes, feeling triumphant. The top was down and a delicious warm wind was blowing on their faces and she realized in that moment that this was it: the Californian Dream. They were living it. Nothing was said, but she opened her eyes and smiled at George, who returned the compliment. They squeezed hands and drove on feeling very much in love.

By following Wolf's instructions precisely they drove up a small street into the hills. It was hard to believe they were in the heart of a city, let alone a capital one. The road was so narrow there were passing places for oncoming cars to park and let you through or vice versa, and the tarmac ran out at some points, reducing it to a single dirt track.

'Hope Wolf's directions are good,' George said, finally voicing his doubts, as they rounded a corner and found themselves on Skyridge Drive, and saw the summit. They needed 8556, which turned out to be a little black-and-white, half-timbered, mock-Elizabethan cottage right at the very top, so tiny, even George agreed there must be more to it than met the eye. It had an awning with scalloped edging shading the door. Polly thought it looked like a pretty odd property and was probably a waste of time, but didn't say so. She just got out and rang the bell.

From somewhere down the hill on the left, a little girl's voice called out, 'Come in. The gate's along here. Walk down and pull the string.' They followed the voice down the road, keeping the unpainted fence to their right. They'd walked a hundred yards or more when Polly spotted a string hanging out of a small hole where a knot in one of the planks used to be, and pulled it. Part of the fence swung back to reveal a small swimming pool in a courtyard. Water tumbled from a lion's head at the far end.

Polly was stunned at the beauty of the place; George by the apparition that appeared before them who had to be the owner of the voice. A manufactured sex kitten squeezed into a minuscule leopard-skin bikini. Manufactured, George presumed, as there was no way those breasts could be real. They were obscenely large, painful to look at, and impossible not to. He stood stock still, the soothing sound of running water now like thunderous cascades in his head. The clip-clop of Perspex high heels accompanied the breasts, which stepped forward and a polite hand was proffered.

'Hi, you must be Wolf's friends. I'm Rhoda Monroe,' the baby voice said.

Polly appraised the situation in a flash. 'Hello,' she said, taking the hand. 'Yes we are; I'm Polly and that's George. What a beautiful place. Is the rest as good? If so, why are you leaving?' she asked, casually wandering behind Rhoda to throw George a cheeky look and draw a square in the air with her fingers, taunting him in his confusion. Tearing his eyes from Rhoda's chest, he mumbled something inaudible, looked away and feigned admiration for a bush.

'Money,' Rhoda replied simply. 'Can't afford it, or I'd never leave. I love it. I mean what's not to love?'

Polly and George looked up to the house and had to agree. What indeed was there not to love? Far from being the minuscule half-timbered cottage it pretended to be, it now appeared to Polly to have been built in reverse, downwards. It clung to the hill like a limpet. The street façade, merely the tip of the iceberg, hid a substantial residence three floors low.

Polly and George had arrived on the lowest level without registering it; having walked down the hill, they doubled back once inside the gate, down three or four steps past the pool, and followed a path on a gentle incline ever downwards to a dear little private garden.

'Golly, it's so secret, isn't it?' Polly said. 'You'd never guess it was here.'

The spectacular views covered the whole of Los Angeles to the sea. Captivated, they stood for a moment before turning and there, like an illusionist's dream, the house revealed itself. Magical. If the interior in any way matched up to the exterior there was a chance they need look no further.

'I know. The cottage is just the foyer,' Rhoda said. 'Here, let me show you.'

She linked arms with Polly, who grinned at George. Typical, he thought. His fiancée had this disquieting habit of instantly bonding with the most extraordinary people, lulling them into an unsuitable familiarity.

The inside of the house was all they'd hoped for. French doors led out of every room either to the garden, a patio or balconies. To George's intense satisfaction there was a manly panelled study and beamed dining room. Polly meanwhile fell in love with the main bedroom – it had a beautiful 1920s bathroom-cum-dressing room en suite, with an elaborate purpose-built dressing table adorned with elegant 'movie star' lights surrounding it. Polly flipped the switches and all the glamorous engraved mirrors on the walls lining the room came alive with the lights from the vanity unit as well as the various wall sconces. It twinkled like diamonds to Polly's eye and she called down to George.

'Georgie darling, come up here. It's fit for Mae West.'

George laughed at her archaic reference, climbed the stairs and walked into the bedroom, where he stood in the doorway rooted to the spot. For there on the walls were hanging large, framed black-and-white nude photographs of the mutant sex kitten in a myriad of soft porn poses.

'Georgie, where are you?' Polly called from the bathroom. He couldn't move. The room seemed to be closing in on him. He stood there with his head pounding for what felt like hours before Polly emerged.

'What's wrong?' she asked. He looked apoplectic. Speechless, he swivelled his eyes wildly around the room at each of the offending objects.

Polly followed his wild stare. 'Wow,' she said.

At that precise moment, Rhoda came through the door.

'Wow,' Polly repeated. 'Are these you? You must be very proud.'

'Yes, yes, they are. And yes, I am. Totally proud.' Rhoda beamed.

George couldn't believe it. 'Proud!' Was his fiancée right in the head?

'My boyfriend gave them to me.' Rhoda lowered her voice conspiratorially, winking at George. 'He took them himself.'

Polly laughed. George felt faint; the whole scenario was abhorrent to him.

'Is that the time?' He looked at his wrist and realized he'd forgotten his watch. 'Come on darling, we don't want to be late,' he said in a strangled voice. They had no appointments but he hustled Polly out.

Back in the safety of the car George exploded. 'I've never been so embarrassed,' he said. 'How could you compliment that woman on those pictures?'

'Oh come on, darling. It was funny and anyway I knew she had to be proud of them. Put yourself in her shoes,' she insisted, refusing to understand his agony.

'Don't be revolting,' he said, 'I most certainly will not put myself in those repellent little fuck-me mules.' The vision of George in Rhoda's frou-frou slippers was too much for Polly and she started to giggle. Then she caught his look of thunder.

'Sorry darling, I'll stop, I swear,' she said but George could still detect her shoulders quivering. It was intolerable.

'Stop laughing,' he barked. 'What's so funny about my discomfort?'

She apologized with tears running down her face that she swore were due to her allergies.

He started the car and they drove on in stony silence. Polly kept sighing deep sighs and wiping her eyes.

Once back at his hotel he was very cold and distant. She, unable to meet his eyes, looked suitably chastened. They retired to their respective bathrooms. Poor little Polly, George thought, lying back in the tub. He'd been hard on her. Never mind. They'd make up over dinner. He'd reserved a table in one of the best restaurants in town. They'd have an excellent wine and he'd forgive her. They'd agreed to meet in their sitting room for cocktails at 7 p.m. On impulse he reached for the telephone and ordered a bottle of Crystal, her favourite. Polly loved champagne. That would start the evening with a bang. He lay back, congratulating himself on his magnanimity.

Polly, meanwhile, lay in her separate bath, looking very far from the beleaguered mouse of his imagination. She too was on the telephone. 'Oh, Wolf, it was so lovely, like being in the country; even George loved it. You are brilliant.' Then she said, 'Rhoda's quite a number isn't she?' There was a pause before she exploded, 'Shut up!' She roared with laughter. 'D'you promise? Oh! Wolf, it's too good to be true. I gotta go, he'll kill me if I'm late on top of everything else. Speak to you soon. Lots of love.' She hung up still laughing and submerged herself under the water, bubbles exploding to the surface as her mirth continued.

Just as George had intended Polly was thrilled by the champagne, as much for the gesture as anything else. The restaurant was superb as expected: the fish so light it melted in the mouth and the wine George chose perfectly complemented it. All in all, the evening was rattling along. In fact, Polly was such charming company, he realized that he'd agreed to the house and completely forgotten her previous heartlessness. 'What about Rhoda then and her giant accoutrements?' he asked, feeling that he'd struck the ideal rakish tone.

'Oh God darling, you don't know the half of it,' she laughed. 'I talked to Wolf this evening.' She stopped. Was that it?

'Well come on,' he said, digging a hole for himself. 'You can't stop now; what did he say?'

'Oh darling, let's leave it. We know how squeamish you are. Don't let's ruin the evening.'

'Come on Polly, Polly, Plop Plops,' he said, digging himself deeper. 'Tell me. I can be as broad-minded as the next man. What did he say?'

'Well,' she said, studying his face, 'don't turn all funny if I tell you. Swear we'll still buy the house.'

'You have my solemn promise.'

'Well,' she said, her eyes lighting up with humour. 'First of all, her name isn't Monroe. That's her stage name. And she's an adult movie star. You know, porn.'

George composed his face to reflect liberal understanding.

'Doesn't surprise me. In fact, I'd surmised as much already and determined to get the entire place fumigated if we bought it. What's her real name then?' he asked with a decided lack of interest.

'That's the beauty of it. Hardhorne! She changed her name from Hardhorne to Monroe? Isn't that priceless?'

'Shows her IQ,' he said smugly.

'D'you know why she has to sell? She told Wolf that the bottom had dropped out of her market. Isn't that just too funny for words?'

'I fail to see why,' he said, getting a little bored with her delight in the seamy subject.

'You do? Oh my God, that's because I forgot to tell you the point. She specializes in anal sex, and she said the bottom fell out of her market.'

George looked at Polly's laughing face. Anal sex. They were buying a house from that woman and she specialized in anal sex and was filmed doing it. This was too much. How could the girl he was about to marry find it so funny? His stomach churned. He could feel the swordfish mixing with the tiramisu: a dangerous combination.

Exorcism. That's what he'd have to do. Fumigate and exorcize. He wouldn't tell Polly, or she'd accuse him of being squeamish. He wasn't. He was just disgusted. And it wasn't the anal sex thing. No, it was the image of those pendulous mammaries, flummoxing about during it that upset him so.

'What? Don't you think that's funny?' she queried.

But he had leapt forward in his imagination to after they were married. Sex with Polly would be different: she had a wonderful lithe body. Of course he couldn't say that to her, or she'd want to break their celibacy vow. Patience was not her virtue. He smiled and called for the check.

'Yes dear, I think it's funny. Let's go.'

The maître d' brought Polly's coat, and George helped her on with it. Fumigate and exorcize, that's what he'd do, he said to himself. Then they'd be happy. For though Polly was undoubtedly wild, he was sure she'd settle down once they had children. Yes, George mused in a slightly self-satisfied way, life really was rather good.

L.A. Mirage

Toby was a beautiful, happy baby born to Alice and Siegfried Moore and raised on an orchid farm near Evergreen, a small town just south of Denver, Colorado. His family hadn't always grown orchids. Their farm, six years before, had consisted entirely of fir trees, but his father, a third-generation German-American, spotted the irrefutable climate change early and cleverly diversified, and now ran a thriving orchid business which catered mainly to Beverly Hills florists all the way over on the West Coast, in Los Angeles, California. Orchids, while being more work-intensive could, by dint of their size, be protected fairly easily against the frost with greenhouses and Siegfried had devised a revolutionary business plan. He'd suspended operations at his sawmills while he took and recycled seventy windows from a failed soft-toy factory that had been a local eyesore and installed them into the roof and walls of the enormous barn that housed the mill's machinery. Then to complete his vision, he'd purchased a highly efficient cast-iron wood-burning stove from Sweden and converted the barn into a vast hothouse for orchids.

Siegfried wanted Gary and Carl, the two old boys who operated the circular saw and planer, to stay on, regardless of the fact that for almost thirty years they had done nothing but produce quality timber from the trunks of trees. They knew nothing of growing and everything about felling and fashioning wood to their specifications, and were therefore understandably nervous about the proposed shift in their employment, especially as they were tantalizingly close to retirement age. Nevertheless, they trusted Toby's father to see them right and remained open to change and willing to learn. Especially as Siegfried assured them that he'd keep all the sawmill's equipment and workbenches in case his scheme went belly-up.

It didn't. From that moment on the entire Moore operation changed from dramatically noisy to remarkably quiet working days and, while the neighbours' plantations languished, dependent on the Christmas trade, when they sold their young trees at a fraction above basic timber prices, the Moore farm thrived year-in and year-out. Particularly during the festive season when their orchids would fetch higher prices and be delivered a far shorter distance to exactly the same star-studded crowd who migrated annually up the road to Aspen, Colorado.

Toby loved his home and would never have left had he not felt stifled by his parents' adoration. Whenever he found some part-time job to supplement the regular income he was paid for working at the orchid farm, his father would try to give him extra, deflating his ambition and defeating the object of the exercise. Then, God forbid, he'd drop an item of clothing on the floor of his room – his mother would have it laundered, starched and returned to his drawer before he could blink. Not good, as he always wore dungarees that looked totally lame with a perfectly ironed crease down the front.

'Mother,' he'd say, an archaic form of address for a young American on the cusp of the twenty-first century, 'I'm no damn banker.'

'No, but you could be,' she'd retort proudly, 'or a doctor. Or a dot com millionaire. Show me the man who says you can't and I'll show you a fool.'

He'd surrender in the face of such indulgence, chill and feel happy. His friends weren't quite so easy.

'Dude! You're missing the world,' Gary would jeer incredulously. 'Hanging in the nest at nineteen – uh-huh. You gotta do things, dude,' he'd urge, as if the fast-food joint where he worked behind the counter, a few miles away in Denver, was Maxim's restaurant in Paris, France. Toby knew his friend was talking bullshit but still, in the end, it was just this type of peer pressure that finally made Toby leave his comfort zone to try living in LA. People of all types were sucked into that city so, by his reckoning, if he went there the world would come to him; saving a lot of time, effort and money.

He told his folks of his intentions and though he could tell by his mother's eyes and father's veiled hints of danger that they were against his going, they supported him in the end, and arranged for him to stay with his Aunt Aloha, his father's sister.

He set off in Sally, the 1956 Ford pick-up that had belonged to his grandfather. He first had to deliver some orchids to the Jerome Hotel up in Aspen. To drive Sally as far as Denver was risky, to attempt to drive her up to Aspen, then across the continental divide and on another thousand miles to Los Angeles, California, was considered insane by everyone except Toby. He knew all the old truck's noises, what they meant and how to fix them. Every inch of her engine was familiar to him. Besides, he had armed himself with water, oil, a good toolbox, fuses, two spare wheels and an extra fanbelt, so felt fully prepared and supremely confident.

The Jerome Hotel was glamorous, sort of grand and rustic at the same time. It was bang on Main Street, in the middle of Aspen, a small, very up-market ski resort deep in the heart of the Rockies, where all – but all – the rich and famous went. The scale of it, built in 1889, differed from all the other places in town with an impressive, twelve-window-long façade. Whenever he saw it, Toby imagined the changes it must have witnessed since the town's initial gold rush days and the inception of the railroad. As he entered the doors weighed down by his orchids, he saw beautiful girls everywhere, glowing from the crisp air of the slopes. They all looked like A-list actresses, or models, and most probably were, who knew? Toby recognized some – not others – but all were babes. His first cousin Michelle would fit in, he reflected. She was only eleven at the moment and already a successful actress. OK, so not yet A-list but certainly hovering around the Cs. Besides, as her mother, Aunt Aloha, always said, time was on her side. One time when he'd been up with a delivery, Toby had seen Hunter S. Thompson, who was his favourite writer; Jack Nicholson, his favourite actor; and Ed Bradley, his favourite newsman, as they watched Cameron Diaz walk by in the lobby. She stopped and gave Ed a kiss. 'Boy,' Toby thought as he put the large cream zygopetalums, their most expensive orchid, into the big brass tub that sat, strategically placed on the dark, heavy sideboard opposite the entrance. 'It must be nice to be an old man in Aspen.'

The journey to the coast, the way Toby was intending to go, normally took one to three days but with Sally he figured it would be more like five to seven, which was cool as it would give him time to think about where he was heading. He was not so green that he didn't realize that to call Los Angeles a city was to stretch conventional wisdom. Certainly the place was much too big to be described as a town, which was a shame, as that would have made it fit the definition – 'Town *n.* a group of prairie dog burrows' – in the *New Webster Encyclopedic Dictionary*, his favourite book apart from the *Guinness Book of Records*.

Was it a metropolis, then? No way. More like a giant suburb than anything else. Or perhaps the entire conglomeration was simply urban sprawl? Whatever – people flocked there and they all had 'a dream'. Toby didn't. Was that wrong, he wondered, to be perfectly content with who you were?

Having nursed Sally over the continental divide, an endurance test which alone took three days, Toby continued by driving all the way down Highway 91, which ate up another one and a half. He stopped early on the fifth day and in the morning rose with the dawn and drove straight through Vegas with no stopping but a lot of looking. 'Tacky, tacky, tacky,' he thought, taking in the glitz, glamour and underlying desperation of the early-morning clientele, who sat blankly staring into their coffee cups at the diner where he stopped to breakfast. On reaching Barstow, he lay over one last time, in the morning picking up Route 66, which carried him into the heart of Los Angeles. A great trip and, apart from the three nights in the Rockies when it was much too cold, he did all his sleeping in the back of Sally, making her comfortable with the quilts and blankets his mother had thrust upon him before he left.

He stopped at the drive-thru, In-and-Out Burger on Sunset and La Brea. He was feeling excited, looking forward to seeing Michelle and Aunt Aloha. He hadn't seen his little cousin in over three years and wondered how much she had changed and grown. He was also curious to spend time with Aunt Aloha's husband, who never came to Evergreen when his wife and daughter visited. None of Toby's family knew much about him except that he was a Los Angeles city employee who had been on a skiing vacation in Telluride thirty years earlier. Aunt Aloha had met him there then married him after a whirlwind romance. It was done and dusted in under a month. After the ceremony she had moved with her new husband from Evergreen to the San Fernando Valley and there they stayed. Their dining set was farmhouse-style, pine and varnished to a high gloss with fancy curlicues carved into the table legs and the backs of the chairs. They'd won it on the 'Newlywed Show' and the whole ensemble had stood proudly in their dining room ever since, a testimony to their happiness.

Michelle, who'd been conceived *in vitro*, hated the house even though she owned it. She, or her company, had bought it from her parents on the advice of her business managers – who happened to be her parents. The problem was the location. Michelle had regular meltdowns on the subject, which ended with her screaming that she had to move, 'I'm gonna sue and sell, soon as I'm able, coz, like, I'm *not* a valley girl. I suffer mental anguish about it daily. You totally don't get it.'

These rants made for an uncomfortable atmosphere as Aunt Aloha and the husband had made themselves slavishly dependent on their hard-won only daughter in their quest for surrogate glory, and although they knew her teenage tantrums were just a callous phase that would pass, she did have a point. Especially since the film *Clueless* had come out, damning valley girls to universal ridicule. So they caved in and said they lived in Los Angeles. Sometimes they even blurted out Hollywood as their address.

Toby arrived at the door of his aunt's house after eight days of hard driving, including the Evergreen–Aspen leg, to be greeted like the long-lost family that he was. The husband wasn't there but he had helped, Aunt Aloha said, to make the den over for Toby. Michelle, who hadn't grown much at all, was totally over-excited and dragged him through to see his room. It had three dark walls made of nameless wood veneer and a fourth of sliding plate glass that opened out on to a kidney-shaped pool. A queen-size bed had been inflated for him. Michelle grabbed his arm and shouted, 'Get a load of this.' On her instigation, together they hurtled headlong towards the bed, flinging themselves on it with great force and a whoop. As they landed on its fuzzy, rubberized surface, it bounced then skidded off across the purple nylon, shag carpet, the terrific friction causing sparks to follow in their wake.

'Cool.' Toby laughed as they gently hit the far wall and came to a standstill.

'Wanna go again?' Michelle asked, jumping up and down. Toby felt a wave of exhaustion come over him.

'Maybe later Mitch,' he said, flopping back on to the bed, surprised to find it incredibly comfortable.

'Oh sure – sorry. Tired eh? Have a zizz; we'll go again later. See ya,' she cried and ran from the room.

Michelle was cool like that. Apart from her occasional bratty behaviour Toby had always pretty much dug his spirited little cousin who, in turn, hero-worshipped him, which, if Toby was honest, most certainly helped.

Michelle acted in a sitcom, which made her the sole diminutive breadwinner in her household. She played Ruby, the only daughter of a widowed rabbi in the half-hour comedy show entitled 'Oy Vey'. It blew Toby's mind. She was only eleven, for Christ's sake. Toby, fascinated, started going to the TV studio, not surprisingly situated fifteen minutes away in Studio City. Michelle worked there five days a week. A script would be delivered to the house on Sunday night in time for the read-through at 10 a.m. on Monday. After which they'd rehearse for the rest of the week, coming in at 9 a.m. and leaving at 6.30 p.m. or later. As the actors left, the writers' work would begin and they'd start making their adjustments into the night, cutting or adding lines to the script. And so it went every day, up to the last moment on Friday, when they'd tape the show in front of a live audience. The next Sunday another script would arrive and they'd start the whole process over again. Three weeks on – one off, for a whole season, which lasted six months.

The show's format was pretty simple. Awkward, widowed rabbi flounders with his young growing daughter's everyday problems. The only brief given to the writers was that at the end of each half-hour episode showing the rabbi's domestic blunders, they must devise a way to produce a life lesson from the chaos. Michelle, as Ruby, would have to drink this in while showing suitable contrition in the face of her father's superior wisdom. Michelle was eleven but played a nine-year-old in the show, the age she'd been when Toby last saw her. Weird.

The so-called comedy wasn't funny – but Michelle was, as far as was possible with the scripts she got given. Toby started to help his little cousin learn her lines. They ran through them together on set before shooting. When she *dried* (actor-speak for forgetting words, Michelle told him), Toby acted out her dialogue as if they were playing charades. He'd use movements to prompt her memory, so the next time it happened she could refer to his action. Like the first week she kept stumbling on 'believe', substituting it repeatedly with 'think' or 'imagine'. To help her out, Toby put his palms together and raised his eyes heavenwards in earnest supplication. On the day of taping, the audience was in and the dreaded word arrived when Michelle began to freeze, until her body remembered what her brain had forgotten, and she too put her palms together, unconsciously finishing off the action by crossing herself like a Catholic approaching an altar. It got a double take from the rabbi which brought the house down.

Toby's clowning loosened up Michelle's performance. It turned out she excelled in slapstick. Her timing, impeccable to begin with, was enhanced by her newfound enjoyment of the physical process. It made her performance infectious and the quality of the writing almost irrelevant.

Props and Wardrobe started coming to watch the cousins rehearse; they'd split before taping began. Together Toby and Michelle were so spontaneously in step they outshone the show. The producers got to hear of this phenomenon and came down from their office on high to watch Toby and Michelle with Esther, an Armani-clad network executive who was visiting. They noted that when Michelle incorporated Toby's shtick into the mix, she elicited longer laughs from the audience, holding them for an average of fourteen seconds. This made her, unofficially, the star of the show and Toby an important component in her success. They were abuzz about him and his positive effect.

Gearhart, one of producers – the money guy – suggested, 'Why don't we offer him a job as Michelle' s assistant?'

'Not cool babysitting your kid cousin at twentysomething,' the arty producer Scott replied.

Everybody nodded their agreement.

'Why not a country cousin for "sweeps"?' Esther cut in, referring to the week in television when ratings are taken. 'No lines, just a walk-on,' she continued. 'Get this: good-looking, six-foot-six, dumb country boy in jeans, versus our very own petite, sassy, four-foot-two, pre-pubescent Valley Girl, Michelle.'

The next thing Toby knew, he was about to be paid to appear on a sitcom as an actor! Wow!!

According to a scientific study once carried out by a broadsheet newspaper in the UK, adrenalin levels in an actor's body on an opening night in the theatre rise to the equivalent of that experienced by someone involved in a major car wreck. All subsequent performances are comparable to minor prangs. Although Toby was not being asked to do theatre, the sitcom was taped in front of a live audience (the show filmed twice before they let the audience in). And when, eventually, there were bums on seats Toby knew he would panic, convinced his nerves were going to trick him into making a fool of himself.

'No sweat. It's already in the can,' the director kept telling him at the dress rehearsal. Toby, in the guise of his character Zachary, stood paralysed beside the fridge in the very realistic set kitchen, unable to open it and perform his one and only action – glugging the entire bottle of lactose-free milk – as he'd done all week.

'It's fine if you goof, Toby,' the director reassured him. 'Good in fact; makes the audience feel special, like they're privy to a private moment.'

That safety net made no difference. Toby remained frozen, fucking everybody up. If he didn't drink the milk, Michelle – as Ruby – would be able to pour it on her Cocoa Pops, and then she wouldn't have to leave the house and there'd be no story.

'You'll be cool, cuz,' Michelle prattled as she gave her cup back to Props to replace on the counter she was standing by. 'You're so like – gorgeous – you'll be totally down with the girls.'

He smiled at her adoration but it didn't help. All week his mood had been lousy. He'd not been able to sleep, unusual for Toby.

At least he was getting good money. Aunt Aloha had seen to that. She demanded and got one thousand five hundred dollars for Toby for this one week's work – incredible. Now he could pay his own way, which was sort of cool. Except he always had been able to, thanks to his parents. Not to quite the same degree perhaps, but it never bugged him, other people picking up the tab if they insisted on going somewhere fancy. Still, fifteen hundred was a hell of a lot of money whichever way you cut it . . . Definitely something he *should* be pleased about, he thought, concentrating as hard as he could on trying to make his soul ambitious.

As he feared, the end of the week came around all too soon and in what seemed like a nanosecond it was Friday, the day they had to perform in front of an audience. Toby's adrenalin surged and if the level didn't equal that of a road accident it must be have been the same as a near miss. He struggled with the fridge, choked on the milk and it didn't matter. The director had been right; the public fell in love with him, roaring with laughter at his every move. They'd been primed by the warm-up guy, who'd told them that Toby was a real, bona fide country boy. Michelle stuck by his side whenever she could, supporting him throughout the ordeal, even after he'd finished his ten-second scene. Toby surprised himself by finding that he'd enjoyed it in a weird sort of a way. He felt kind of elated, like he'd conquered or climbed to the summit of something.

The bigwigs at the network were delighted by the way this laconic boy had been received. There was something irresistible about his innocence. 'The kid's a natural,' Gearhart stated.

'True,' Scott replied, 'but he's not interested, is he? He's just hanging with his cousin until something better comes along.'

'Let's be that something better then,' said Winter Hardrock, who was the biggest wig of all.

The network approached Aunt Aloha and asked her if Toby would consider doing another episode. Who was he to consider anything, she thought, and negotiated on his behalf.

This time they gave him a line. Only a single word, 'Yup.' After the rabbi asked if he'd closed the door. Of course he hadn't and, when the rabbi's back was turned, a dog snuck in and ate his bowl of chicken soup and matzo balls. A safe laugh as the audience always went for a live-animal gag. But for Toby, that one small syllable was enough to start his nervous system surging up the massive roller coaster of his angst once more, giving him that adrenalin fix again. Getting him hooked.

'It's karaoke-acting kid,' the rabbi said kindly. 'Just say the word and take the money.'

Toby heard from the prop department – always first with the news – that the rumour was, he was going to be made a series regular if he didn't mess up. Bob, head of props, said it was a sure thing.

To be made a series regular is, by any standards, hitting the proverbial gravy train. Toby amazed himself by being thrilled at the prospect. He craved the heightened sense of realism, to feel the fear course through his veins again. The latent desire for success that hung in the air all around him proved contagious. Toby wanted to know precisely what time that train came in the station, and how he could hop on board.

'Hurry up and wait,' Bob said with a wink, his favourite cliché for referring to the baffling pace at which his world in Los Angeles moved. Up until now it had been precisely this never-do-today-what-can-be-rescheduled-tomorrow attitude that Toby liked about the place; it suited his own easygoing ways. But now the star system sucking him in began to make him impatient.

He didn't have long to wait. 'Faster than a speeding bullet,' Bob said in comparison to the way these things normally panned out. In less than three weeks Aunt Aloha hammered out a contract with the network and Toby was making $6,000 a week. An unheard-of sum. That was $6,000 to the lowliest member of the cast. Heaven and Aunt Aloha only knew what Michelle was grossing. It was incredible. He'd hit the mother lode.

When you have more money you're not richer, you just spend more, and when you spend more people notice. That's how Toby got his posse. They were rocking. Together they hit the hotspots. The Billboard was his favourite; it always played good live music and had the advantage of a balcony to which you could escape when the throng of crazies got too wild. As soon as Toby was spotted approaching the club, Mark the doorman (another new friend) would part the hopefuls waiting on the sidewalk to clear a path for Toby. LA really worked when you were hot.

Everywhere they went they were snapped by a barrage of photographers. 'Quid pro quo for the six thousand,' Michelle said, when he told her about his wild nights being captured on film. 'Go for the gusto,' she insisted, 'being dogged by them is good. OK? Jeeze Louise, it's when they stop that you worry.'

Toby did what he was told and went for the gusto and, for a while, he dreamed in strobe lighting.

Soon he needed his own place. It wasn't that Aunt Aloha and the husband weren't cool. This was about Michelle. She was a piece of work, and had taken to bursting into his room any time, night or day, without knocking, and, hey, he was a wanted man now, a chick magnet.

Scott – the artsy producer – and Toby's favourite – found him a place over the hill from the studio in Whitley Heights. It was the ballroom belonging to a grandish, Spanish house from the twenties. Separated from the main building by a terraced garden and pool. The ballroom's entrance was next to the house, through a wrought-iron gate that led down a long perilous flight of stone stairs, originally built for tradesmen to deliver ice. There was no bedroom to speak of, but a minstrel's gallery up at the far end of the vast space had been partially enclosed by a mahogany partition. Behind which, in solitary, if somewhat cramped splendour, stood an ornate Spanish bed. Four grotesque hunchbacks about four foot tall carved from single blocks of wood looked out from each corner, turning the bed into a quasi-four-poster. This beguiling edifice was reached via a spiral staircase. Underneath the gallery there was a small kitchen, separated by a wall with a serving hatch, 'So as you can ice champagne and pass it through,' Scott said wryly when he showed it to Toby.

The house had been built by the legendary producer, A. J. Godt. His wife Lottie still lived over in the main building and Toby had yet to meet with her approval. Scott warned Toby to smarten up and mind his manners, as Lottie could be tricky. But she just peered at him briefly from the top of a sweeping staircase, then turned and nodded at Scott from behind a large crisp white handkerchief, saying she felt 'under the weather'. Scott said that meant he'd passed muster and was in. Toby put down $3,000, standard, Scott said, as in the first and last month's rent, plus a deposit and signed a month-to-month lease. The move was completed within the week.

Toby had never heard of A. J. Godt. Still, he must have been something at the height of Hollywood's glory days. It was like the whole place had been pickled in formaldehyde. Trophies from epic movies were everywhere, if you knew what to look for. A couple of days after Toby moved in Lottie told him that his bedposts were the actual gargoyles from the studio cathedral, in the 1939 film of *The Hunchback of Notre Dame*, in which the actor Charles Laughton (another unknown to Toby) had played Quasimodo. The staircase was from the *Bounty* (as in *Mutiny on*), also starring this Laughton guy as Captain Bligh. Laughton had been a good friend to both her and her husband, Lottie explained.

Toby thought the history of the place genius, and Lottie awesome. She must be at least eighty, he guessed. Her face fascinated him; it was covered in fine lines and looked like one of the pages out of his Rand McNally road atlas. Only her lines represented a comprehensive map of life. Early each morning, she'd waft, very slowly, down through the garden to bathe in her grotto-style pool just below Toby's window. He could tell she had once been a beauty. She still was, actually, always immaculately turned out in something loose, like a high-neck shirt and wide, flowing silk pants. Her grey hair would be scraped back into a severe bun, showing off her high cheekbones, and she invariably had one or two pieces of chunky, vibrantly coloured jewellery hanging about her neck, ears or wrists.

'Don't peek,' she'd trill in case he was awake when she passed. So he didn't. Suspecting – rightly – that she swam naked.

Living alone for the first time was right on. The market was a trip. He couldn't believe it when he went there to stock the icebox – the machine in the tiny kitchen back at the ballroom, although electrified, was way too old to be called a fridge. He'd gone for beers and pre-packed pepperonis, but ended up spending an age at the refrigerated dairy section studying the products. They made him think of his Mom; she would have loved the fat-free cream, butter and mayo and low-cal sugar hanging by the side of the display. Everything she yearned for with none of the calories. Chicks, you had to love 'em and their endless diets, he thought, tickled by the craziness of it all.

Take-out and delivery ruled. As did drive-thru. All the rest of the shit was taken care of by the studio. The props department became his handymen. The show's electricians created seductive lighting for his crib. Even the wardrobe department pitched in and did his laundry every Monday, rendering Aunt Aloha obsolete. So although he sometimes missed the rough and tumble of family, everything was hunky-dory. He saw Michelle every day on the set anyhow, and Aunt Aloha visited often. So truthfully, the pluses (i.e. privacy for sex) far outweighed the negatives, usually . . .

Until months later when, early one morning, he found himself lying in bed with the umpteenth, identical babe of the week. He said identical but who knew? Not Toby. He had little or no memory of the night before and since he couldn't see her face, only her ubiquitous blond hair splayed out across his pillow, she could be one of the million interchangeable women who gravitated to LA. Whatever. The point was, she was snoring and it was bugging the hell out of him. He didn't want to wake her, as he was bored stiff or limp – with fucking. He couldn't hiss her name because he didn't know it. He said 'Hey!' abruptly. Not a flicker.

Understanding there was no hope, he bailed, slithering out of the bed. He tiptoed down the stairs and flopped on to the sofa, where he lay inert, irritated, staring blankly at nothing and grinding his teeth. His eyes were resting, without purpose, on a very long break in the ceiling. It looked like a piece of two-by-four floating independently in the plaster. He saw that there was a millimetre or so of space all around it. Odd, he thought, focusing. 'What the fuck?' Now that he was looking properly, he noticed that there was a sort of step in the ceiling. His interest piqued, he crossed the sprung dancefloor and stood directly beneath the strip. It had to drop down, whatever it was. 'Hold it just a second. Could it be?' He looked up at the panelled partition that hid the bed and for the first time spotted that one square was smaller than the rest. 'You have got to be shitting me,' he thought and went to quiz Lottie.

It was getting light and he hoped she wouldn't be long. He sat poolside surrounded by a luscious mix of roses, ferns and succulents. The garden, created in the thirties, had been tended ever since by the same devoted Japanese gardener. The sunrise reflected against the pool's surface and played on the green of the foliage. In the stillness of LA's early morning, Toby's mind free-floated, landing back at the fat-free foods in the market. How did they suck the fat out anyway? He'd somehow got used to all that kind of artifice, but it was most definitely out of whack, he decided. Like Hollywood. You never knew the skinny in this place. Loads of things, tits, lips, hair, identity, all these everyday things you could name, in this town probably wouldn't be real. OK. So – go figure – not his problem. He lay back and surrendered to the pleasure of the incremental warmth. At least the plants were honest. They got their light from the sun, processed it and grew. No artifice there. On cue, a small breeze rustled through the colossal leaves above his head, flapping them gently. Like elephants' ears. Toby had loved elephants ever since he first saw one in Denver Zoo. He closed his eyes to savour this sublime moment.

'What the fuck,' he thought. His brain and body snapped to attention at the same time. No artifice? What about the water for this abundant *nature*? It came from halfway across the country. Stolen from *his home*, Colorado, then piped hundreds of miles to feed plants that shouldn't be here in the first place. He sat up to examine the garden. Hardly an indigenous species in sight, apart from the sage and that was in a pot! It wasn't Lottie's fault. Her roses were old plants – real humdingers – that had to have been planted when the water was plentiful. Possibly even before the Los Angeles River had been diverted. Anyway, she didn't have acres of thirsty, manicured lawn like the ones that disgusted him every time he drove through Beverly Hills. Toby came from a working farm, even though his family had diversified. Those acres of lawn in the middle of a desert totally shocked him. Conservation was – *so* – not happening here.

Toby's ruminations were cut short moments later as the sun hit the pool fully and Lottie appeared, glorious in an orange caftan with enormous green bangles on both arms. She passed without seeing him and stopped by the diving board, bent forward, crossed her arms and, accompanied by the clanking of Bakelite, grabbed the caftan to pull up over her head. Before it reached her knees, Toby called out in a nervous falsetto, 'Did the ballroom used to be a screening room, Lottie?'

'Why, good morning Toby,' she said, dropping the folds of orange in a delectably demure fashion. 'Yes, yes it did. Well, it was both.'

'Neat.' Toby was grooving on the prospect.

'I had it taken out,' she continued.

'Why?' he cried, bummed.

'The studios used to send us – well, send AJ,' she corrected herself, 'the first print of all the movies. We'd screen them evenings and weekends. Then AJ died.' Toby caught the sorrow in her voice even though the man had been dead like, fifty years. 'I had the projector removed. Come, I'll show you,' she said. 'The projector's still in its box, hidden in a panel behind your bed.' She started walking towards the ballroom.

'Jeezus. Don't bother on my account,' he said, thinking of the blond head on the pillow.

Lottie didn't hear him, she was far too busy remembering. 'I had cards printed up, you know, stiff ones.' She threw Toby a mischievous look. 'I had them hand-delivered to all the studios, informing them that Mrs Godt no longer wished to receive films. I let it be known that I had converted the screening room into a ballroom. I was damned if I was going to allow those young whippersnappers to drop me – it was only a matter of time.'

Lottie really was cool. The nerve of it! To have cards printed up. Genius. He was so busy admiring her, he clean forgot to stop her, and before he knew it, she'd drifted into the ballroom through the door he'd stupidly left open and, being surprisingly agile, was halfway up the spiral staircase.

'Oh shit,' he hissed, drawing in his breath as he saw her stop dead in her tracks on the top step.

'Ex-cuuuuse me,' said an unknown voice in an accusatory tone. Then silence.

Then Lottie's voice: 'Anna-Savannah! Can that be you?'

'Lottie?'

'It is. Well what a turn-up for the books. I haven't seen you in an age,' Lottie cried. She looked down to Toby who was waiting on the bottom step. 'Toby, you dusky mustang.' She went on to ask, 'Where did you find my little friend?'

'Your f-friend?' he stammered.

'Yes, we were at school together.' The blood drained from Toby's face. Lottie burst out laughing. 'Don't look so stricken, silly,' she giggled, 'not at the same time. She was just starting when I was finishing.'

As if that made anything any better. Just then an Ancient with flowing blond hair poked its head over the balustrade. The full, pouting lips parted and to Toby's absolute horror they said, 'Morning, lover.'

'Why don't you two get dressed and I'll make coffee,' Lottie trilled, descending the perfect little stairs towards Toby. Passing him, she shook her head, smiled, winked and patted him, very lightly, on his butt.

Since it was Sunday he couldn't say he was late for something. It was only ten after six in the morning, and he couldn't even pretend he had lines to study because the show was on hiatus, giving them a well-earned break before embarking on another season. If, that is, they got their contract renewed. Nothing was clear-cut in Tinseltown. He didn't want to diss Lottie, but he sure as hell didn't want to go up and confront the Gorgon just to get the rest of his clothes.

'Let me,' he said to Lottie and scuttled, still in his boxers and T-shirt, to the back of the ballroom, where the New World gas stove sat waiting to be lit. Miraculously, when he opened the icebox, he found no milk. 'Can I fetch some from the main house please?' he asked Lottie.

'Surely,' she said sweetly, 'help yourself.'

'Thanks,' he said. Casually sauntering to the door, he fled into the garden. Once out of sight, he collapsed. How the fuck had this happened? Eleven, twelve years younger than Lottie still had to be close to seventy. It just had to be. Jeezus.

When Toby returned to the ballroom, Lottie had already made the coffee and was bringing it out on to the patio, where the small table had been laid with three floral, porcelain cups and saucers. Toby always drank his coffee from a thermal travel mug and never used the china. He nipped up to the scene of the crime and quickly dressed, then came back down to the table and drank his coffee. It didn't feel like he was sitting in his own place at all.

Lottie and the Gorgon were so phenomenally pleased to see each other that they practically ignored him, giving him all the time he needed to study his disaster. He'd fucked up, he could see that, and he could also see why. Anna-Savannah, though almost wholly concocted by the plastic surgeon's knife, had remained, by the skin of her teeth (a horribly apt simile, Toby thought, and shuddered) on the cusp of plausibility. At least he now understood the loss of his sexual appetite and blessed his dick.

First opportunity he bowed out of their reunion. The Gorgon freaked him one last time by calling out as he left, 'Love you, mean it,' in a totally insincere yet lascivious way as he walked out the door.

It was crystal clear to Toby that he was going have to rethink everything. So . . . totally rattled, he hightailed it to Aunt Aloha's and, as he drove Sally into their carport, felt like he was coming home. He hadn't been back in months, since the move in fact, and was excited to be there. No one was up, but that wasn't surprising. It was still only 7.45 a.m. He'd never surrendered his key, which was cool, since he could let himself in. He shut the door behind him and felt his body uncoil as he exhaled. Jeezus, that had been tense. He was doubly grateful for the normality of Aunt Aloha's. No old dames posing as teenagers here, he thought, and giggled at the image.

Going straight through the kitchen to the pool, he stripped off and swam seventy-two lengths, thinking hard all the way, and by the time he stopped he'd reached a decision. He was going to have to leave Lottie's. Boundaries had been blurred. Look at the way she'd patted his butt. It became essential that Aunt Aloha take him back. He didn't anticipate a problem, but what if there was? He tried to see into his old room. Was it empty? It was hard to tell as the sun shining on the glass made it impossible to see through, unless he pressed his nose to the pane, and that, Toby thought, was the way a guy gets shot in Los Angeles. He looked up at his aunt's closed drapes. He needed her awake. How to sell his homecoming? The truth was so humiliating. Maybe he was just going to have to eat craw. Tell it like it was, and beg.

Coffee. The smell of it was sure to seep into one of their dreams and bring them down. He could also help disturb their slumber by opening the doors in the dining room; they squeaked badly in their runners and were right below the master bedroom. He left the water, grabbed a towel and went inside. After flipping the switch on the coffee machine he went on through to the dining room. Empty. Where was the dining set; had they moved it to another room? Only the den was big enough to accommodate a table and six chairs. He went and tentatively stuck his nose through the door. No sign of it. At least he was able to verify that there was no one in his room or . . . was he in the wrong house? Beginning to feel a little panicked, he raced back to the pool and got dressed, then to the entrance hall to check the mail. He saw Frattini in black and white on an unopened bill, so what the hell had happened? He ran upstairs and knocked on Michelle's door. Not waiting for her to answer, he went straight in and found her asleep under her pink satin counterpane surrounded by an array of garish cuddly toys.

'Hey Mitch,' he whispered, shaking her gently.

'Hey cuz,' she croaked, 'what's up?'

'Where's the newlywed stuff?' he asked, coming straight to the point.

'Gone,' Michelle said and turned over.

'Why, where to? When?' he continued, pushing the issue.

'Daddy left, OK? Wanna know why?'

Toby nodded his head vigorously.

'OK,' she said, sitting up in bed, yawning. 'So, like it turns out he was a little light in the loafers. He's been having an affair with a guy in Water and Power. Anyway, Mom was pretty cut up and threw him and the dining set out.'

'How come no one told me?' Toby demanded, miffed.

'Hiatus,' she replied simply.

'Yeah, OK but . . . hello . . . I've still got a cell,' he snapped, wagging his phone in her face. He was trying to stay cool but failing miserably. It was too much on top of everything he'd gone through that morning.

'Whatever,' Michelle shrugged. She pushed him out of the way, heading down to the kitchen, where she poured herself a cup of fresh brew and started weeping.

'Jeez,' he breathed, at a loss as to how to deal with her. 'I'm sorry, Mich,' he said. 'Not cool. You've got enough going on, without me wigging out on you.'

'Will you come with me tonight?' Michelle asked between recuperative gulps and little sobs. 'Daddy was going to . . .' she trailed off and then added, 'It's important and I don't want to go on my own.'

'Where?' he replied; then feeling guilty for asking, said, 'Sure.'

She brightened up considerably.

He spent all that day with Michelle and Aunt A. The husband was never mentioned. Spooky – but that's how they were playing it. He felt sad for them and wasn't so convinced about the moving back thing any more. Sure, he would if they wanted him to, but that wasn't the vibe he was getting. It felt more like they needed their privacy, so he never mentioned it. He didn't need to; he could always sleep in the back of Sally. It wouldn't be the first time.

The 'important' evening turned out to be the opening of a shoe store on Rodeo Drive in Beverly Hills. Toby couldn't believe it. It seemed like a new low to him, and that wasn't all. As they drew up Michelle jumped out of Sally and hit the pavement ready to pose. The photographers obligingly clicked away and called her name. Just before they swallowed her up in their frenzy, she half-turned to Toby and whispered out of the side of her mouth, 'I'm cool. See ya inside.'

He thought that she'd needed him. Wrong. He handed the keys of the pick-up over to the valet parking, who arrived seconds later, with the instructions not to rev her too hard, then sloped around the throng outside the shop, to the top of some low steps just inside the door, where he waited and studied his little cousin basking in the media glare. Some sort of photosynthesis was taking place under the flashes of the cameras – she was growing visibly, inclining towards the light. Craving it, like a plant does the sun. When the photographers had enough, she came towards him glowing.

'Sorry about that, cuz,' she said, rolling her eyes, 'needs must.' Whatever she meant by that, it was bullshit. There was no needs or must to the opening of a shoe store, but he let it slide and took her for something to eat. She had to be pretty broken up, he figured, and gave her the benefit of the doubt.

They went to one of Toby's favourite haunts, Kosta's, a dilapidated Greek restaurant off the beaten track. Perilously close to Lottie's, but too low-rent for her to frequent. They settled into a circular booth facing a large, poorly painted mural of muses dancing around fluted columns in ruined Grecian temples.

'Hi, I'm Wes, your waiter for the evening.' The blond youth fiddled with the place settings while he sized up Toby in a predatory fashion. 'Do either of you guys care for a cocktail before you start?'

'Beer for me. What's yours, Mich?' Toby said, smirking while offering his cousin this under-age opportunity. But

Michelle remained stony-faced, seemingly studying the menu with disproportionate interest.

'One beer coming up.' The flaccid boy minced off to the bar, reappearing almost immediately with the desired beverage and an iced glass tankard. 'Has the lady made up her mind?' he addressed Toby before he deigned to turn to face Michelle. 'How about a nice glass of Retzina? Or maybe an ice-cold Domestica?' he cajoled, performing a full body shiver, presumably in an attempt to make it more appealing.

'How about, like, food, yeah?' she retorted bluntly.

'One moment and I'll be right back to take your order,' he simpered and sashayed off behind the mural, only to re-emerge laden down with plates that overflowed with sizzling skewered meat, which he carried out to the trellised car park that passed for a patio. He stayed out there, hovering around a table pouring drinks, clearing plates and occasionally letting out a scandalized shriek at some comment from one of the all-male diners. He returned to the bar and took them fresh drinks, then hummed a Gladys Knight number as he did a samba around the tables. He was making his way back towards the mural and the kitchens when he was intercepted by Michelle.

'Excuse me,' she called out across the room, knitting her brow as if remembering his face in some elusive memory she'd yet to locate. 'But are you, like, an actor?'

'Why, yes I am,' he replied, coming over to their table, puffed up with pride. She had to have recognized him from his advert for 'Jock itch' playing on cable.

'Good,' she whispered sweetly, breaking into his reveries, eyeing his jugular, 'then please do your job – like *act* – like a waiter.'

The poor guy had no Uzi or bullet-proof vest: it was an easy kill. Looking devastated, he took out his notepad and stood there mute, waiting for them to order.

'Hey dude, do me a favour and come back in a couple, will ya?' Toby asked softly, smiling at the boy and reaching out to pat his arm. The waiter swallowed, acquiesced and shuffled off. Toby turned to Michelle. 'What the hell, Michelle?' He was disgusted. 'That was the brattiest thing I've seen you do. And believe me I've seen some.'

'It was just a joke,' Michelle said. Toby's face remained unbearably cold. 'Look, cuz,' she tried, 'it's just like – I don't need his attitude – OK?'

'What attitude – the gay one?'

'It's got nothing to do with that. I was just goofing.'

'What! Goofing like he's a waiter and can't answer back?'

'I love waiters, OK.'

'Like fuck.'

'Yeah, like fuck. I've known more waiters than I have people in my life.'

'Go to hell,' he said, losing it.

'Come on Toby. Let it go, he's cool.'

'No, Mich. He's not cool. It's not cool. You can't crap on every gay guy in town just coz your Daddy's lied to you.'

'I said it's nothing to do with that,' she shouted.

'Get your coat,' he ordered, finding a five spot to give the poor kid. Michelle started to bawl, but this time he wasn't going for it.

'Please, let me explain,' she blubbed, as the tears, predictably, tumbled from her eyes.

'It better be good,' he said.

'It is,' she replied. Just before her Dad left, the studio had rung her Mom and said how the network weren't going to pick her contract up. 'They think I'm too old,' she whimpered, 'and, like, I'm only twelve, OK? But they still think I'm, like, eleven. Mom fiddled with the birth certificate to keep me under five, OK? And they still don't want me.'

He didn't know what to say. He shunted over and put his arm around her. Over the hill at twelve: it had to be rough.

'So when the waiter offered us drinks without ID-ing me,' she went on, 'I freaked.'

Ironically, had the network seen her now, looking beyond young and vulnerable, they would have signed her then and there. No comfort, especially as he didn't tell her. No point, it could only prolong her agony.

After dropping Michelle back at Aunt A's, Toby went on, ostensibly to return to the ballroom. Instead he drove up to Mulholland Drive, his favourite road; it wound along the spine of the Hollywood hills. A full moon was shining, giving everything a perfect, albeit blue, clarity. 'Genius,' he thought. Indigo photography. He parked at a bend in the road where he could see the lights of Los Angeles shimmering on one side and those of the San Fernando Valley on the other. Pasadena and the San Gabriel Mountains were more than visible across the valley. Even the snow on the faraway peaks was distinct, like white under ultraviolet lighting. He kicked back in Sally and closed his eyes. What, he wondered, should his next move be? He understood the pull of celebrity, he was certain he'd felt that same chemical change he'd observed in Michelle working on him, and he wasn't sure he liked it. He realized if he hung about much longer he'd lose the luxury of choice. Buy into a class-A drug for too long and you get hooked. Buy into the concept of class-A celebrity and who knew? Besides, if 'Oy Vey' had no Michelle that should mean no show in Toby's book. She was blood and blood mattered.

'Needs must,' he remembered, trying to smile for the cameras.

'Hey,' they called out, vying for his attention.

Knock, knock on glass. He turned this way and that.

Knock, knock. The glare made smiling harder but he kept trying. KNOCK, KNOCK. The lights were blinding him.

'Hey.'

'Hi,' he said, putting on his best matinee idol smile.

'Put your hands where we can see them and step out of the vehicle.' The voice was accompanied by the sound of Sally's door being wrenched open and the unmistakable click of a revolver's hammer as it pulled back. Toby entered full consciousness to a maelstrom of activity. The cop's flashlights were trained on his eyes and the helicopter's searchlight was sweeping the hillside for accomplices. He stumbled out and was frisked by strange hands. The voice belonged to a mean-looking cop. When he spoke again the hysteria had gone. 'We need to see a driver's licence and insurance.'

'Got it,' another voice said.

Toby squinted out of the harsh pool of helicopter light and saw a kinder-looking man holding documents he'd retrieved from the glove compartment. He was studying Toby with curiosity. 'Hey, aren't you the kid from that show . . . what's its name?'

'Doesn't matter – but yeah – yeah I am,' he mumbled.

'Well, you can't sleep here, son,' the soft cop said.

'We got big stars here,' the mean one continued, presumably trying to diminish Toby. 'Jack Nicholson, Marlon Brando, and they don't need bums on their doorstep.'

His uncalled-for hostility was beginning to get to Toby when the good cop cut in. 'Just move on, kid, and don't let us find you here again.'

Toby saw sense. He obeyed the order and drove away, more empty than angry. He was heading towards the mountains and he drove as far as Pasadena without feeling any desire to stop. He crossed over to the Golden State freeway and kind of doubled back on himself, to the 99, following signs for Bakersfield. He didn't know where he was going, nor did he care. It didn't matter. He had a full tank of gas and he needed out.

The further he got from LA the better he felt. He saw signs pointing to places he couldn't trust, like Magic Mountain or Pyramid Lake, and weirdness like hilltops sliced off and replaced with pre-fabricated houses covered in orange stucco. They didn't exactly bother him, but were pretty gross and did make him wonder, momentarily, what kind of person would choose to live there. Maybe they caught the breeze up high, he thought, stopping for a piss in the sweltering stillness. Then Sally started to climb and climb, straining as much as she'd ever done. They were attempting the Grapevine Pass, quite a thing for a 1956 Ford and when, valiantly, she made it to the apex, he stopped to give her water and rest. He took out his sleeping bag and made it into a cushion for his back, so he could lean against the rock that held a plaque telling them they'd climbed to the summit. He scanned the horizon for the city he'd left behind. The sun was just starting to rise on his left and he thought he could make out the shimmer of lights way, way off, in the far, far distance – or was it a heat haze. As he stared, he felt strands like cobwebs straining, breaking throughout his brain. A dense fog was lifting and a certain clarity returning. Up here the question of what he should do seemed easier. Whether to return to Los Angeles or not became an irrelevance, as the very existence of the place was being put into visual question. Perhaps far from being a city LA was simply an amalgamation of everybody's imagination. OK, Toby thought, running with the concept, that would make it like . . . hey . . . wow . . . what *was* that?

Jack

Ellie was over twice his age when they first met at her house in north London, a mother to two young children, Louis and Maria, while Jack was her son's best friend.

She'd been happy with her lot as a mother, even though she'd had to give up music, which was her passion, to raise them. She still played the violin, just never attained her dreamed-of career. She rationalized her loss, admitting to herself that she most probably wouldn't have been a success anyway. How many from the conservatory were? Only one student had stood out, and she'd married him. No, Ellie was competent, but that was about it.

Music had always played a large part in their life as a family. Even the children's names were taken from two of their favourites, Louis Armstrong and Maria Callas. Hal, her husband, was a top-notch conductor. He used to organize acappella sing-songs with the children, when they'd harmonize as only blood can, four facets of the same voice. It made the hairs on all who heard them stand up with its perfection. Then there were the hoolies, as Hal liked to call them, when friends of all ages, creeds and colours came to visit and everyone would pick up an instrument, even if it were only a tambourine, a pot or a pan, and play and sing into the night. Ellie would lose herself in the fiddle on such occasions, playing as if her life depended on it. Those were the times when her children saw her for the person she felt herself to be, rather than solely as their mother. She never realized it, but that's what happened.

When Jack started coming round, he had just turned fifteen. A shy boy of no obvious merit, save a gentleness that perhaps belied a mild form of autism. This seemed to contribute to, rather than detract from, the fact that he was a musical prodigy. For when you set him before an instrument, any instrument, he came alive, and that's how, flying in the face of peer pressure and ridicule, he'd grown close to her nine-year-old son. Jack needed musical companionship and Louis – a bit of a prodigy himself – despite the six-year age gap, provided it. Unusual as their union was, Ellie ultimately approved of her son's odd, silent, older friend.

Her life had proved a happy swap: passion, recognition and glory for family, love and security. The only trouble was, glory and recognition had come to her husband in spades, and now as the children were leaving her, so was Hal.

She could of course have gone with him, to Vienna and Paris, to New York or Milan, but when she tried, it awoke in her the uncomfortable unknown emotion of envy. Not a feeling she espoused with gusto and, as Hal's work took precedence, he gradually became an absentee husband.

It didn't matter that much as the children had grown up and their job as parents was now effectively done. Still, it was the first time in her life that Ellie had been alone, having gone straight from home to marrying Hal. Louis was on a world tour, playing lead guitar in a band opening for the Rolling Stones, and Maria, a medical undergraduate, had volunteered to work for ASAP, an African-based charity, in her holidays. Consequently, Ellie was rightly, if cautiously, proud of her them and although mindful of the fact that pride really does seem to come before a fall, as far as she could see – and she'd looked pretty hard – they seemed to personify happy, rebellious, gilded youth.

She'd let them go, relinquished them at the appropriate time, and though it hurt to do so, she was comforted by the near certainty they'd return home if they were in trouble.

On her own for the first time, she was horrified to admit that she felt just as convinced of her own inadequacies, no wiser or better equipped to deal with life than she had been at age seventeen. Without the constant responsibility of Hal or her children, physically present for an anchor, she felt every bit as adrift. Left to her own devices, she started getting up late and stayed in her pyjamas, erroneously thinking they could pass for clothes, wearing them to the Portuguese patisserie on the corner, where she'd have a cake, then return home and not necessarily bathe each and every day as she'd been wont to do her whole life. Not that she let herself go or was dirty, she thought. No, she'd just become a little more relaxed, that's all.

Enjoying her own company, she began to spend more time at the weekend cottage in Shropshire. She read a lot, a luxury, as any mother would acknowledge. Then, branching out, she obtained satellite television and quickly became obsessed. It was her introduction to the onslaught of the junk-culture she'd fiercely guarded her children against. Knowing it to be addictive, she'd always imposed a strict limit on their viewing hours when they were still at home, realizing that however good the programme, their imaginations would serve them better, and should be encouraged in any way possible.

She watched 'Jerry Springer' and the Hallmark channel for three months solid. Then, reluctantly surfeiting, she came out the other side, which is when she returned to music, and Jack came back into her life.

Jack and Louis had grow apart when the six-year age difference became a chasm that couldn't be bridged or ignored, but they joined back up again on the other side as young adults, although never, quite, obtaining the same degree of closeness. Their musical tastes had diverged: Louis's had stayed purely rock and roll, while Jack's encompassed jazz, bluebeat, classical – the lot, in fact. So while they'd remained good friends, their lives no longer followed the same paths, nor did their aspirations.

Jack hadn't achieved, or sought, the high profile of Louis. He wasn't a performer, but a composer and session musician, one of the best, in constant demand, paid handsomely for his talents and more than happy to stay in the background, writing the songs that others sang. She'd hear of his progress via Louis, and then one day he turned up on her doorstep.

Having been commissioned to write a rock opera, no less, and finding it a daunting task, he'd decided to isolate himself, and took a cottage over the hill for three months. After a couple of days of fruitless toil he thought that perhaps physical exercise might unlock the muse and walked over to see the place that housed so many happy memories of his youth, not expecting anyone to be there mid-week. Cresting the brow of the hill, he'd been intrigued to see smoke billowing out of the chimney from the cottage below and went down to investigate. Ellie was delighted and invited him in immediately.

And in this innocuous way, a new and rare friendship formed, an adult one. It was a first for Ellie, one that took some getting used to. She'd never known that transition when children become peers, and she found it hard not to mother this young stranger. Seeing Jack as a child still, she retained the compulsion to entertain and nourish, as if time on his hands, a missed meal, or the lack of stimuli, would stunt his growth or lead to trouble as it invariably does with most adolescents. But over time she relaxed and they sidled into a friendship that shared as a basis a common love for her children. Jack was someone she could talk to when she missed them, he understood the family shorthand, knew Louis and Maria almost as well as she did, and could swiftly allay her fears about them with the aid of his own insider knowledge. They started having dinner together most nights. Afterwards they played music, backgammon, gin rummy or scrabble, watched TV, or swapped favourite books, which they'd sometimes read to each other aloud. Gradually it began to dawn on her how much she enjoyed his visits; she had almost come to rely on them, which in turn made her nervous.

Why did he come here most evenings? What did he want, apart from food? He ought be going to the local pub or something, mixing with people his own age. A small, almost imperceptible tension crept into the relationship, yet still he turned up on her doorstep, and still she invited him in. The unease grew, but there was nothing she could put her finger on and ask him without feeling foolish and running the risk of losing her new friend. Yet surely there was something wrong when someone she thought of as a boy, even though he must now be well into his late twenties, was spending the majority of his time with a woman of fifty. She let it slide, as much out of loneliness as anything else, and decided to live in the moment. Life, she figured, had a way of righting these things all of their own accord.

This state of affairs carried on for six weeks, the ignored tension growing worse every minute. They both knew they were dicing with danger, yet both studiously ignored it.

Until one evening, as they sat, bellies full, around a crackling fire. A storm raged outside. They were sitting there all toasty when the lights went out. A power cut. This happened quite often and Ellie went to the kitchen for the candles she stored in the drawer by the sink. It was empty. Annoyed with herself, she returned to the room where Jack was sitting silhouetted against the fire to enlist his help. There was a kerosene lamp in the attic, but the extendable ladder providing access was perilous, unless someone was holding it, she said, especially without light. Asking as nonchalantly as possible for his help, Ellie tried to ignore the unmistakably charged atmosphere in the room. He answered in the same vein and together they climbed the narrow stairs.

How it transpired, she wasn't sure. Although with hindsight the danger had been obvious. 'An accident waiting to happen' she thought, watching him sleep. She replayed the events in her mind. He pulled the ladder down on to the tiny landing at the top of the stairs, and she had to squeeze her body past his to climb it. They had been forced to touch.

But neither forced what followed. With that one spine-tingling moment of physical contact they'd turned into animals, each as fevered as the other. There was no question of stopping. Passion, lust, hunger and the desire to satiate all three took over. They made love for hours, each delighted with the other's pleasure, and when at last they'd had their fill and fallen asleep, their bodies intertwined, they were filled with the calm that good lovemaking can bring.

Now it was 4 a.m. and here she was, hunched on a wooden, straight-backed chair in the corner of the bedroom, as far from him as possible, filled with remorse and guilt. Jack was a baby, for God's sake. She was definitely to blame. It was practically rape, she convinced herself in her turmoil. What now? She must definitely wake him up and explain the dreadful error they'd made, the carnal sin they'd committed. She looked at him for a long time, lying there, naked, in deep repose, so beautiful and peaceful, his angelic face framed in short, soft curls with one perfectly defined arm flung out across the vacant pillow, as if waiting for her.

Taking a deep breath, she steeled herself, crossed the room, sat on the very edge of the bed as quietly as possible and began to whisper his name. Getting no reaction, she leaned over and gently pushed the curls back from his brow. 'Jack,' she said again, as softly as before. He mumbled something, swallowed, turned his head from side to side, fighting his way out of the inky pool of sleep into which he'd sunk. Then suddenly surfacing he saw her, and his face switched from passive tranquillity to active joy in the matter of a moment. 'Good morning, beauty,' he said, pulling her to him.

'Jack,' she said with an effort, turning away.

'What is it, my love?' he said, kissing the back of her neck.

'This wasn't the plan,' she thought, as she succumbed and they started all over again.

Over the next month she tried to muster her resolve and block him out of her life. Then he'd appear at her door and she'd invariably melt with little or no resistance. He was like a drug. All her life she'd had only one lover, her husband, and never found sex that pleasurable. Now it was patently clear to her that she had never experienced an orgasm until Jack. Which made it near impossible for her to give him up.

The time was fast approaching when Louis would be coming home. She longed to see him and hear all his adventures, but what about Jack? Louis, hopeless at keeping in touch, had made it easier for Ellie to forget the reality of sleeping with his best friend. To ignore the reality, more like. Now it was upon her; the tour had only three more dates left to play. The penultimate one, in the NEC Arena, in Birmingham, was at the end of the month and she'd promised to see it.

'We'll go together,' Jack said.

'Are you mad?' she replied.

'Why? We're in love, aren't we? Louis will be happy for us,' Jack said in all innocence.

Ellie felt panic at the thought of her son finding out. She started to breathe too fast, too many shallow gasps. Each was inadequate, never filling her lungs. Tears threatened; she blinked them back furiously. Jack saw her difficulty and came over to comfort her, stroking her hair and shushing her as if he were her equal, his face a picture of naïveté and optimism. 'It's OK, darling. We always used to talk about how badly Hal treated you, all his affairs and everything. We felt so sorry for you. He stifled your creativity, made you a dull housewife when you should have been an artist.'

'What?' Ellie said, aghast.

'Louis hated it,' Jack went on, 'said if Hal hadn't been his father he'd have killed him. So don't worry about him, he'll be thrilled.'

She couldn't believe what she was hearing. This boy and her son talking about her . . . always. Labelling her a dull housewife and discussing Hal's affairs?! Something snapped. Guilt at their forbidden sex, mixed with lust and frustration over her lost career and the shock at being cuckolded, rose up in her throat like bile and she broke under the poison.

'Who in God's name do you think you're talking to?' she snarled, quivering with humiliation. 'What do you think I am? Oh yes of course, some "dull housewife"! Well for your information I've always known about Hal,' she lied. 'Just as he's known about me. None of it mattered, they were just diversions on both sides. Like you are now.'

Jack looked incredibly contrite and laid his hand on her shoulder. 'I'm sorry, Ellie,' he whispered. 'I've hurt you, the last thing in the world I meant to do. That was stupid of me.'

'You said it,' she spat, swiping away his hand. 'And while we're on the subject of who said what, we always said you were simple . . . autistic. We laughed together over Louis's idiot friend.'

'I am,' he replied simply, 'slightly. I've a very mild form of Asperger's syndrome but it's manageable, and I love you. I always have and I think you love me and I don't believe you laughed.'

This was too much: this dear, sweet, shy boy, getting it so right, taking her insults and willingly admitting something so momentous to ease her pain. It was disarming, and made her want to hold him in her arms and kiss away her cruelty. This made her panic worse, which in turn made her more vicious.

'Love you. You really are simple, aren't you? Can't you get it through your thick skull that you're just an amusement? Now get out of my house,' she screamed, hitting him again and again, unable to stop.

'I'll go,' he said, locking eyes with her and demanding the truth. 'But first give me one good reason why, apart from Louis.'

An inhuman calm descended on her. 'Listen carefully then,' she said precisely, holding his stare, 'everything I ever found attractive or delightful about you now repulses me.' A wicked, wicked lie. His eyes flickered, lost their fatal hold, his head dropped and he turned and left. She sat down trembling from head to toe, yet curiously devoid of emotion; it must have been scared out of her, she thought.

That afternoon she left the cottage, and returned to London. The fortnight leading up to Louis's triumphant homecoming passed in a lethargic haze. Horrified into inertia, each and every day seemed interminable. She could neither eat nor sleep and felt like a somnambulist, senselessly floating through time. She replayed the events of that morning over and over, disgusted at her own villainy. Ironically these were also the only times she felt alive, when she was reliving those ghastly moments or when she was so tired, she let herself remember the good times they'd had together. She must love him, she thought again and again. Then again and again she rejected the feeling. It wasn't possible. It would be too great a sin.

All too soon it was Louis's day. She had to drive to Birmingham that evening, see him play before bringing him back home. Dreading it, she summoned what little strength she had to bathe and dress. Looking at her reflection in the full-length mirror she was shocked by what she saw, a shadow of her former self. She must have lost a stone at least. Her eyes, accentuated by the surrounding dark circles, had sunk back into her head. She looked ghastly and did her best to camouflage her appearance by carefully applying make-up, then, with little or no enthusiasm, set off up the M1.

Arriving at the NEC she almost turned to head back for home; it was so crowded and she felt sick. Remembering she hadn't eaten, she went to the concession stands and purchased a pint of Guinness and a hot dog. She took one bite before she retched and threw the rest away, although downing the entire contents of the plastic beaker containing the black liquid made her feel immeasurably better. Her stomach calmed and a tingle of anticipation at the thought of seeing Louis perform crept up on her. Guinness really is good for you, she thought, buying another and making her way into the auditorium. She kept drinking to keep it from spilling, no hardship as every gulp made her feel more three-dimensional, more able to cope. She hadn't felt so good in ages. Eventually locating her seating block, she excused her way past the people already settled in her row, focusing on the spot her son would soon occupy. His guitar and microphone were already there waiting and, when she arrived at her allocated seat, she found it was perfectly positioned to see him play. No doubt he'd arranged that when he gave her the ticket.

The stadium began filling up. Louis had told her this had started to happen, that his band, Narik, had gathered a following by word of mouth during their months on the road. The audience began a slow handclap. They were ready for something to happen and so was Ellie. Until, all of a sudden, she was acutely aware of the vacant place next to hers, the only empty seat in her section. It could be for only one person, she realized, and passed out.

She was startled awake by the crowd's chanting 'Sympathy for the Devil'. Disorientated, she took it personally and, stumbling to her feet, fought her way along the row of enraptured fans in their seats like a thing possessed. Halfway she realized the chant was simply a request for one of the Stones' songs, although in her present state she still couldn't help feeling the demonic words were a sign, an omen directed at her, and battled her way against the flow of people, to ask an enormous security man the way backstage. She wanted protection from her son, whose performance she'd completely missed.

After she had shown him her 'All Access' pass and identified herself as Louis's mother, the man introduced himself as 'B. C.' and escorted her to her son's side. He was standing in the dark on the side of the stage, watching Mick Jagger's performance. The noise was deafening and Ellie had to tap him on the shoulder to be noticed. 'Mum,' he screamed, hugging her. 'Did you like it?'

'You're wonderful,' she bellowed truthfully. 'I'm very proud of you.'

He beamed, scanning the dark recesses behind her. 'Where's Jack? He promised he'd be here.'

She shrugged, feeling queasier than ever, and put all her concentration on the stage.

The drive back proved surprisingly easy. Ellie had been nervous about it for weeks, sure she was going to be in for the third degree, but Louis was so full of himself and his last six months on the road, all the countries and in-house scandals he'd experienced. It had been an enormous operation involving a relatively small cast of incestuous characters, and even she found herself vaguely diverted. While she was intensely relieved that he didn't notice the enormous change in her, she also couldn't help feeling a tiny bit resentful. Yet what child would notice, she reasoned. You saw your mother as a constant source of stability and that's the way it should be.

Down at the cottage that Sunday, she cooked Louis his favourite lunch: slow-roasted lamb with a couple of tins of flageolet beans emptied into the juices of the roasting dish after the lamb was out, then put back in the oven to warm through while the meat rested on the side for ten minutes. She followed it with treacle sponge and double Devon cream.

'Cool. Thanks Mum,' Louis said as he saw the steaming pudding. 'I've been dreaming of eating exactly this for the last six months.' He got up and gave her a big hug and a kiss.

The telephone rang. It was Hal calling for the first time in ages. He wanted to know if Louis was safely home and to talk to him. His production in Madrid was passable, he told Ellie, fun enough but not worth a trip and he couldn't wait to get back home soon . . . he hoped. Some girlfriend was delaying him no doubt, she guessed, finding it hard to believe that she'd never suspected him before, and her kernel of resentment grew. She passed the receiver to Louis, who wandered out in the garden to talk to his father in the sunlight.

Clearing the kitchen, she acknowledged the part she had played in facilitating Hal's behaviour by refusing to accompany him abroad. There are classical groupies too, she thought, recalling her son's tales of a musician's life on the road with all its temptations. She loaded the dishwasher as her inner monologue swung back in her favour. He didn't have to be so blatant though. Louis knew and gossiped with Jack about how pathetic she was. Did Maria know too? No, not her daughter, who checked in without fail from God knows where every week. She couldn't. Or, maybe she did and also thought her mother was just a joke, a stupid, downtrodden, cheated-on, old joke. That wasn't true. Ellie remembered the unsolicited hug Louis gave her ten minutes ago, just in time to save herself from descending into unreasonable paranoia. No. It wasn't they who had changed, but she, herself. Having given Hal his freedom, he had gratefully taken it and now she must bear the fruits of her benevolence and, truthfully, lack of interest.

A few days before Hal did eventually return, Louis came in full of the news that Jack had a girlfriend. 'I'd never have believed it of him,' he said, roaring with laughter. 'He never showed any interest in anyone, girl or boy . . . except . . . well, to be honest, I always thought he had a crush on you.'

'Don't be silly,' she said and went into the laundry room, turned on the dryer and cried.

The girlfriend was someone Ellie had seen around for a long time; she'd always been on the periphery of Louis's gang. Tam was her name. Louis used to say she was on the make, an aspiring singer, not quite good enough, always trying to worm her way into different bands he knew. She was of mixed race, pretty enough and usually wore a turban, which had struck Ellie as affected even before she started hating her. Jack would be invaluable to a girl like her, Ellie thought bitterly, a brilliant musician happy to stay in the background and let her shine. 'Stop,' she reprimanded herself, 'it's not right to be jealous; I'm old enough to be his mother. Tam's perfect for him; they're the same age, share the same interests, for heaven's sake.' Even so she wanted to ring him and try to get him back. 'You're disgusting,' she argued. 'Be happy for the boy and, anyway, I can't. He's Louis's friend.'

She bumped into them once, in her local street market. It was awkward. Tam draped herself all over Jack as if some sixth sense told her she was under threat. Ellie feigned enthusiasm at their union, while Jack seemed desperate to prolong the meeting. Or was that her fond imagination? It didn't matter as she could keep up the front only briefly before saying in a light-hearted way, 'You should come over. Hal's back and I know he'd love to see you. Bring Tam.' She walked on with an unmistakable bounce in her step that disappeared the moment she rounded the corner. 'Stupid, stupid, stupid thing to say,' she thought and crept into a pub, where she ordered a double brandy and sat staring blankly at the walls for a long time.

When Hal did finally come home Ellie was waiting and set on him, ravishing him in a way he could never have imagined his wife of twenty-six years capable of doing.

'Ellie,' he moaned, 'I should go away more often.'

She was too busy to answer, trying – and failing – to fuck the anger and heartbreak out of her system.

The next morning she told him she needed a divorce. She wanted nothing, she said, except the cottage.

'But why?' he asked, taken completely by surprise.

'Because I know everything,' she answered.

And that was it. He acquiesced with no more discussion, save of how and when to tell the children. What in heaven's name had he been up to, she wondered? But not for long as, honestly, she didn't care.

Her life now officially in ruins, she retired to the cottage to try and find a way to carry on. Louis and Maria came down and did their best to be supportive. They were adorable and though she was touched by their concern – Hal had told them that their mother was going through the change of life, and Ellie had refused to be drawn on the subject – neither knew the real reasons behind the break-up, therefore how could either help?

Each day Ellie wanted to ring Jack, tell him she was free and prepared to face her children and the world with him by her side, but she didn't. She did, however, inquire of him through Louis on the phone. She couldn't trust herself to ask in person. 'He's still with Tam, Mum, can you believe it?' Then, being the loyal friend he was, Louis caught the tone in his own voice and added, 'I've come round to her a bit, been laying down a guitar track for them. Jack's recording a couple of his songs with Tam singing . . . they're not bad.' Ellie could tell her son was lying, but didn't press him further.

Early the next morning, sitting at the window in the cottage, drinking coffee while staring out and trying, as she did every morning, to find some motivation for the day, she spotted someone up on the top of the hill. It looked remarkably like Jack. Her heart leapt; she stood up and went to the door, shading her eyes with her hand against the morning sun. The figure stood still, looking in her direction, she thought but couldn't be sure, then turned and walked away. She wondered whether to go and check the cottage he had taken in the spring, before deciding she was crazy. He was happy, as she knew all too well, recording his songs with that vile woman. Why was she torturing herself?

A few mornings later, she imagined she saw him again and this time determined to go and speak with him. Quickly perfecting a casual, I-happen-to-look-like-this-every-morning sexiness in the hall mirror with the aid of some lip balm and a little rouge, she opened the door to catch him, when who should draw up, scuppering her plan with his mid-life-crisis red roadster but Hal, parking between her and the figure on the hill.

She hadn't seen or heard from her husband for weeks. He opened the car door and, before getting out himself, passed her a tin of caviar, a bunch of flowers (very excessive and incongruous for the cottage), and a bottle of vintage – he was careful to point out – champagne. She could tell he was taken aback by her appearance; the children had probably exaggerated and told him that she was neglecting herself. Clambering awkwardly out of his status symbol, he scuffed his feet on the gravel, hugged her, then asked if they could talk. He needed to, he said. Over his shoulder Ellie saw the figure on the hill turn and disappear.

As much as she didn't want to, she felt she had to invite Hal in. Accepting with alacrity, he went straight, unbidden, to the kitchen, where he sat down, opened all the gifts that he had taken back from her at the door and proceeded, while eating and drinking voraciously, to tell her how much he missed her, although she had been right about the other women.

'*Women*,' she thought. 'Jack was right. *Was* that him on the hill?'

'They mean nothing to me,' he said. 'It's the challenge, a sickness, the thrill of the chase, simply that, Ellie. Nothing more, I promise.' Then he tried to explain that what they had was different – special. 'Love is like a cruise around the world, darling, on a beautiful sailing ship and my peccadilloes are simply ports that I occasionally have to pull into overnight, to replenish the stores.'

Though singularly unmoved by the analogy, Ellie almost fell for the effort Hal put into telling it. After all, that's how he'd won her in the first place, by spinning fantasies. He'd never grown up; look at him now, sitting opposite her in the little kitchen, so desperate to try to sell his absurd theory that she found herself comforting him. One thing inevitably led to the other, they were so familiar with each other and it seemed churlish to refuse. Besides, old habits are hard to break and they ended up in bed together. He tried to deliver her to ecstasy with hitherto unheard-of solicitude, but for all his efforts their lovemaking left her cold. She made the excuse of being hungry to leave the bed and went down to the kitchen.

It was still only about 1.30 on a beautiful English summer's day. She put a pan of water on the stove and sat in her customary place, waiting for it to boil, gazing out of the window to where she thought she'd seen Jack, wishing she could run from the house and go to him. She remembered poor Hal upstairs. She knew he loved her in his way, and realized their separation was ruining his life, depriving him of a wife to cheat on. Who was it who said, 'When you marry your mistress you create a vacancy'? One of those Frenchmen, she'd wager.

Amused at her own objectivity, her train of thought was abruptly broken by a shy little brown bird, of no obvious merit, save an inquisitiveness verging on stupidity, which permitted it to hop in through the window and brazenly stand on the draining board watching her, tilting its head every which way, ostensibly to study her better. She watched it watch her, each one as fascinated as the other. After a moment or two it hopped chirruping from the draining board on to the far end of the table where she sat. She could hardly believe its boldness and held her breath while it came forward. The nearer it came the more she was awed; such a cheerful, inquisitive, bright little creature with its touchingly nondescript plumage.

'What do you want, little thing?' she asked, as it hopped around, chirping at her as if trying to communicate. 'Are you hungry?' she asked, remembering as a child how she'd nursed baby birds that had fallen from their nests, but this was an adult. 'I have no worms,' she said, 'perhaps you'd like milk?' As quietly as she could, she went to the fridge and filled a saucer with some milk, crumbled bits of bread into it and placed it at the end of the wooden refectory table. Slithering back down into her chair, she edged the saucer slowly forward, towards her unexpected guest. The bird was not at all put off by the movements of this giantess and continued to watch her with an intensity that more than puzzled Ellie. It half-jumped-half-flew over to the saucer, examined the poor fare she'd provided and stuck its beak in, apparently out of sheer politeness, for it didn't appear to take any, then hopped ever closer.

'You must be tame,' she said, but could see it was wild. 'Maybe you're hurt?' She knew it wasn't. 'What's wrong with you, eh?' She picked up the saucer and put it on the window ledge outside. 'Don't you know how to escape?'

It followed the saucer, but showed no desire to go further. She shut the window, leaving it on the outside, and they both stayed looking at each other through the pane of glass for a while, before it flew off. 'What a curious little fellow,' she thought, reopening the window as the water boiled.

'It's nearly ready,' she called up to Hal, putting the pasta in the pan, and getting out a jar of pesto. Poor Hal, she thought, picking up where she'd left off before the strange visitation. She was going to have to tell him their ship had been dry docked or sunk or something. He appeared at the door, confident she was his once again and that life, as he knew it, was back to normal. How was she to disabuse him? She had no wish to crush him, any more than he did her. Hal had deceived her, yes, but he'd never been intentionally cruel.

Ease into it, she thought, and started to tell him of the strange little bird, intending to work her way around to explaining how happy she was on her own in this cottage with only nature for companionship. This was, after all, the truth – if she couldn't be with Jack. Barely had she finished her description, when the bird flew back in through the open window and landed as before, on the draining board. Only this time it was singing a very different song, one of fury. There was no mistaking the tone and it seemed to direct its ire at Hal.

'Have you ever seen anything like that?' she asked. 'I'm so frightened it'll hurt itself. I've put it out once. What can I do?'

'Get a cage,' Hal replied, damning himself further in Ellie's eyes. She reminded herself she was going to be nice whatever the provocation.

'I suppose if it doesn't want to leave, I could get a pretty little cage but I'll never ever shut the door,' she said firmly and placed two full plates of pasta on the table.

The little creature flew up on to the wooden clothes rack that hung above the Aga and sat there watching them. They ate in silence. Ellie never said any of her intended speech, she was afraid there might be a row and didn't want to disturb the little bird. Instead she waited until they'd finished, then made do with asking him to leave, saying she had things to do, and suggested, politely yet pointedly, that Hal ring the next time he was thinking of coming to visit. She'd deal with it then, she thought, shutting the front door on him without a kiss.

She couldn't go to Jack now, if indeed that had been him on the hill, as she was sure she had the aura of sex about her. Whether or not she had found it enjoyable was irrelevant. How could she look him in the eye so soon after the act? She returned to the kitchen. The little bird was still there and flew down to hop about, chattering happily while she washed up.

'I wonder if you would like a little cage,' she said. 'I'll try and find one tomorrow. Look at me, I'm talking to a bird.' She shook her head in disbelief. 'You know I do love him, Jack that is, not the man who's just left, although he is father to my children. Do you think that's wrong? Loving Jack. He's very young, and my son's best friend, but he makes me feel . . . Oh I don't know, but I definitely love him; is that crazy?' She started laughing. 'About as crazy as me talking to you. OK, little friend, I'm going to Shrewsbury to buy you something to eat. And stuff for Jack and me. God willing he's there. Be safe and please, please stay. You'll love him.'

She left and drove straight to the tiny health food shop in town, presided over by Debs, the owner, a dear old hippy, who'd been her friend for years, ever since the early days of recycling when Ellie, as a fledgling customer, had seen a stacked pyramid of brownish loo rolls, a banner swirled across each packet announcing that it had been used before. Fantastic, Ellie thought and bought the entire stock to distribute among her friends, vastly relieving Debs as it had sat gathering dust on her shelves for months. Debs wasn't in, but as Ellie suspected, the shop did stock millet, and she bought a bag, before going to see if the antiques shop had a birdcage. Drawing a blank, she returned home filled with anticipation at tomorrow's potential reunion with Jack.

As soon as she entered the kitchen the bird came flying down from his perch on the clothes rack. 'Oh good, you're still here,' she said, unpacking the stores. 'I'm going to make a stew for tomorrow, Jack's favourite.' The little thing chirruped. 'You like it too? Well look at this.' She opened the bag of millet and decanted some into a sugar bowl. The bird fell on it, eating some, then jumping into the bowl to whoosh the rest all over the place. Really comical. She enjoyed her evening with the bird, cutting up onions to the beat of Prince Buster's greatest hits double CD, which played as she cooked. The bird watched her antics with interest until, satisfied with her preparations, she decided to have an early night. 'I'm going to bed now,' she announced. 'You're welcome to fly up; I'll make a nice little nest for you on top of the cupboard if you like.'

She left the room and climbed the stairs, half expecting it to follow. Of course it didn't. Leaving the door open in case it changed its mind, she lay in bed thinking of Jack and her little friend downstairs. They'd love each other, she smiled. Supposing Jack wasn't at the cottage? She quickly wiped that thought. If he wasn't, she'd go to London and find him. She was determined to try and make a go of it. 'I love him,' she confirmed to herself before falling asleep.

The next morning she was awake by seven, jumping out of bed straight away, like a little girl on her birthday. She went downstairs to see the bird. Where was it? She looked absolutely everywhere. Gone. Bitterly disappointed, she scoured the garden, dreading coming across its lifeless body. It must have been damaged. How stupid of her not to have known and taken better care.

The telephone rang and she ran into the house, frightened by such an early call. 'Yes,' she said, grabbing the receiver. 'What?' She couldn't hear any words, just high-pitched sobbing. 'Maria, is that you, are you all right?'

'Jack's dead,' Louis said, in a voice so distraught it was almost unrecognizable. 'He hung himself. Something to do with Tam, Mum.'

Ellie collapsed on the floor, unable to credit what she was hearing.

'She was fed up that Jack wasn't glamorous and tried to change him. When she couldn't, she stole all the recordings they'd made together, saying they were hers. He was depressed. He'd got it all out of proportion, Mum. Everyone knew they were Jack's songs. He'd nothing to worry about.'

'Jack's dead?' Ellie said.

'Said it had nothing to do with the stupid music,' Louis continued, not hearing his mother's query. 'And that I didn't understand, but he wouldn't let me. I begged him but he wouldn't tell me anything, Mum.'

'Why didn't you ring me?'

'You?' Louis perplexed, sounded momentarily normal. 'Why? What could you have done?'

That's right, she thought, why tell her? Thanks to her idiotic pious secrecy. 'I don't know, but you should have tried,' she reiterated.

'Anyway, he said he was going to deal with it himself and went back to that cottage over the hill, the one he rented while I was away. Do you remember I told you about it?'

'Yes,' she answered, numb from the shock. 'I remember.'

Her son's voice broke. 'I was so worried about him I rang his mother. She went there and found him last night. He was still warm.' Louis started crying in earnest. 'Oh Mum, I knew what a state he was in. I should have done something.'

'It's nothing to do with you.' She was emphatic. 'Don't you dare blame yourself. D'you hear?'

'Yes,' he mumbled, 'but it's hard . . . I'm so sad.'

'I know, darling, me too. He was a wonderful boy. Where are you now? I'll come.'

'At home . . . thanks, Mum.' He hung up.

Ellie replaced the receiver, opened her mouth and let out a cry that lasted until she was up on her feet and out of the door, where she stood under the clear blue sky and howled, fists clenched, toes curled, rigid with horror. She could see it all. Hal arriving in that stupid fucking car, herself running out, happy to see Jack, Hal intercepting her with a hug. How could Jack have known that that picture was a lie? He'd walked away with an image that reinforced the lies she'd told him before. Utterly crushed, yes crushed, ironically, by her for a second time. Ellie cried until there were no tears left, when her body heaved great dry sobs she still couldn't stop. It was she who'd killed Jack, just as surely as if she'd shot him.

She must go to Louis. He was suffering enormously, blaming himself for his friend's death. She would be guilty of ruining two young lives if she didn't take care. She wanted to tell Louis it was her fault and explain why, but instinctively knew that would only be to salve her own conscience. Coming clean wouldn't help her son, in fact it could only harm him. Imagine finding out your mother had slept with, then effectively killed, your best friend. No, the time for confession had passed.

Consoling Louis was a relief; he was so bewildered by his first experience of death that she was plunged back into a role she understood, that of mother and protector. Maria flew back from Johannesburg for the funeral. Hal paid for her ticket and the whole family stayed together in their London house for the last time. She must confide in someone, but whom? There was always Father John, the local priest, whom she talked to once in a blue moon, but only ever about small stuff; besides, she wasn't religious. And even if she had been, how would it be possible to admit, let alone atone for, such a vast crime? In the end she told no one, fearing that if she did, it would betray Jack's memory.

When the funeral was over, Maria flew back to South Africa; Hal to New York; and Ellie stayed on in town for another ten days until she felt Louis was back on his feet. Paradoxically, the stronger he felt, the weaker Ellie grew and the more she needed him. She had to go before he realized. After extracting a promise that he'd come down if he got too depressed, she left. Parting from her son was very nearly too much for her and she almost broke down completely as she kissed him goodbye.

The cottage was grim. There was a power cut; it made her remember the night when she and Jack first made love. She looked at the flowers, dead in the jug on the table, and the stew still festering on the side, stinking to high heaven. Everything she'd prepared for Jack had died with him, due to her cowardice.

Spring cleaning – an occupation she hated beyond most, and never did, even before she could afford to pay someone else to do it for her – was the only option: mindless, useful and somehow appropriate. She set about it, starting in the bedroom with a burning Lady Macbeth-type urgency, and worked her way down through the house like a cyclone until finally she arrived in the kitchen, where she was stopped in her tracks by the bag of millet she'd brought for the bird. She'd forgotten all about the little fellow. Somehow it was the last straw and triggered all the grief that she'd managed to suppress with her furious activity. She sank into a darker place than she had ever known existed. It frightened her. She could see no way out. Debs. That's where she'd go. Visit Debs; she would possibly know some herbal remedy that could nip her nihilism in the bud.

Sitting in the back of the little shop with Debs, sipping a cup of tea, Ellie described her little feathered friend with what, she realized, would sound like disproportionate sorrow. Debs was bound to think she'd gone mad to be so distraught about a bird. On the contrary, her story was met with an unexpectedly serious response.

'Do you know anyone that's died recently?' Debs asked, concern creeping across her florid countenance.

'Why?'

'Oh nothing, it's just an old American Indian thing. They say the souls of those who never got to say goodbye come back as birds to those they love.'

'What a wonderful idea,' Ellie whispered, challenging her tears to remain dormant and hugging her friend. Making some excuse about being late, she left the shop with her head spinning. Debs had provided her with one, albeit meagre, consolation. When she had been talking to the bird in the kitchen she had set the record straight. Mad as it was, she now believed that the bird somehow had been Jack. The whole incident had been so remarkably odd; what other possible explanation was there? Still, it was just as hard to continue the everyday business of living. Where was the point to any of it, even her children? What would they do if she died? Miss her for a bit, but they'd get over it. The days rolled over and she remained mired in suffocating melancholy, susceptible to every dark temptation, all prompted by her own immorality. Try as she might, she could devise no appropriate penance.

It wasn't until months later, when Maria telephoned to announce her pregnancy.

'I'm longing for you to meet Paulo. We're so good together, Mum, and he's going to be a great dad to your grandchild.'

Ellie had never heard her daughter happier and understood like a bolt from the blue. Her punishment became clear to her, as plain as the nose on her face. The day Jack died she had been sentenced to life.

Angels

When Tarquin Lamort, aged fifty-two, moved to Los Angeles the intention was to change his life completely. But seeing as he shipped all his carpets, New Age crystals, wind chimes, mandalas and paranoia into another apartment, generically indistinguishable from the one he'd just left behind nearly three thousand miles away in New York City, his plan seemed destined to fail. He had always lived cocooned by his genius. His implausibly high IQ made social interaction elusive. He couldn't catch the subtitles of society's dance, nor understand his starring role within it.

As an only child he had been devastated to find himself orphaned aged nine when his father, an uncompromising industry baron, and his mother, untarnished in Tarquin's memory as forever beautiful, young, loving and kind, were both killed in a car wreck. The vehicle had veered off the road for no apparent reason, according to eye witnesses, turned over three times, before bursting into flames and burning fiercely for a full twenty minutes before any rescue vehicle arrived. The coroner returned an open verdict in his report. Tarquin's father had been driving and the accident had occurred at 3 a.m. after his parents had been seen jiving at Truman Capote's

Black-and-White Ball. The question of his father's sobriety had haunted Tarquin ever since.

The next seven and a half years were spent as a full-time boarder at Amply School, near Newhaven. Because of his misfortune and the fact that his father was an alumnus, Amply allowed Tarquin to enrol a year early. They bent the rules and squeezed him into a class composed of children eighteen months older than himself.

This worked well academically, as he was exceptionally bright. Socially it was a disaster. Tarquin was always the first with his hand up for the teacher, earning him the name, among his peers, of the 'Oily Fucker'. He made no friends and his lessons bored him. Science was the only exception; he found the subject mesmerizing from the moment he learned about the existence of the quantum theory.

Whenever possible Tarquin stayed on at the school, through the holidays. Everyone else went home to their families or to exotic climes, apart from an apparently unwanted Arab princeling and a skeleton staff that had been retained especially to oversee the two boys. Tarquin didn't mind; he liked the freedom it gave him. He was allowed to use the school laboratories to conduct physics experiments on his own. As he had no relations to visit, he felt that this was just fine. His only other option was a visit to one of his trustees, in his view more boring than death itself – something Tarquin now measured everything against.

Graduating from Amply meant leaving the one constant in his life. He was about to turn eighteen years of age and inherit everything that was coming to him, which was a great deal. Thrown alone into the deep end at such a tender age was hard; he was an introverted boy, and the dollars, of which there were millions, made him even more so. He became defensive and suspicious of people who tried to befriend him and lived his life alone for the next thirty-four years with surprising success, absorbed by his own health and the projects he'd devised for himself. These tasks ranged from posting conspiracy theories on the Web, to writing a book on his soul, and painting self-portraits in oils. Apart from his intricate rambling on the Internet none of his other efforts saw the light of day, as he would squirrel them away in his storage unit the moment they were finished. Unencumbered by other people's opinions he did as he pleased, and remained alone, marooned by his wealth and intellect.

The act of unpacking his possessions in the spartan apartment he'd taken by the sea on Ocean Boulevard was like reading a diary of his loneliness. There were hardly any sentimental keepsakes given by loved ones or relations. He was an orphan and a loner and always would be. He'd been trained that way. Unwrapping an ornate glass bong that he'd acquired in Morocco, he remembered the toothless old man who'd sold it to him. 'It is the very healthiest way to smoke hashish, sir,' the vendor screamed. 'You see, the hashish and tobacco passes through the water, yes?' He filled his lungs on a demonstration model. 'All impurities are removed,' he croaked, exhaling a stream of pungent white smoke. 'And that, my friend,' the old merchant shouted, sounding extremely volatile, 'keeps you sane.'

Tarquin started to fix himself a hit of the finest Humboldt mixed with the contents of a Lucky Strike and packed the bowl to light the pipe. Inhaling deeply, he lifted an oval Fabergé mirror out of a box of polystyrene pellets. It was his most treasured possession. Faithful replicas of morning glory flowers fashioned in exquisite silverwork grew around the mirrored glass as a frame. Wherever he moved, it was always the first object to be unpacked and hung in pride of place. He carried it carefully through into his bedroom to hook on to the nail he'd drilled and rawl-plugged earlier, then stood back to check the positioning. This mirror was a tangible memory of his mother. He could see her now, sitting in front of it at her dressing table smelling delicious. Still thinking of her, he was caught unawares by his own reflection. A sorry sight, his face peeking out from beneath a bird's nest of hair, cheeks puffed up, half visible above an unkempt beard and his lips, mid-toke, pursed unattractively with the effort of holding the smoke inside his lungs. Exhaling, he ruminated on where life had taken him and was saddened by the obvious lack of change or growth in his persona.

The sea, only three blocks from his new home, was the one changing element in the middle of this ocean of self-imposed sameness. Deciding to take a walk, he donned his sunglasses, even though it was the middle of the night, and stepped out to stroll down to the surf. Maybe the wind would blow the desolation from his psyche.

She, meanwhile, was running to meet him as fast as her legs would carry her, which wasn't very fast at all, as the legs she had were faulty in a way she couldn't quite put her tongue on. Whether the trouble was a lack of mental co-ordination or a genuine physical disability hardly mattered; the fact remained that if she couldn't get them to move a little faster, she was going to miss the appointed hour, and heaven only knew when the next chance would be. She smelt a rat. The very whiff of it swamped her with loathing and indignation. Rats weren't allowed in the same vicinity as Hands, and they knew it. 'Where rats run disease spreads,' she remembered by rote.

Locating the revolting creature wasn't difficult. Even on the move, she just had to follow the odour-band to its source and find the glittering red eyes she knew would be there. And sure enough, scanning the darkness from where the smell originated, there they were. Two little red pinpricks following her progress, chock-a-block with malevolence, daring her to deviate. Pathetic creature. Did it think she was born yesterday . . . literally?

Summoning the wisdom of ages, she prioritized, ignored the rat and hurried on with little or no regret; after all, she was enjoying herself. It was a grand Boulevard to be running down after so long, even if she was, by necessity, blinkered against looking around at all the exhilarating changes she passed. Unread news hung everywhere, tantalizing her. It was on the lamp-posts and the hydrants, lying in gutters, floating in the breeze, but she didn't have time to stop. If she missed him she'd be stuck – unable to move up, down, east or west. The concept renewed her resolve, propelling her around a corner and down a side street, where she spotted Tarquin at the far side of the next avenue. He was already at the traffic lights and had passed the interception point; to make matters worse, he was walking on at a healthy pace and the road between them was in the process of being resurfaced. A new layer of tar had just been laid, and huge men stood poised in the shadowy streetlight, ready to rake out the gravel–pitch mix that was being spewed out of the back of a truck. They might have researched my route better, she thought, looking up at the dark sky reproachfully.

She cried out for him to wait. He didn't hear. Then with the spectacular courage that's born of desperation, she launched herself in front of an oncoming roller that was bringing up the rear to flatten the newly laid uneven surface. She somersaulted, with the consummate ease of a gymnast, across the new sticky-sharp stuff, ending up on the pavement on the other side of the street. Springing up, she staggered. What was wrong? Her legs seemed to be functioning worse than ever, if such a thing was possible, and her coat was covered in noxious goo. It was burning through to her skin. She fought the pain and persevered, each step a more monumental effort than the last.

'Wait,' she called out again and again. A shortness of breath seized her oesophagus, shrinking the air passage. She crashed on to the sidewalk. She was gulping. She needed oxygen.

He stopped, turned to see what the commotion was, saw her fall, heard her gasps, and ran back.

'Thanks be to the Powerful One,' she wheezed. Now, even if it cost her this life, the mission would count as a qualified success. They wouldn't strand her. Evolution was once again possible. She accepted her fate, and let go.

When she regained consciousness, she was insulted to find herself lying on a cold metal trolley, being forcibly restrained by a Hand (male) while another, female in gender, stuck a twig up her backside. Such a wholly insufferable assault on her dignity called for desperate measures, and she lashed out with her mouth, the only body part left under her control. She screamed and screamed, trying with all her might to bite the Hands. Until she remembered – what? Nothing. She couldn't remember a thing, who or what she was, her parents, her childhood or why indeed she was here in such an uncomfortable and demeaning position. How long had it been? she wondered. How long was a yard of sausages, come to that? No, sausages had nothing to do with it. With what? She was puzzled. She couldn't recognize her thoughts.

Tarquin spoke: 'You all right, boy?' When she heard his voice it activated her brain, which scanned straight to a memory cell where she found: 'T. Lamort intersection Venice and Ocean 11.45 p.m. May 15th 1999'. That's right, she thought. He's it. The reason for her being. Of course she had no memories of this life – there weren't any. But she did now know exactly who and what she was.

A Korean Jindo of royal stock, and a direct descendant of the first, great immortal Jindo Quint, whose exploits had been recorded by Hands in a twelfth-century manuscript ostensibly concerning the fabled isle of Jindo and its inhabitants but which, in fact, was a simple, elegant tract paying homage to Quint, to his mythic powers and heroic feats, to his qualities as handsome, valiant and brave. Hangwen Kang had summed up his oeuvre by stating that Quint was the embodiment of all wise Jindos, for they were well known to be dogs of a rare and honorable breed. Kang's brush strokes, recognized as the most delicate of his age, produced faultless calligraphy, which meant this important artefact had been preserved up to the present day, and now lay guarded behind glass in a private house in Seoul.

Now she knew what she was, she then remembered who. And, since she had come down through the western hemisphere her name would be the Poppulina, as always. Much easier for the occidental to pronounce than Princess Ulteoug Hau-Pai.

Feeling better now that she'd regained her identity, she understood everything; the twig must be a thermometer, and the Hand (female) had to be a vet-doctor. She'd been briefed that this would happen if the first phase was successfully completed.

The vet-girl and Tarquin were only acting with the best of intentions. She forgave them. It wasn't their fault. They'd been born on a lower rung of the evolutionary ladder and were too dense to realize that any species other than their own could suffer humiliation. This was precisely why she'd come, to show him that each and every living organism possessed feelings, humour and a soul, as well as the inalienable right to use all three. She stopped her plaintive cries and lay limp.

Tarquin relaxed his grip. 'That's right. Good boy. No more barking, the nasty part's over,' he whispered.

The vet-girl corrected him. 'He's a she, and we can't risk more solvent on the poor little thing. Her skin's raw enough as it is. At least she can breathe.' She scraped very gently at a patch of the black sticky macadam seared on to the skin of the Poppulina's back. 'Just feather out any more of the tar you might find with a penknife or something. Like this.'

'I'm sorry,' he declared. 'I think there's been a misunderstanding. I can't keep it. I'm not equipped for a dog.'

The vet-girl deflated. 'Oh,' she said, despondent, 'she'll never make it through the pound. No one will take her looking like this.'

The Poppulina was indeed a pitiful sight. She appeared to be suffering from mange, lumps of her coat were missing, her back right thigh muscle was wasted, and the leg looked atrophied.

'Maybe she was hit by a car,' the vet-girl ventured. To top it all off the Poppulina had been afflicted with a nervous tic that made her head bob up and down like those toy dogs in the back of cars. The vet-girl confidently diagnosed this as a symptom of distemper tremors. 'Never goes away, but don't worry. It won't get any get worse either,' she assured Tarquin.

He stroked the velvety little head ruefully.

The Poppulina was exhausted yet compos mentis enough to spot an opportunity when she saw one. She craned her neck, licked his hand weakly, then gazed up at Tarquin from beneath her eyelids, in what she hoped against hope was a beguiling manner. In any case it was the best she could muster under the circumstances, as the physical exhaustion brought on by the perpetual twitch, coupled with the effort it had required to achieve this preliminary stage, was making her shake uncontrollably.

'I suppose I could take her for a week or two,' Tarquin ventured tentatively.

'Fantastic,' vet-girl replied, brightening up beyond all recognition, instantly transformed into proficient-vet-in-charge-of-happy-dog-with-contented-owner. 'Her second set of shots are due March sixteenth. Avoid letting her mix with other dogs until then. She's prone to infections right now.'

Tarquin was alarmed. The vet was still talking to him as if he was master of the mutt. 'Whoa there, I said a week or so. March sixteenth is seven weeks away.'

'Don't worry,' she countered. 'I'll put her on the Web. Look at that face. Someone will fall for her.'

The Poppulina looked at the vet-girl and she looked back. Was there complicity in the look between them, Tarquin wondered? No. Was he mad? Collusion between a human and a dog? What in God's name had he been thinking?

The Poppulina lay in the back of Tarquin's SUV, happy to be leaving initial obstacles behind her. All is good now. Rendezvous completed, she thought, reporting up. But for how long, she wondered privately, would it stay that way?

'You all right, boy?' the T-voice said.

She saw his eyes looking at her in the rear-view mirror. The whites were yellowing and traversed by tiny red spider veins.

'Liver,' she diagnosed, perfectly sanguine. 'Healthy body . . . promote healthy spirit,' she recited to herself in staccato Korean. She had to get Tarquin on a regime a.s.a.p.; only then would she be able to gauge the amount of work that lay ahead. Armed with a plan, she relaxed, allowing herself to revert to the common or garden dog that she used to be in the carefree youth of her first life on earth many, many moons before. She promptly fell into a deep sleep for the rest of the journey.

'Here we are,' Tarquin announced, closing the door of his apartment and bending down to release her from the ignominious blue nylon string he'd used to lead her up the stairs.

So this is where she was going to live . . . what a horrid place. Nice things though, good smells to read. Her body tensed autonomously and her hackles rose. She saw danger in a smell and, baring her rotten teeth, turned the corner of the flimsy wall separating the bedroom from the living space and saw the Siberian wolf that she already knew was there. It was lying on Tarquin's bed bold as brass and she attacked it before realizing it was long dead. Tarquin was using the pelt as insulation for his body. 'There is more to protégé than meets eye,' she thought, looking back at Tarquin, who was laughing at her. Impressed with his courage she covered her embarrassment with solemnity and continued her investigations with great dignity, acquainting herself with the origins of each and every object in Tarquin's apartment. She sniffed, then lay down on her favourite, an oriental carpet, whose smell readings transported her back through the souks of ancient Persia, even on to the time of its creation, when it was woven on a loom constructed of rosewood so pliant it could safely stretch the finest gossamer threads with no fear of their breaking.

Then a strikingly peculiar thing on the other side of the small room took her attention. An eye on a table trapped in translucent casing with no smell attached. It stood next to the transparent wall that cut them off from the ionized sea air. Not possible. She inched her nose further forward, trying to inhale some small clue. Nothing. She limped nearer – not a whiff. 'How have they done it?' she asked herself. 'Smell can sneak through anything.' She stood there, head bobbing up and down, completely stumped by the lack of any odour. Never once, in the hundreds of years visiting life-on-earth, had she come across such a thing. It appeared to be the eye of a Hand. Not Tarquin's, but some Hand-person nevertheless. It was certainly Hand-sized, and the iridology confirmed her guess-work. She pressed her nose to the Pekinese-sized mystery. No smell. She sniffed it from the front, then the back, from under the table and then from above. In short, she scrutinized it minutely from every conceivable angle, with every form of sensory perception available to her. Nothing. She could make neither head nor tail of it and sat down defeated. Her bad back leg stuck out at a peculiar angle making balance on her one good haunch appear precarious. Oblivious of her handicap and the comical aspect it lent her, she sat there, proud, lopsided and perplexed, looking from the smelless eye to Tarquin, and back again.

'It's a hologram,' he said. 'Do you like it?'

Hologram? The Poppulina knew about telegrams – they had been all the rage on one of her previous visits – but holograms?

She had to hand it to these Hand-people; they really were fiendishly clever. No one in her Jindo homeland had succeeded in transporting the metaphysical imprint of a smell-image. The finest brains had tried and failed. To this day you still had to pick up a smell-image from source. Yet here were these creatures succeeding where far greater minds had failed. Completely missing the point. I mean what's the use of a transposed snippet-of-a-smell, without the actual reading to digest? A concept the Hand-people, of course, couldn't conceive of. Once they'd evolved and grown hands they'd stopped listening. Armed with eight fingers and two thumbs they'd become arrogant, puffed up with their superior dexterity. If they'd only remember to interact with the universe they'd be invaluable. Instead they remained gluttons and greedily sucked the very planet on which they depended dry, regardless of natural lore or limits.

'Oh dear, the folly of the Hand-people,' she thought, struggling up to buckle down to the task of enlightenment. Tarquin needed to be reacquainted with the elements. Hopping on her three good legs to the front door, she began to whine.

'Want to go out, boy?' he said.

She turned, fixing him with a look. 'I am not a boy,' she communed, 'I am the Princess Poppulina, Miss Popular for short.'

'Come on then, boy,' he said, bending down to re-attach the grimy blue string to her collar.

Emanating discreet authority, she made a show of lifting her bad leg pathetically and willed physical contact.

'Oh look, what's wrong?' he said, taking the little damaged limb in his hand and examining the paw. 'Got something in it?'

She wagged her tail.

'There's a good girl,' he said. 'Now let's see, what shall we call you? We're in California, you've got orange hair . . . What about Poppy?'

Close enough, she thought, leaning all her weight against him, weak with relief to discover she hadn't lost her power to communicate.

'Poppy it is then,' he said, ruffling her head and throwing the blue string aside. 'Let's go, shall we?'

She trotted out, a spring of satisfaction in her step. The work of rehabilitation had begun.

After the first twenty-four hours the Poppulina knew she was safe and that Tarquin would keep her. She became known as the bouncing puppy and she transformed his life. They were well suited and became highly attuned to each other's individual needs. Take the incident with the neighbourhood cats. Vicious rumour-mongers, slinking around, forever stirring up unrest and scavenging from all the local boardwalk bins, which drove the Poppulina to distraction. Their latest piece of venom reported back to her by the chocolate Labrador that lived next door was to brand all canines the ultimate Hand Parasites. Incensed, Poppulina challenged them, demanding an explanation of their disgusting habits, such as the use of litter trays.

'We are independent, self-sufficient,' three of them caterwauled in unison. 'We shit where we please, when we please, and catch mice, lizards and moths. While you are merely an inferior inconsequential creature like the feathered life force to be found hitchhiking on the back of hippopotami, except you choose to leech off the Hand beings.'

'What gives you the right to scorn Hands?' the Poppulina growled, prowling forward into their rubbish-strewn alley. 'Hands are good, they're just in need of a little guidance.'

The insolent felines stretched detestably, purring. 'In need of guidance? Really? We don't think so,' they sneered. 'Hands worship us. Have done since time immemorial. The Egyptians . . .'

Enough was enough. To get them out of her sight and squash her base instinct to practise genocide, the Poppulina sprang at them snarling. She realized, clever as she was, that if she had to hear once more about their bloody feline immortalization on the walls of the flipping pyramids, she'd go rabid. The cats scattered, and in their wake the Poppulina peed a declaration of war across the entrance to their alley. From that day on, whenever he had time, Tarquin had the sensitivity to drive the twenty minutes it took to reach Topanga or the Palisades, where he walked the wild, uninhabited stretches of canyon and let the Poppulina hunt, keeping her free from a life fraught with old urban enmities and territorial wars.

She in turn enabled him to come out of his shell. He loved the white-rabbit-like qualities of the Poppulina, discovering that he could hear 'I'm late, I'm late, for a very important date . . .' in the rhythm of her step, as she ran from one bush or burrow to another checking for any changes or signs of life, reading the smells, moving on, rushing back officiously to double-check. She'd always enticed him to walk further than he intended, cunningly entertaining him at the precise moment he was about to turn for home.

Gradually, Tarquin's monastic car-home-car regime began to be replaced by *life*. He noticed the subtle changes of seasons in the Los Angeles basin, and became interested in identifying the different herbs and wild fuchsias that grew on the hills. With each new name some small part of him healed. His feelings of wellbeing grew in tandem with the sage. He stopped taking his vitamin pills and started to prepare food for himself from which the same were derived. Unbeknownst to him he was re-establishing fundamental connections. A process that, once assimilated, would begin the slow restoration of his soul.

For the Poppulina, the training of Hands was easy. Still, she always found herself amazed by their capacity for learning. She'd noticed they possessed a love of the ridiculous, yet they liked consistency, and long ago she devised simple regimes that incorporated enough fun to keep them amused while they studied.

The Poppulina watched proudly as Tarquin blossomed. She knew that in addition to many other things, having her by his side as a companion at parties – nightmares he called them – gave Tarquin the courage to attend and engage in healthy interaction with other Hands. If she sensed him conjuring up his imagined inadequacies she would limp over or pant furiously demanding attention and break his downward spiral by making him turn his attention to her. He'd have to check she had enough water or some other invented need, giving him the time to recover his equilibrium and return to socializing, as a good Hand should. He began to smile; this restored his physiognomy to what it always had the potential to be. To reward him the Poppulina stopped bouncing.

Tarquin noticed a change but couldn't work out what it was. He took her to the vet-girl, who was thrilled. 'Look, she's still. The tremors are gone,' she exclaimed. 'It's incredible, a medical impossibility. It has to be due entirely to your love,' she said, impressed.

Tarquin shrugged, apparently unmoved, but secretly he could see no other possible explanation and was so proud that he went to a barber and had his hair cut off . . . beard, moustache, the lot. His naked face proved engaging and he began to acquire a moderate popularity, a first in his lonely life. The years passed and the bond between man and dog grew. Now that Tarquin had been socialized and grasped the elemental basis of being, he had a girlfriend.

The Poppulina knew this signalled that it was her time to move on. She hated this bit, and never got used to it. She'd been warned ad infinitum not to become emotionally involved, and she always tried hard. Avoiding too much nuzzling and patting, rationing it to a paltry twenty minutes morning and evening despite Tarquin's pleas for more. Even so, he'd managed to worm his way into her heart with his funny little quirks and simple enjoyments. And here she was, yet again, unable to say goodbye.

It had to be done, she resolved. She'd taught him all she could. To stay would put him in another rut. Furthermore, she was needed elsewhere by some other lost soul.

The form of farewell was left up to her but, as usual, not being able to decide on which was the least painful for Tarquin, she couldn't face making the choice. And so the Powers that Be did it for her by starting the decay of her body.

Tarquin tended to her for the next six months, buying a little red waggon to take her on walks when her legs began to give out.

The end was agonizing for the Poppulina. She clung on until Tarquin was ready to let go, even though, impatient for her return, the Powers had started accelerating her decomposition, initiating growths that protruded through her coat. Then they made her lose control of her own bodily functions, and without one iota of joy, they doggedly proceeded to reduce her life to misery.

One evening, Tarquin was lying next to her on the floor, caressing her and trying without success to tempt her into eating chicken, her favourite, when he suddenly got it. ‘It’s humiliating for you, isn’t it? D’you want to go, my baby girl?’ he asked, feeling sadder than he ever remembered being. Unwillingly the Poppulina let him know that it was indeed the time. Tarquin never left her side that night.

The following morning they went together to visit the vet-girl one last time. The Poppulina tried to eat all the usual treats on offer so as to comfort Tarquin, but she was too weak and nauseous to keep them down. Finally, he held her in his arms, and with the aid of the vet-girl’s injection let her spirit go. The Poppulina watched over Tarquin for seven days and seven nights, allowing him time to regroup. Then she was ordered up. Never to see him again . . . officially.

But no one could blame a Jindo dog for taking a sneak peek once in a while.

The Wind in the Willy

Arthur's wind-on-willy thing had just seemed sweet when he was little. Someone should have spotted it for the potential powder keg it was. After all, the family had always had their fair share of quirks: some nice, some not.

Like the father's boyhood habit of drinking foetid flower water. He'd been caught by the priest during mass, a straw in his mouth sucking the floral arrangements dry, not only hazardous to himself, but downright embarrassing and offensive to others.

No one checked Arthur's behaviour even though, if anyone ever went to his house, they would always find him dressed only from the waist up. Throughout the long English winters, his parents kept the heating turned up insufferably high to accommodate him. Still, no one questioned his habits.

Later, pre-pubescent and able to articulate, Arthur lit on a new word. Constricting. 'Air ... Air ... I need air! I'm constricting!' he'd scream in blood-curdling agony if anyone dared approach him to offer any conventional covering for his genitalia.

'D'you think he's quite right in the head?' asked the father, who was a brigadier.

'Shhh, don't make him self-conscious, you'll break his spirit,' the mother answered.

Arthur had a sister Jody, who was older than he.

He started to steal her clothes, a great irritant to the obsessively neat little girl's sensibilities.

The mother decided that Arthur had been put on this earth to, as she put it, people a new enlightened generation. To spread their seed. And so, to this end, she should give his precious seed the room to grow and flourish, without the dreaded constriction he so rightly feared.

After a great deal of thought, she decided to paint Arthur's life anew and invented – *Scottish ancestry.*

Arthur was deliriously happy with his new heritage and when next in London they went immediately to Mary Quant's boutique in the King's Road, where they bought her entire range of mini-kilts for him to wear.

Thirty years on, although he has not peopled a whole new generation, or indeed grown that much physically, he has become a mogul, married for love and adopted a child on whom he dotes.

He still fits into and proudly wears those original Quant kilts whenever he wishes to dignify a special occasion. Admittedly they may now be a tad too short and strain a little at the buckle. But they still serve as, if nothing else, a reminder of his humble Sassenach roots.

Chemical

Having lived and worked all of his forty-seven years in Boyne, Indiana, Paul had finally galvanized himself and moved into a loft in New York's garment district. He'd often visited Manhattan before, always accompanied by his wife Patsy and always with a meticulously planned agenda. They'd stay on the Upper East Side for a maximum of three days, during which time they'd catch a show, visit museums, eat well and leave.

Now Paul had the seductively named Tribeca, Alphabet city and the Village lying at his feet to sample at will. His dream come true. Be careful what you wish for.

Ever since the onset of adolescence, he had imagined himself as a painter manqué. Throughout his life he'd dabbled with the brush and easel, gone to endless life classes where he learned to draw and received praise from tutors and friends alike. Still, he'd never dared do it to the exclusion of everything else. Then, a couple of years back, at Patsy's instigation, they discussed the possibility of his taking a year off to follow his passion. She'd act as his mentor/agent, she said, make him follow through. Both made good money in their jobs, she in real estate, he in insurance, and since they planned to have a family, they had been careful to put some aside. They could afford to gamble on him, Patsy insisted when no children arrived. She had problems conceiving. That's how they found out. When she'd gone for a D and C scrape and haemorrhaged.

Don't go there, he thought, looking around the big bare loft he now called home. It was a marvellous space. Light flooding in everywhere through wall-to-wall windows. An easel and orange plastic chair stood next to a trestle table, on which were propped a selection of brand-new, stretched-to-drum-tension canvases, brushes of varying sizes, and countless pristine tubes of paint. A dilapidated panel of oriental fretwork, which Paul had found in the street on the day he moved in, divided the space and gave it definition as well as partially hiding the poignancy of his single, unmade bed. On the far side of the screen were the only other essentials in his life: a drip coffee machine and a large, plain white, porcelain mug that he'd already, annoyingly, chipped, luckily not on the drinking side. Both sat on a small fridge beneath the bank of windows that faced south. Everything he needed was there. There were no more excuses, he thought. The time had come to see if he had talent.

He remained modest in his ambition and harboured no Julian Schnabel-type aspirations. He'd been thrilled to spot the painter/film-maker in a little café called Tea and Sympathy that he'd discovered on his first week in Manhattan. Struck by the sheer presence of the man, he recognized how low he'd set his horizons. If he could garner any interest in his painting after one year, a self-imposed deadline made in honour of Patsy, that, he accepted, would be more than enough for him.

Very serious about his new incarnation as an artist, he quickly settled into a routine, getting up at around 6 a.m. To catch the light, he told himself importantly. He'd paint for an hour then, at 7 a.m. sharp, walk the seven blocks down Seventh Ave: 777. Auspicious, he liked to think. To a cosy French bistro he approved of because it let dogs in. Not that he owned one. Sitting by the window, he'd read the *New York*

Times, bought en route, and consume a croissant with one café-au-lait. He often wanted another, but too many coffees in one go made him jumpy; he didn't like that. Walking back up Broadway for variation, he'd take a break at Madison Square Park, sit on a bench to smoke his pipe and read any unfinished article that had caught his eye earlier or merely observe New York life as it bustled by. Without fail, 9.30 a.m. found him at his easel, where he stayed religiously until 3 p.m. Then, depending on whether or not the work was going well, he'd carry on, or go exploring armed with a small bottle of water, a sketchbook and his little tin palette of watercolours.

On one excursion to the farmers' market in Union Square, he spotted a stall laden with Heritage tomatoes, bright red, orange and green. Reassuringly misshapen, they had to be bought. Inside the brown paper bag their colours appeared even more vibrant. Paul stuffed his nose in and inhaled; it was the aroma of his youth. His father had grown tomatoes and, up until this moment, he'd forgotten how much he loved their smell. Store-bought ones never had it. Flooded by memories, he opened his eyes, and found himself looking directly into others – large, pale blue, with black rings around the irises. They were fringed by long, dark lashes and belonged to a fellow shopper – female – who was smiling at him. 'Delicious, aren't they?' she said, referring to the jewel-like fruit.

'Yes,' Paul agreed, shocked by the proximity of the stranger. She was beautiful, and Paul found himself intrigued by a woman for the first time in the eighteen months since the merciful death of his wife. The day Patsy did eventually leave him, Paul, who had nursed her through long and painful months, slumped into a lethargy that knew no bounds. If they'd only had children maybe he wouldn't have felt so utterly dispossessed. He wasn't sure. But to find himself alone for the first time in twenty years was a devastation too far. Seven months later to the day, on a fine, crisp morning, a large cheque arrived in his mailbox: Patsy's life insurance. This seemed to be the final insult. He remembered their taking it out on his insistence. A joint policy so she'd never have to worry, he'd said, never for one moment imagining himself as the beneficiary. Now that he was, guilt and sorrow overwhelmed him. He would have taken his own life, had it not been a mortal sin, prohibiting entry to heaven, where Patsy would surely be waiting.

His lethargy intensified over time into severe depression. After a year even Patsy's mother got fed up. 'P wouldn't want this,' she said, invoking her daughter with the passion of her own bereavement. 'She'd want to see you happy, for Christ's sake.'

It was true, he thought; she'd hate to be the cause of his pain. Recalling their shared dreams, he decided to act on their favourite. Packed all his possessions into storage. Sold their home and came to live and paint in New York City. His dream supported by her misfortune. Life was cruel.

All this passed through his mind as he stood motionless in the open market, staring vacantly into the eyes of the mystery beauty and clutching his small brown paper bag of tomatoes in front of him like a shield for protection. Still smiling, she moved past him. Conflicted by the small stirring of guilt and pleasure she produced, Paul dismissed the encounter. Until he saw her again, a few weeks later, across a sea of people at a gallery opening that he'd walked in, off the street. Deciding to approach her, he made his way over, but by the time he reached the spot where she'd been standing, she'd disappeared.

This set off a small obsession. He wondered who she was, and what she did. Was she married, did she have children? She certainly seemed happy. Radiant, that was a good word to describe her, he thought, as he painted the urban view from his window.

Three weeks later, 9 a.m. sharp, Paul, fortified by his quotidian routine, waited at the entrance of his building. Three large men obstructed his progress with a blood-red brocade sofa that they were trying to ease through the door. Managing to slip by, he went for the elevator and was just in time to see it close, fully occupied with a piano, a large Venetian mirror, and two more removal men. Seeing no other option, he cursed and began the long walk up the twenty-nine floors. Maybe he could intercept the elevator; he should have asked the men how long they were going to be. Who was the new tenant, he wondered? Or the old one come to that. He realized that in the two months that he'd been living here, he'd never seen another living soul, apart from the surly superintendent.

Rounding the stairs on sixth he caught sight of a man's back disappearing through a door, situated coincidently where his was, only twenty-three floors lower. He checked his watch: 9.10 a.m., not too bad, except the elevator was jammed open by the piano. He tried to push it aside, but it was much too heavy for him alone. Red in the face, he called out for assistance. No response. The door of the apartment the men had gone into was still ajar. He knocked and it swung open. 'Hello, is there anyone there?' he hollered. Nothing. Upon entering he was surprised to find himself at the top of a long dim corridor with rooms on either side. He'd expected something large and airy like his place. Beginning to feel uncomfortable with the direction his morning was taking, he proceeded with caution, calling out, 'Excuse me . . . Hello', as he went. Suddenly he was confronted by the radiant one. She was right there, in front of him, standing like an Amazon, brandishing a poker in a threatening way inches from his head.

'Can I help you?' she said, defiant.

It was so unexpected he let out a yell and jumped back, tripping and falling over a box. She came forward, loomed over him, the poker still firmly in her hand. 'Who are you and what do you want?' she asked, imperious this time. 'Answer please, the cops want to know.' She waved a cordless phone in her other hand.

'P-P-Paul,' he quavered. 'P-Paul Rice, I live on the twenty-ninth floor, and I th-think your piano's blocking the elevator.'

The hand with the phone shot up and covered her mouth. 'Christ, so it is. I'm sorry, I'll get it moved straight away.' She turned and shouted into the room behind her, 'Hey guys, you're blocking the elevator.'

Two of the three men Paul had seen earlier emerged from the room, looked down at him still prostrate on the floor, then at each other before lumbering past him to deal with the problem. 'It's completely my fault,' she said disarmingly while helping him up, 'I persuaded them to hang an enormous mirror for me,' she went on. 'See, doesn't it look grand?' She dragged him through into the room the removal men had vacated to admire the large Venetian mirror, now hanging above the marble fire mantel. Paul nodded without seeing. Abstracted, he was brushing straw and other unidentifiable bits of packing fodder off his trousers.

'Oh dear, are you hurt?' she said. 'Can I get you some coffee? I just unpacked the machine and cups – and I've got fresh milk,' she ended with pride.

'No, no, I'm f-f-fine, I should get on,' he answered.

'Oh please,' she said. 'It would make me feel better, after giving you such a fright.' She was so earnest it made him smile.

'All right,' he said, 'but I can only stay a minute.'

'Great,' she said, and led him down the corridor into a light kitchen, where she put the phone down, and started trying to assemble a fancy hi-tech coffee machine.

'You're my first guest,' she told him.

'Don't you think you should tell the p-police,' he said, indicating the phone.

'No need,' she said. 'I was bluffing. It's not even connected yet.'

'I'm impressed,' he said. 'I believed you.'

'Big mistake,' she laughed and returned to the coffee machine, twisting up her mane of hair, using two pencils to fix it in place like a geisha girl. 'This is a fiendish thing,' she wailed. 'How could anyone be expected to put it together?'

Up close she was lovelier than he'd remembered. In her late thirties, he guessed, tall and willowy, with tiny bones. He wasn't at all surprised to learn that she'd been a model, but had given it up. 'Boring,' she said simply, blinking back wilful wisps of hair, and trying to focus her enormous eyes on the machine.

He watched her struggle with what seemed to him a perfectly easy task, until he could bear it no longer. 'Here let me,' he said, taking over and snapping all the bits together easily.

'You are wonderful. Where did you learn to do that?' she gushed, spooning coffee grinds into the filter.

'I don't know, probably a left-brain thing,' he said, feeling very masterful.

'Hunter-gatherer,' she said.

'S-sorry?' Paul queried.

'Hunter-gatherers. Men like you. Such a relief.'

He knew she was flirting and liked it. 'Is there anything else I can help you with?' he asked, buying into the image.

'No, nothing, but thanks,' she said, switching on the coffee. 'Do you want to see the rest of the place while we're waiting?'

'Love to,' he replied.

She took him through to the sitting room.

'Actually, there is the sound system,' she said helplessly, 'but don't worry, I'm sure I can work it out.'

He sprang at the opportunity. 'L-let me.'

She looked dubious.

'Honestly, I'd like to,' he insisted.

'Well . . . If you really don't mind,' she said. 'I'll just carry on, shall I?'

Without waiting for an answer, she upturned a box filled with cushions and linens. 'Wrong box,' she said, and moved on to the next. By the time he'd connected the wires and mounted the speakers, the radiant one had emptied six large boxes into jumbled heaps all over the floor and moved on to 'unpacking' the kitchen. Heaven help the kitchen, was all he could think.

'Shall I order lunch in?' she called through.

He looked at his watch. Ten to twelve. He'd never goofed off before, 9.45 a.m. was the latest he'd ever begun, and that was because he'd cut off the tip of his thumb, opening a tin of varnish, and now because of . . . Paul realized he didn't know what she was called.

'What's your name?' he asked, getting up and going to join her in the kitchen.

'Is that a prerequisite for having lunch with me?' she teased.

'N-no. But it would be nice to know who I was lunching with,' he parried.

'Oh, good. We're on. What shall we have?' She beamed. 'I know a delicious place that's fast. Now where's the number?' She turned to the only vaguely organized corner of the room. Papers flew everywhere. He was daunted by the chaos.

A cyclone later, she emerged triumphant, waving a menu. 'Have a look. I want Salad Niçoise. It's the best.' It would be hard to start painting now, he rationalized. The sun would have left the view.

'Suits me,' he said.

'Great.' She grinned, and grabbed the phone to dial. 'Shit, I forgot,' she said, waving the dead phone. 'What shall we do now? Where's my cell?'

In for a penny in for a pound, he thought, dreading the onslaught of mayhem her cellphone search was sure to produce. 'We could call f-from my place,' he suggested.

'Wonderful. Let me just go check on the state of play and tip the guys,' she said and disappeared, returning a few minutes later.

'All done, come and look. I'm starving, aren't you?' she said.

He wasn't, but nodded as he followed her back into the room where the piano now stood, reflected in the newly hung mirror.

'Sunshine,' she declared, when they were out in the hall waiting for the elevator without a window in sight. Paul looked at her.

'My name,' she explained. 'But everyone calls me Kate. Guess who had hippies for parents?' she continued. 'That's what whacky-baccy does. Makes you give your children names they get crucified for. I can't stand the stuff.'

It was a shame everybody called her Kate, he thought. Sunshine suited her.

She loved his loft, particularly his bit of broken screen, which she identified as Rajasthani, and she was very complimentary about his paintings, even wanting to buy the one of Madison Square Park. 'S-sorry,' he said, 'I'm not s-selling yet,' and offered to give it to her as a housewarming present, which she accepted to their mutual delight. The food arrived. She was right. It was delicious, but while he ate all of his, she barely made a dent in hers.

'I thought you were s-starving,' he said.

'I know, must be the excitement of moving or something. I'll take it with me for later,' she replied. 'D'you think I could make one more call?' She was already picking up the phone. 'Then I promise I'll leave you in peace.'

'P-please do,' he said.

She went to the far end of the open space. Yet he could still overhear her say she wanted to see Charley now, and repeat her address. Charley had to be her boyfriend, Paul thought. At least he'd found out early. Of course, a beauty like her would have one. Well, things change. Besides, who knew how committed they were? What the hell was he thinking about anyway? 'Sorry P,' he whispered, patting the breast pocket of his jacket where he kept his dead wife's photograph in the wallet she'd given him. Kate hung up and, true to her word, left, hugging him on the way out, and saying how fantastic it was to meet him on her first day. A new-old friend was how she put it.

When she'd gone, Paul went and lay on his bed and, for the first time in months, felt faintly less than happy with his solitary life as a painter.

Still, it was nice knowing someone in the building, and their lives did inevitably become entwined to a certain degree. She, completely independent in one way, was totally helpless in another. Anything technical was lost on her, right down to the DVD. On the other hand, she seemed to be very high-powered, at what he wasn't sure, but she was always busy, rushing about making calls and appointments she found hard to keep. The perpetual threat of lateness seemed to haunt her days. One evening he asked if she would play the piano for him, and learned it was inherited from her grandfather, a concert pianist. And although she loved to play – not that well, she assured him – she hadn't touched the keys since his death. 'It's just too sad-making; he was my rock, my inspiration,' she explained. 'But don't worry,' she giggled, 'I promise you're not missing much.'

Physically she was frail, and he worried about the way she caught more than her fair share of colds and flu, and too often had to take to her bed. He'd ply her with vitamins and syrups, which she'd swallow dutifully, looking pathetically vulnerable between snuffles and sneezes, and Paul's heart would melt with concern.

She let him call her Sunny. No one else was allowed to and that pleased him. Sadly, though, there was no hint of romance. He had kissed her once, but she'd said they mustn't. Because of Charley, he supposed bitterly. He had met some of her friends over the months, none that he could honestly hold his hand over his heart and swear he cared for. Never Charley. Charley wasn't good for her; she lived on her nerves constantly waiting on him to arrive. And as far as Paul could see, Charley did nothing for her that required a man's strength. Paul had to do all that stuff. All this, combined with Paul's growing infatuation for Sunny, made him dislike Charley more than anyone else he'd never met before.

Then, one day in late April, as he was dropping off Sunny's mail, a favour he often did, as she was a late riser, Paul was dismayed to see her door wide open. He told her repeatedly that she was too lax about security. They were living in New York, for God's sake. He heard the piano playing Beethoven. Amazing! Sunny had been lying about her abilities; it sounded beautiful. Sneaking in, he leaned against the wall of the corridor to listen to more. It finished and he broke into spontaneous applause, calling out 'Bravo' as he walked into the room, then stopped, embarrassed to see not Sunny at the piano, but a man he'd never laid eyes on before. Charley, he thought. Charley could play the piano.

Paul was utterly crushed. 'Exc-c-cuse me, I thought you were S-Sunny,' he stammered, 'I mean K-Kate,' he added as the man looked blank. 'I'm her vertical neighbour P-Paul . . .' he said.

The man's face broke into a smile of recognition. 'Hi, yea,' he said. 'Kate's taking a shower. I'm her brother, John. She won't be long. I've heard a lot about you.'

Paul would have liked to return the compliment, but it wouldn't have been true. He had no idea Sunny had a brother, or any living relatives. For some reason he had always imagined her alone in the world. Hadn't she'd told him that? Obviously not. He could see the family resemblance now. It was a masculine version of the same lovely face.

'You play well,' Paul said.

'Not really. It's got a perfect tone, make anyone sound good,' John replied, fingering the keys.

'Not me, I can't play,' Paul laughed. 'But I agree it is a beautiful instrument.'

'Yeah, I was with Kate when she bought it. All fired up ready to learn . . . Yeah, right!' John rolled his eyes. 'She left it upstate with me for three years. I miss it, but I've got my own and who knows? Maybe she will start now. I hope so, it'd be good therapy for her.' He stood up and carefully closed the lid.

'Bought it? I thought it was your grandfather's,' Paul said.

John froze. He looked pained. 'My grandfather?' His eyes shot to the door.

'Yes, the c-concert pianist,' Paul confirmed.

'The concert . . . ? Is that what Kate said?' John's eyes widened.

Paul nodded.

'Well, if that's what she told you, I guess it must be so,' he spluttered, ducking out of the room. 'Say I'll phone her later, yeah?' And with that he was gone.

How weird was that? John had definitely been put on the spot. He didn't have a clue what Paul had been on about. But why would Sunny spin such a story if there were no truth in it? It didn't add up. What would her reaction be, he wondered, when she heard he'd met her brother. Well, he was about to find out, as here she was. She took his breath away with her beauty sometimes, and this was one of them. Her hair, wet from the shower, accentuated her eyes and high cheekbones. Barefoot, and dressed in a simple, white cotton shift, it seemed to Paul as if an embodiment of spring had entered the room.

'I just met John,' he said, watching her face carefully. What he saw was unadulterated pleasure and anticipation.

'Where is he?' she cried, clapping her hands.

'He said he'd call you later,' he replied.

'Damn, damn, damn. I was as quick as I could be. He might have waited. Did he say where he was going?' Nothing surreptitious there, he thought.

'No, but he did say he'd been with you when you bought that piano,' he said, more as a challenge than a fact.

'That's right.'

'I thought you said you inherited it from your grandfather,' he persisted.

'An inheritance that I had to pay his bloody-bimbo-bitch-of-a-jail-bait-wife for,' she spat with such venom it shocked him. Then, quick as mercury, she was all sweetness and light again. 'Look Paul,' she said softly, 'do you mind if we don't go into this now? It's long and ugly, and I'm late.' She slipped on her high heels as she spoke, and grabbed her purse. Tears were welling up in those sapphire-blue eyes, threatening to spill out over the long lashes and perfect cheekbones.

'No, no, of c-course not. It's none of my business. I'm s-s-sorry I mentioned it,' he said, horrified to have pried into such a patently delicate subject.

'I'll tell you about it one day, OK?' she whispered in his ear, kissing it and giving him an instant hard-on, to his intense embarrassment. 'Be an angel and lock up, will you? I'll ring as soon as I get back.' With that she turned and ran.

He heard the door slam, leaving him alone for the second time in twenty minutes.

Back up in his loft, he went over the whole thing again in his mind, step by step. It made no sense whichever way he looked at it. He felt he was missing a vital piece of the puzzle. He saw no duplicity in Sunny's eyes, just pain, which made him feel all the more protective of her. In fact, hadn't John mentioned something about therapy? He couldn't remember the context, but the way he escaped rather than face the sister who so clearly adored him at the mere mention of the grandfather's name made Paul certain of one thing, and one thing only. The siblings had some nasty skeletons in their closet.

From that day on, Paul accepted that Sunny was scarred from some dark history he wasn't privy to, and he tried to be understanding. A difficult thing when you're utterly in the dark as to what it is you're being understanding about. Gradually he came to realize there was little or no consistency between word and deed with her, and he began, slowly, to register how many times she'd let him down. Not that any of it was important, but it was boring to make a plan, no matter how trivial, only to be stood up, usually with no prior notice. Or, if she did bother to call, it was to regale him with lies that were so transparent that he couldn't help but be insulted by her estimation of his intelligence.

Over the next couple of months their easy-going relationship degenerated to such a degree that not only did Paul's infatuation for Sunny subside, he actually started to think of her as a virtual millstone around his neck. She was still utterly adorable at times, but he paid for those times with the duties he was expected to perform. The name 'Paul' became synonymous with 'slave'. 'Paul, could you just . . . Paul, will you please . . .' Bottles of water or giant, economy packs of detergent, anything remotely heavy, had somehow become his responsibility. Having once made the mistake of cleaning the squalor she called her kitchen in order to be able to enjoy a clean glass of water, that too had come to be expected of him.

John, her brother, often came in from Rhinebeck to visit his sister. Paul had made friends with him one evening, when John had arrived and found her out. With no alternative plan he came upstairs and knocked on Paul's door to see if he could leave his bag. He needed to eat. It had been a good day and Paul was only just cleaning his brushes. Being hungry too, he suggested they go down to his dog-bistro on 22nd where they could have dinner together while waiting for her to get back. Before leaving they pinned a note on her door saying where they'd gone. Over dinner they discussed a wide range of topics, forgot that they were waiting and enjoyed themselves. It made a nice change for Paul who, thanks to his self-inflicted work ethic, hadn't made many friends in the three months he'd lived in Manhattan. She stayed out till 2 a.m. that night. By the time she got back her brother was asleep at Paul's on the sofa he had secured for $22 at the auction rooms on East 16th. Far from being grateful and apologetic, Sunny acted hurt. As if she was the one who had been stood up. Like they had in some way betrayed her by having a good time. That's when Paul decided that John was by far the easier sibling.

Thursday 23 November was a red-letter day, made so by an acquaintance of John's who was coming to look over Paul's work. Sagat MaCaw was a quasi-gallery owner in Manhattan's meat-packing district. It was more of an empty space than anything else, according to John, but as the guy was looking for artists to show, he'd thought it was worth a try. Sagat MaCaw was an odd-looking individual with a very large nose. He examined the contents of Paul's fridge, before offering him a show at the end of January. Three months inside his year's deadline. Paul, ecstatic, accepted without the hint of a stammer. As soon as Mr MaCaw had left, Paul went and bought a bottle of champagne at the Broadway Baby liquor store. Rang Sunny and invited her up to celebrate. She appeared in a moment, if anything more excited than he was. They toasted his achievement, and went on to finish the bottle before, on Sunny's instigation, to Paul's complete delight, they made love in his woefully inadequate little bed. What a day. Paul couldn't believe his luck. Everything he'd fantasized about for so long was happening all at once. She lived up to all his expectations. He fell in love. The stars had to be in very serious alignment, he decided with delight.

Over the following weeks, when Paul went somewhere, Sunny went with him. She helped choose which frames to use on his paintings and gave him lots of starry names and addresses for his opening night's guest-list, still possessing an enviable address book from her modelling days. As ever, she created every bit as much chaos as she solved. Still it was all fun, and the pre-show nerves that threatened to make him ill were dispelled by her enthusiasm. The only blot on his landscape was that she refused to make love to him again. He wanted to and tried to kiss her. She turned away, saying it had been a one-off, a unique celebration that they'd shared together in honour of his impending show.

'Is it Charley?' he asked.

She looked shocked. 'What do you know about that?'

'Only that he's no good for you,' he replied. 'Leave him,' he pleaded. 'I'll look after you.'

She softened. 'You're sweet, don't ruin it.'

Show day dawned. He hadn't slept a wink the night before, tossing and turning. Occasionally he'd look over to where the invitation should be pinned to the screen. There it invariably was, so he'd quickly look away, filled with simultaneous relief and dread. Sunny rang early. She was bubbling. How was he feeling? She had got him something. When should she bring it up? 'Immediately,' he replied, and up she came carrying a suit of the palest duck-egg blue, almost no colour at all. A perfect fit. It was shockingly flattering, and transformed his appearance, giving his neglected mop of dark, curly hair a romantic quality and his complexion, contrasting with the whisper of blue, lost its sallow pallor and took on the appeal of alabaster.

She adjusted the lapels and brushed her lips over his. 'So handsome,' she said, and leant into his chest. He enveloped her in his arms. 'I've gotta go, sweetie,' she said, pulling away. 'I'm late.' Then she solemnly promised to meet him at the gallery no later than six and ran.

He was down there by five, double-checking everything. At seven, people began turning up in twos and threes. At one point there must have been about thirty people. At 7.25 he sold a painting. His first, a banana skin at sunset. Still yellow, it lay discarded in Riverside Park, crumpled on the grass with the shoreline of New Jersey, all pink, red and yellow in the background. As luck would have it, the young lady who bought it, Sagat's niece, came from New Jersey and lived in one of the buildings that Paul had particularly concentrated on. Her kitchen curtains were clearly visible in the finished painting. He was longing to tell Sunny. Surely it might warrant another 'unique celebration'. Two more red dots materialized, meaning two more paintings had sold. One of them might not really count, as it was of Patsy and bought by her mother, who'd flown in for his big night. Paul, deeply touched, tried to return the money, to be met with blank refusal. The other was smaller, an urban view which had gone to a bona fide stranger. He didn't care and kept looking over to the door, expectant . . . waiting.

What should have been a triumphant evening was ruined by Sunny's absence. Dinner with his mother-in-law afterwards was awkward. He sat there turning his cellphone over in his pocket, not listening to her congratulations, or news of home, or managing to engage in any way. He couldn't believe it. Sunny hadn't even bothered to ring and explain. A relief in a way; who knows what he would have said, he was so angry and hurt, and anyway, if she did call, he knew that it would be to tell more lies. So fuck her and her selfishness, he thought, paying the bill.

Since moving in, it had been Sunny's habit to bother him at least once a day, regardless of time. The concept had no meaning to her, and she was as likely to pester him at three in the morning as she was that same hour in the afternoon. Since his show, however, there had been nothing. For a while the silence was a blessed relief. But after a week went by, he started to worry. He understood someone as beautiful as she must be used to forgiveness, and imagined that she would try to wheedle her way back into his good books. 'I'll wear earplugs if necessary,' he promised himself, expecting the phone to ring and hammering to start on the door any second. 'Whatever she tries I'll stay focused,' he thought. She didn't try anything and the lack of harassment disturbed his equilibrium, preyed on his mind. He did his best to concentrate. Build on the success he'd achieved. It was impossible. Even his beloved routine now appeared pretentious to him. He'd chosen a solitary life when Patsy died and congratulated himself for his success. Too soon. Sunny had pierced his isolation and created a new void in his emotions. He felt if something had happened to her he'd never forgive himself.

Morbid fancies of accident and illness niggled at him, until he stopped the painting he was doing of the neon lights across the street. Left everything and went down to quiz the superintendent of the building. He wasn't in his office, so Paul continued searching, eventually finding him outside, cowering in the porch against the rain, smoking a cigarette. 'Have you seen Miss Palmer from 6A?' he asked with no preamble.

The little man bristled and took on the mantle of a martyr in uniform. 'Not seen her,' he said. 'Heard her though. A lot more than I'd like.'

'She's in then?' Paul said.

'She's in all right,' the officious man sniffed. 'Has been all week, making all kinds of racket. Mr Gandolfi in 6B asked me to do something. So I went up and she started yelling at me through the door.'

Paul's heart sank. He'd known it; a nagging voice in his head kept saying something dreadful had happened. He'd been too wrapped up in his own bruised ego to listen.

The super was still talking: '. . . her all-night parties, disturbing the other residents, I'm gonna have to report her to the board. "It's none of your business!" That's what she yelled at me.' The very memory of this insult made the little man go red in the face and he began to yell himself. Paul watched him dispassionately. 'It's precisely my business what goes on in this building,' he ranted on. 'Who does she think she is? She's got no right talk to me like that. Little tramp.' He hadn't and obviously wasn't about to draw breath.

Paul cut in. 'Here,' he said, slipping the aggrieved pedant a twenty-dollar bill. 'Wait 'til we see why. I'll go up.' The nasty wannabe official took the money and moved away from the door. Paul turned his back to the wind and increasingly horizontal rain to light another cigarette from the stub of his last.

In the elevator Paul fingered the key on the ring in his pocket, Sunny's. She had a copy of his. They'd exchanged after the John débâcle; it made sense for emergencies. Neither had ever used them and Paul didn't intend to now. Arriving at her door, he knocked, waited. Knocked again, twice more, each time harder than the last. Finally, putting her key in the door he let himself in, or tried to . . . Someone had wedged the door shut, not very well and Paul squeezed his face to the open crack. Instinctively he recoiled from the rank stench that hit his nostrils. Taking a gulp of the relatively clean air on the landing, he tried again, this time calling her name. The long hallway looked messier than ever; it didn't feel right. Had she been robbed or something worse? The urgency of the situation made him ram his shoulder against the door. Whatever the obstruction, it gave way and the door flew back. Paul walked in, leaving it open behind him in case he needed a speedy exit.

The place was in a dreadful state, even by her standards. Venturing further, he peered in every room. All the curtains were closed, but he could see how trashed they were. The kitchen defied imagination. Filthy broken crockery and unfinished fast-food cartons, now ashtrays, mingled with bowls of swollen cereal floating in rancid milk, growing mould, also used as ashtrays. Gagging and now seriously concerned, Paul went back into the hallway and flipped open his cellphone to call 911. He saw the door swing shut out of the corner of his eye. Whirling round, he squinted into the corner behind the door and there was Sunny curled up on the floor, shivering in the half-light.

'Sunny?' he whispered.

She jumped up, eyes wild, urgently shushing him quiet. She was rail-thin, covered in cuts and bruises and appeared to have lost her mind. Rushing past him into the piano room, she peeked out from behind the closed shutters, all the while babbling about being under surveillance by the FBI.

'Shall I get John?' he asked.

'It'd be no good. He's under surveillance too,' she confided. 'Come and see.' She dragged him across to the window. When they reached it she pulled him back, 'Careful,' she hissed, 'don't let them see you.'

This was terrible, what was he to do? he wondered. 'Come on, Sunny.' He made his voice as reassuring as possible. 'Let's go upstairs, they'll never find you there. You can clean up, have something to eat. What d'you say?'

She turned on him. 'You don't believe me, do you?' she screamed, spinning back to the window. She checked her watch, and went tense. 'Wait a minute. There. See for yourself, they've been doing it all week.'

Catching her paranoia, he flattened himself against the wall and peered out of the window, paramilitary-style, to see . . . 29th Street. Nothing struck him as out of the ordinary. But then, this was New York, so that would be, by the city's very nature, a tall order at the best of times. Which this wasn't.

'I can't see a thing,' he said.

'There,' she hissed behind him, taking his head in her hands and jerking it to the left. Her trembling finger pointed over his shoulder to a white car passing in the street. 'Amos school of driving' was written in red along a triangular advertising block that ran the length of the car's roof.

'What?' he asked, perplexed. 'You mean the student driver?'

'Get back,' she rasped, pushing him away from the window. 'It's a cover, the fuckers. They circle every hour.' She really was crazy, he thought. He needed help with her.

'OK,' he said, trying for just the right conspiratorial note. 'I know someone on the inside, I'll find out what's going on. Stay here, don't open the door to anyone till I get back.' He put his index finger along the side of his nose and winked at her, the way he'd seen spies do in B movies. Sunny must have seen the same movies, as she nodded, suitably impressed, and let him slip out.

He waited impatiently for the elevator, then used the freestanding, aluminium ashtray to jam the doors on his floor. He had to talk to John. He rang and the answering machine picked up. 'Hi,' John's recorded voice said, 'leave a message or try my cell. Yeah, I finally succumbed and got one: 917-324-4170. Hope you do. Bye.'

Paul searched for a pencil, a pen, scrap of paper, anything to write with or on. The loft, now an archetypal artist's mess, defeated him and he grabbed the brush, still sticky with the vermilion he'd been using earlier, and daubed John's number across the roofs and pale blue sky of his carefully executed city landscape. He dialled and when John answered Paul's relief was immense. 'Sunny . . . fuck, I mean K-Kate's gone c-crazy, she thinks the FBI are out to get her,' he blurted, then remembered. 'S-sorry John, it's Paul. Hi.'

Without missing a beat John's voice said, 'Has she been doing Charley?'

Even in the midst of his hysteria, Paul was nevertheless shocked that anyone could refer to his own sister's sexual activities in such a casual way. 'Yes, I think so. I mean I don't know. I've never been under the bed for verification, but I know she's always waiting for him, and that upsets her. What's the story with those two anyway?'

There was what seemed like a long, long pause, before John's voice said, 'Hang on Paul, I'm in the city. I'll be there in fifteen. Keep an eye on her, will you?'

Paul, happy to see the light at the end of the tunnel, said, 'Yeah, sure. I'll go right back down, but please hurry.'

The nineteen minutes before John arrived were a nightmare, not that they got much better after, just weirder. It turned out – as any simpleton would, Paul thought, have known – that Kate was a recovering drug addict, clearly not recovering very well. Cocaine had been her drug of choice, Charley, of course. Paul was mortified at his own stupidity. It wasn't as if he hadn't done the stuff himself, in fact he'd stopped only after developing an allergic reaction that made his nose swell up like Karl Malden's if he so much as looked at the stuff. Truth to tell it had been no great loss; he'd never really cared for it, equating it with a good time only because everyone else had. It was all so eighties. It'd never occurred to him that anyone could be so downright passé as to get strung out on it any more. OK, some people still snorted it occasionally at a party or wedding or something. Even he'd rubbed some on his gums once in a blue moon. But descend into coke paranoia? He'd thought that a thing of the past.

The moment John arrived, carrying a bottle of water, he took control, walked straight over to Sunny, who was still kneeling by the window spying on her imaginary spies. 'Take this,' he coaxed. Sunny heard and, still on her knees, shuffled around to face him. Put her head back as if to see him better and opened her mouth. He placed a little white pill on her tongue and put the neck of the open water bottle to her lips. She drank. Paul watched this scene unfold silently in front of him. It was surreal and reminded him of church. It was like John was the priest giving Sunny, the innocent, her first communion.

'Come,' John's positively pastoral voice said, 'let's get you to bed.'

Paul was amazed to see Sunny rise from her knees, as elegant as all get-out, and glide gracefully from the room. The vestal virgin has left the building, Paul thought, reminded of Elvis for some peculiar reason.

He could see all this had happened before. 'I'll be upstairs,' he said to John. 'Call if you need help,' and left them to it.

Back upstairs, for diversion, he went to clean John's cellphone number off his canvas, but was captivated by the violence of the vandalized painting. His angst over Sunny appeared so clearly in those jagged numbers. It was real, he thought, a reflection of himself at the moment of painting. Inspired, it set him off down a whole new, and infinitely more interesting, he thought, creative avenue. Sagat MaCaw was not convinced.

John came up later that night and told Paul the whole of the Sunny saga. It was bad; she had been in and out of rehab since she was sixteen. Never stayed the course. 'Never hit rock bottom I suppose,' John said. 'I've offered to pay for her to go again. It won't do any good,' he added blankly, 'but what can I do? I have to try. She's my sister and she's killing herself.'

'Will she go back?' Paul asked.

'No,' John said, 'I don't think so. She's already insisted she can go it alone with her Narcotics Anonymous meetings.' He shrugged at Paul and attempted to smile. They hung out for a couple of hours. Not talking – there wasn't really that much left to say – but they very deliberately drank a lot of whiskey. At four that morning John, like an errant schoolboy, went back down to his comatose sister.

That night marked the beginning of the months of hell for everyone involved with Sunny. She didn't attend her meetings – not that anyone thought she would – and her lies got progressively more convoluted and pointless. Any friends to whom she had given objects of any value, and this included Paul, were now accused of being thieves who had stolen those things from her. Paul saw a cruelty emerge in her character which he hadn't noticed before. As her finances depleted, her viciousness grew. Six months later, Sunny was broke and forced to move out of her apartment. The first Paul knew of it was when he found her piano, for the second time, occupying the elevator, ready to start its journey back to John in upstate New York. It was a sad day for Paul and a positively gleeful on for the beleaguered superintendent.

Over the last few months of her residency Paul had tried to help her, but Sunny was gone. It transpired she didn't just take cocaine but anything she could lay her hands on. It broke his heart. Not hers, she was too lost in the miasma of her chemicals to notice Paul's growing alienation. She continued her downward spiral, congratulating herself roundly for handling every day with such tactful aplomb.

For Paul, Sunny's tale had no end. He couldn't bear to stay in touch and see it. Even John, much as he liked him, proved too much of a reminder of his failure with Sunny. So, with a heavy heart, and a laudable sense of self-preservation, he cut them both out of his life. He'd gone through one agonizing death with someone he loved, and he knew he didn't have the strength to endure another. More importantly, he didn't think

Sunny wanted him to. In one of her lucid moments, she acknowledged how far out there she'd gone and attempted an apology. He wanted to believe her capable of recovery but he couldn't. It was too obvious: her sensibilities had been addled to such a degree that she didn't have a clue how to start. Or a wish to.

Silver Spoon

Jennifer was born with a silver spoon in her mouth which, upon her reaching adolescence, was ripped out with such force it nearly broke all her front teeth. The rot began a year earlier on the day of her fourteenth birthday. That was the day her father chose to desert their home and leave her in the care of her pill-popping, alcoholic diva of a mother. For the eighteen months prior to this cataclysmic event they'd all been living at the Regency. Jennifer had her own room, as did both her father and mother and her mother's lady's maid, Blossom, who had a poor little room in the back. All the other three were resplendent, decorated with French plasterwork of escalating extravagance, culminating with her mother Sarah's, where the candlelight bulbs in the wall sconces reflected into infinity against the antique, mirrored walls. Jennifer thought that room embodied unadulterated sumptuousness.

The Regency, one of London's grand, and once ubiquitous, residential hotels was situated in Belgravia. It offered a choice of either rooms for the usual traveller passing through or fully fitted apartments for the long-term guest. Renowned for its sympathetic attitude to those of an artistic temperament, it was the obvious place for Sarah Lawrence, Jennifer's mother. Sarah was one of those Judy Garland-type stars who demanded fanatical adoration and got it. She needed more pandering to than ever at this juncture of her life as, together with her sycophantic piano player, she'd written a one-woman tribute-to-herself for the West End stage, now in the middle of rehearsals, opening in three weeks' time and already sold out. The pressure was on and the atmosphere volatile in Sarah's inner circle. Especially for Jennifer, who was doing her best to blend in at the American school in London. It was bad enough being Sarah Lawrence's daughter, without any of her new friends finding out how crazy her mother really was.

Their apartment at the hotel was on the fourth floor, usually reached via the elevator, a rich mahogany and brass affair, fitted with a green velvet bench to rest on as you rose through the building. Jennifer loved it when the doors opened to reveal the azure-blue Axminster carpet with a border of golden scrolls, shaded for a three-dimensional effect. Deep-pile, it ran luxuriously from the bottom step in the lobby, up the entire stairwell to the very top floor. Each landing – Jennifer had explored them all – was squared off with the golden wool. After school she liked to huddle up, hidden away on the flight above their floor, leaning against the meticulously maintained wood of the liftshaft. The faint, slightly antiseptic smell of beeswax made it a special place for her to do homework or read a book, undisturbed by her mother's tantrums. Blossom would nip out now and again to bring her a cup of tea and a slice of cake or a sandwich. Then Jennifer would picnic on the stairs while she waited for her father to return from his club, where he spent most of his time. A professional poker player, he often didn't come back all night but, if at all possible, he would try to see his daughter at the end of her day before returning to the game. Blossom was invaluable to Jennifer, who could confide in the eccentric creature and know her secrets would go no further. A lunatic in her own right, Blossom always wore a hat, in the house and out, usually flowery or fluffy, a bit like the Queen Mother's, and she'd stuck with Sarah through two marriages. A creature of habit and a snob, she continued to call her 'Your Ladyship', even though Sarah's wedding to Lord Sneed had been over sixteen years ago and lasted a mere fortnight before being annulled. 'I was with her Ladyship before you were a twinkle in anybody's eye,' she liked to say to Jennifer. Or if Sarah was being a nightmare she'd sympathize with the daughter, trotting out her other favourite: 'Her Ladyship's a lovely woman,' she'd announce, 'just not all there upstairs, if you know what I mean.' And she'd tap her cranium with her index finger to illustrate her point.

One afternoon, Jennifer was eating a cheddar cheese and honey sandwich in her hidey-hole and the lift doors opened long before the expected time. She sprang up, readying herself to jump down and surprise her father, and was instead electrified to recognize the great Natalia Nablova being ushered by the hotel manager into the only other apartment on their floor. Jennifer was an ardent fan; she attended the Ballet Rambert three times a week for classes in an old church in Notting Hill Gate and for her Miss Nablova was the greatest living ballerina. Plucking up courage, she came shyly down the three steps from her sanctuary, proffering her maths exercise book in an awkward way, and asked for the great lady's autograph. Miss Nablova, who was staying for four months while she danced at Covent Garden, graciously acquiesced and a bond of sorts was struck, with most of the adhesive being provided by Jennifer.

Well trained by her mother to gush appreciation for the smallest glimpse of anything approaching talent, Jennifer proved agreeable to the genuinely gifted Natalia Nablova, who invited the intense ribbon-of-a-dancing-schoolgirl to practise bar with her in what she called her studio.

Mirrors lined the walls, as they did in Sarah's room, but this one was empty save for a ballet bar, retrieved from the basement where it lay waiting for the ballerina's visits, which had been pushed into the middle of the floor and had its wheels locked. In this hallowed space the endless reflection lacked any suggestion of the *poule-de-luxe* decadence of Jennifer's apartment. On the contrary, it was a picture of diligence: two figures clad in leotards and leg warmers intent on perfecting the domination of their muscles. At the end of each punishing session they'd sit starving together at the kitchen table, impatiently waiting for Miss Nablova's Hungarian maid Tilda to serve up lovely big bowls of goulash, pasta or some other energy-giving carbohydrate such as Wiener schnitzel with mashed potatoes. While gobbling the resuscitating fare they'd talk, in a very maudlin Russian way, of the harshness of love or their aching muscles. Once Natalia poured a small tot of vodka for Jennifer, explaining that it was imperative she drink in order to join her in an old Russian toast to eternal friendship – it was Jennifer's first taste of spirits and, given by such a sophisticated grown-up, made her feel very important. The great ballerina, in a magnificent gesture, threw her head back and drank her much larger shot in one, then hurled the glass into the lit fire and Jennifer, thrilled, did the same. Heady times and by far the best part of Jennifer's life.

Her fourteenth birthday dawned and she did four jetés across the landing to see her friend and mentor. Would she get a gift from her heroine? Of course she would, but what, was the question pirouetting around her brain. Any old bit of signed memorabilia would be best. A programme from *Giselle* perhaps? Maybe, just maybe, a pair of the ballerina's old points? They came from Freed's like Jennifer's, only hers weren't points yet. They were pink satin, though, and Natalia's were only leather. If it were her old shoes, she needn't even sign them; they'd be imbued with her genius and treasured for ever, Jennifer thought, positively brimming over with expectation. Catching sight of the watch on her arm, which was raised and about to knock on the Great One's door, she saw it was 8.35.

Damn. She turned on her heels and clattered down the stairs. It'd have to wait till after school, which meant excruciating expectation all day. At 5.30 that afternoon Jennifer spun back through the revolving door, ran past the reception waving at her friend the concierge and, much too excited to endure the stately ascent of the lift, leapt up the four floors almost as fast as she'd gone down them earlier. Letting herself into Natalia's, *comme d'habitude*, she made, as she always did, for the guest bathroom to change for practice, but something in the echo of her footsteps on the parquet flooring kept her walking down to the kitchen at the far end of the hall, where she found no Tilda, no shoes, no nothing in fact, except a shock. The place was empty. All the personal embellishments had been stripped from the walls and counters. Natalia Nablova and Tilda had obviously left the apartment.

Flying back across the landing, she burst into her mother's room to tell her of the devastating discovery. On receipt of this information, obscene invectives came tumbling out of Sarah's slack mouth, culminating with the threat of shaving Jennifer's head for collaborating with the enemy. 'Your great cunt of a ballerina, has, with your father, but no warning to *me*, up sticks and gone.' Slurring, she put particular emphasis on the word *me*.

'What d'you mean?' Jennifer asked, already crying.

'The concierge saw them into a car together with all their bags. Fucking spineless worm, all he left me was a note,' she said, howling. 'Can you imagine someone doing that to *me*?'

'Or me,' Jennifer blubbed.

'Why *you*? He's not even your father,' her negligent mother growled. Only to deny the venomous bombshell five seconds later, saying she was drunk, which, while being true, did nothing to make anything better.

Jennifer went into the back quarters of their apartment and sobbed to Blossom, who couldn't help. No one could. The damage had been done. The seed of doubt planted. From that moment on, with both females feeling terminally betrayed, their diminished household grew grim.

Her mother basically went to pieces. She quit her one-woman show, reneging on her contract, and lay in bed eating chocolates, ordering room service and watching TV. A constant fleet of doctors, conventional and homoeopathic, swirled through their apartment, along with psychics, acupuncturists and masseurs. 'They're bleeding me dry,' Sarah wailed to Blossom to explain the dearth of her wages, 'scalping me, simply scalping me.' The devoted enabler took no notice and simply plumped up her mother's pillows.

'You need them, Sarah,' Jennifer said. She'd always had to call her mother by her Christian name.

'That's the truth, M'Lady,' Blossom agreed.

'I know sweeties, but the money . . . Well, we'll just have to tighten our belts, that's all.' Springing out of bed as she said this, she clinched both her hands around her still tiny waist to mime asphyxiation and made them all laugh.

No speeches on economy amounted to a hill of beans in the Lawrence household, as Jennifer knew. Sarah was accustomed to pampering; she needed the ministrations that the many practitioners gave her. More importantly still, she needed their undivided attention to stop her sliding into one of her even deeper depressions. These black holes invariably ended with an attempt on her own life. Jennifer had, in her fourteen years, witnessed Sarah being carried out, apparently lifeless, on a stretcher three times. Not counting the numerous lesser attempts – usually on school nights – when she'd have to march her mother up and down, plying her with coffee to bring her around, or the interminable hours she'd spent crying and pleading through a closed door, to persuade her mother to unlock it without hurting herself. So, for her, they were a small price to pay to keep Sarah stable, and she remained grateful to and blessed each and every one of the many charlatans who pitched up at their door.

Finances were finite. Jennifer's schooling was secure, paid for by a trust that her maybe-father had set up at her birth. Also, when he left he'd sent her a Lloyd's chequebook with her name printed on each individual cheque. The accompanying note told her she had five hundred pounds in her very own account and that it would be topped up by the same amount every three months. The note suggested that she keep her good fortune quiet from Sarah, which Jennifer had to admit was pretty sound advice. She wanted to hate him, but this was a pretty great thing for a father, who-maybe-wasn't, to have done, she thought, pining for his presence.

Sarah dug in and refused to work and three short months later they were forced to decamp from their lovely Regency rooms and take up residence in a borrowed basement off Paulton Square in Chelsea. This move proved to be an unexpected blessing, as their benefactor, Marco Shields, an elderly stately homo, was an ardent admirer of her mother's. He also lived in the house above them in splendiferous camp. Calling her 'the divine Sarah Lawrence', he lavished indiscriminate adoration on Jennifer's mother, thereby satiating, momentarily, her bottomless craving for attention. With the heat off Jennifer and Blossom for a while, things ran smoothly in their subterranean habitat.

After two months of living there, Jennifer was killing time one afternoon lolling about on the sofa in the front room when the telephone rang. Sarah was out and Blossom didn't pick up, so Jennifer answered. 'Hi,' she said lazily.

'Jenny, darling?' It was the voice of her father-who-perhaps-wasn't. 'Thank God it's you.' He sounded happy. Jennifer felt every muscle in her being tense. 'I'm in America with Natalia and we both miss you dreadfully.'

This was the first time she'd heard from him in five months. What was she supposed to say? She remained silent.

'I'm sorry I left like I did, Jenny, but you of all people know how impossible your mother can be. It was the only way . . .'

His voice trailed off, then came back all jolly and asked, 'Can you come and visit us in the Easter break?'

Jennifer was incensed by his admission of cowardice. He recognized the hell he'd abandoned her to, which made it much worse. She didn't, as she wanted to, ask him if he was her biological father or not, as she couldn't manage to form the words and instead mumbled something about seeing nearer the time. Secretly, in her heart, she refused to pardon him and firmly took her mother's side from that moment on. Nevertheless, she did write his New York number down on a scrap of paper and stored it safely in her mirrored box. It used to have a beautiful little ballerina that popped up and twirled around when you opened it, before she'd ripped it off its stand. Blurting out 'I love you Daddy,' she hung up. No, she thought trembling, she would not visit them for the Easter break thank you very much.

Seven months passed before another ordinary day began in their basement flat and at 8.30 in the morning, Jennifer, after breakfasting with Blossom in the kitchen, left for school *as usual*, kissing her mother goodbye on the way out *as usual*, and that's where all the *as usual* stopped for good, only she didn't know it at the time.

Arriving back that evening, she put her key in the lock and it didn't work. The door remained shut. After banging and hollering for what seemed like an age, Jennifer got her mother to come to the door, staggering a little. She'd obviously been drinking, as her face was flushed and her glazed eyes had a familiar, yet disconcertingly absent quality to them. Steadying herself in the doorway, Sarah effectively barred Jennifer's entry, acting distracted as if she'd been interrupted from a very important meeting. 'It's the fledgling!' she cried, as if genuinely surprised to see her own daughter back from school. 'You flew the nest. Deserted us. Gone.'

Bonkers, her mother had gone bonkers – again. Jennifer knew that arguing would only make matters worse. Sarah could be an ugly drunk when she got going. Still, being looked squarely in the eye and told that she'd 'flown the nest', when she was clearly standing there, satchel in hand, tired and hungry after a long day at school, seemed so utterly unfair that she forgot to tread on eggshells, and blew her proverbial gasket, thereby sealing her homeless state. With no potential apology possible until Sarah had slept it off, Jennifer went to stay with Alana, a schoolfriend who lived on a houseboat down the road. Believing Jennifer's excuse – she said that Sarah's singing was driving her mad – Alana thought her friend's predicament glamorous rather than desperate.

The following day, with the help of Blossom, Jennifer managed to negotiate a stay of execution. Six weeks to find alternative accommodation. A period dictated by Sarah's absence; she was going on a mysterious cruise aboard a private yacht. This deadline was relayed through Blossom, as Sarah refused to discuss it openly with her daughter. When she returned she was sorry, she told Blossom, but Jennifer would be on her own. Strict conditions were attached to Sarah's maternal largesse. One, all rooms except Jennifer's own were to be locked and two, Blossom was to keep all the keys about her person at all times. Even as she listened to 'her Ladyship's' instructions Blossom, devoted as she was, realized that Sarah had gone too far. It wasn't right to starve a growing girl, she thought, and for the first time she uncharacteristically and flagrantly ignored Sarah's instructions, leaving the kitchen door open, with some soup, stew or casserole ready and waiting for Jennifer to warm up when she came back hungry.

Blossom, always the only clue as to what was going on, remained true to form. Through her, Jennifer found out the state of play. Her mother was hoping to remarry, for the third time. 'It's his age that's the problem,' Blossom whispered confidentially, 'only twenty-eight. Couple that with the divorce not yet come through from your father' – Jennifer hadn't known that one was in the offing – 'and you can understand why her Ladyship's so nervous.' Jennifer should have guessed;

her mother's passions had always been at the root of family problems. Even when her supposed father was still there, Sarah had retained her so-called 'swains'. She understood the implications of what Blossom was trying to convey. If the prospective husband was twenty-eight years old, who knew what age Jennifer would have to be to fit in with her mother's tangled web of fiction? Any, she was prepared to bet, except a physically precocious fifteen-year-old. Naturally she had to be banished, she thought, empathizing, as usual, with her mother's predicament.

Left to her own devices, Jennifer turned out, necessity being the mother of invention, to be a rather resourceful girl. She managed, with the aid of Blossom's introduction, to rent a room from a woman living in a mock-Tudor, half-timbered apartment building near Regent's Park. 'Anything for Blossom,' Celestine, the owner, said when Jennifer asked. 'The best maid I ever had. She knows I can't bear to see a girl in trouble.'

Jennifer paid fifteen pounds a week, and although the nondescript council flat was small and her room minuscule, she loved it. Heavily disguised, with lamps dotted about which glowed seductively from beneath fringed shawls of reds and orange. More of the same hung from the ceiling in the main room, transforming it into something like an Arabian tent, under which squashy velour, beanbag seats and what appeared to be a couple of mattresses covered with purple fabric, as well as oversized cushions, surrounded the coffee table, a large brass tray on a low stand. This shabby, bohemian style of living was all very original and wonderful for Jennifer. On top of which Celestine's flat was much nearer to the American school in St John's Wood, meaning Jennifer could wake up later. The one drawback to living at Celestine's was her constant entertaining, when Jennifer would have to stay in her room. Still, it was a small price to pay for security.

The remarkable thing was that no one, not Blossom, not Marco, not even her father – if indeed he knew the situation –

and certainly not Jennifer herself, thought, at any stage, to remonstrate with Sarah or report her to the authorities over the deplorable treatment of her under-aged daughter. Instead, everyone tried to cover for her. The Divine Sarah Lawrence was not as others and, as such, seemed to receive leeway from the real world. Marco was terribly upset that such goings on were happening in his house and gave Jennifer his brother Bill's number, since Bill lived near Celestine in north London. 'Ring him for anything dear, any time, he's such a comfort.' Marco's voice was emotional as he shuffled, carrying her suitcase to the black cab he'd called for her. He slipped a fifty-pound note in her hand before closing the car door. 'Don't worry, dear girl,' he said, looking terribly old. 'You just have to give her a little breathing space; the divine aren't as others I'm afraid.' Then, sighing, he gave a sad little wave and turned to go back in the house. Jennifer peered down through the railings to their front window; Blossom's face was there. Was she crying? Jennifer couldn't quite tell and blew her a kiss as the taxi drew away from their door.

Settling back in her seat for the journey across London, she thought of Blossom and Marco and how sweet they'd been to her over the last couple of weeks. She kept telling them it wasn't necessary as she felt quite all right about everything really. She had her chequebook and was determined not to mope. So what if the father who left her wasn't her father, or her mother was insane. As long as she focused, her life could still turn out all right. 'That money talks I can't deny. I heard it once; it said bye-bye.' Her mother's favourite rhyme went around in her head as she watched the meter tick over, reminding her that it could disappear. She'd already squandered most of her quarterly five hundred pounds on frivolous purchases typical of a fifteen-year-old. 'If I'm to be on my own now, I suppose I'd better get a job,' she thought as the fare clicked into double figures.

'Don't look at me,' Celestine said, when Jennifer repeated

this intention to her. 'Blossom would never forgive me if I got you working.'

'I wasn't,' Jennifer shrugged, 'I was going to ask if I could use the phone.' It was raining outside and she didn't want to go to the box on the corner.

'Go ahead, dear,' Celestine replied and continued painting her toenails. Jennifer fished Marco's brother's number out of her coat pocket and rang Bill Shields, who owned Treasures, an antiques-cum-curio shop, nearby on Sutherland Avenue.

'Marco told me all about you,' he said. 'I've been waiting to see if you'd like some part-time work, helping me in the shop.'

Bingo! They made a plan to meet at Treasures after school the following afternoon. Bill, who wasn't gay but was archaic-looking, with horn-rimmed spectacles and a big bow tie, turned out to *really* need her help to bring his shop to order. It was so higgledy-piggledy you could hardly walk through it. There was some polishing to do too.

'An hour after school's fine with me – and maybe some weekends?'

'Great,' she said.

'When could you start?' Bill asked.

'Right now,' she replied and he handed her a cloth, some Brasso and a small metal object. It was a figure of a woman wearing a turban and swathed in folding fabric from the waist down. About three inches high, she was crouched on the top of a pair of slightly longer, lozenge-shaped brass plates that were criss-crossed with deep, rounded ridges and fixed together with bars through which Jennifer could see a metal ball the size of a marble. Holding on to the brass figurine, which had cleaned up a treat and fitted comfortably into the palm of her hand, Jennifer asked, 'What is it?'

'Indian, for washing clothes,' Bill said. 'The ridged underside is meant for rubbing soap into the cloth. The ball creates a rhythm while the women do their scrubbing.'

Jennifer wondered about people who would make such a beautiful thing for such a utilitarian purpose.

She liked being paid for her work; it made her exist somehow, and every new day became a challenge or a revelation to be absorbed or surmounted to the best of her ability. For instance, her landlady was a prostitute. It took more than three weeks for Jennifer to rumble to the fact and when she did, she only thought the better of her. The way Jennifer saw it, Celestine worked really hard for her money – she should know from the hours she spent shut in her room – yet was still magnanimous in her benevolence. It was a lesson in generosity to Jennifer, who duly took it in. Before simultaneously beginning to worry: why wasn't she passing judgement? Did she lack moral fibre? Possess no standards?

Obviously not, as she stopped living there only nine months later after Dave, a friend not a customer – Jennifer could tell them apart now – dropped by one day when Celestine was out. 'I'm in a hurry,' he said. 'Can't wait around. I'll just leave it in the usual place . . . eh?'

While asking her this, he removed his Mr Freedom platform boots and pried off the soles, revealing two well-wrapped cellophane bricks of compressed white powder, each the exact size of the cavity in the fake wedges. Jennifer was both relieved and disturbed. Relieved, because she'd thought him such a wanker, wearing those ridiculous boots. To discover they were purely practical and not sartorial, a necessary tool for his profession as a drug runner, pushed him up a small notch in her estimation. Disturbed because she didn't like drugs. Having been repeatedly shamed by both her parents as they'd snorted, dropped or smoked all sorts, she'd become pragmatic beyond her years and couldn't see the point of being busted for something she didn't do. Packing to leave Celestine's made her sad, not least because she would have to find somewhere else. Bill was looking on her behalf. 'It's in my interest,' he said when she thanked him. 'I like having you help in the shop.'

Contrary to all expectations held by Sarah's stalwarts, Jennifer did not sever ties with her mother, and instead did her best to visit her whenever she could face it. If the fiancé, Mathew, was around she'd pretend to be her mother's niece. She didn't much mind. It was low on the list of lies she'd participated in for peace.

Turning up one Sunday lunchtime, she found Blossom in a high state of excitement; she could hardly wait to tell Jennifer that her mother had landed a wonderful film role. 'She's to star in a musical based on the life of Lucrezia Borgia, dearie, and swears the script's better than *Evita*.'

'Fantastic,' Jennifer exclaimed.

'Yes, she's ever so happy. I shouldn't wonder if this wasn't an opportune moment to put in a bid to come home.'

'But it's his room now. She'll never let me back,' Jennifer said, referring to her old bedroom, which was now Sarah's fiancé's.

'No dear, she never would, not here – but we're about to expand, you see, into a large house, gorgeous with a swimming pool, in Hampstead. Think of it, dearie, we could all sit around in our Kafitans under lovely Parasolas and drink champers.'

Jennifer hugged the funny little woman. 'Good old Blossom,' she thought and went straight through to find Sarah. 'Hi, it's me,' she said, bouncing in and kissing her mother on both cheeks. 'I hear you've got a really good job.'

'Lucrezia Borgia,' Sarah sang in an operatic shriek, adding, 'warts and all.'

'Wonderful. I'll let you know where I'm going and come to the set if I can.'

'What? Going where?' Sarah asked.

'Not sure – Liverpool maybe.' Where did *that* come from? Jennifer thought. No matter; it did the trick.

'Why Liverpool?'

'Oh I don't know, I've got to move out of Maida Vale and Liverpool's cheaper. Anyway I'll ring and let you know.'

'Blossom!' Sarah bellowed. The devoted little woman sprang into the room a little too soon, if Sarah had bothered to notice.

'Yes, M'Lady,' she said, bobbing in a semi-curtsy, the turquoise flowers on her hat all of a tremble.

'Do we have a room for Jennifer in Hampstead?'

'Four on the top floor, M'Lady, she could have her pick.'

'That's settled then. Good. Let's have a gin and tonic, shall we?' This was not a question. Summer with a swimming pool then, Jennifer thought, relieved to have it all sorted out.

The one proviso was that she must not, under any circumstances, disturb her Uncle Mathew. This proved harder than it sounded, for he persisted in disturbing her. Not in any creepy way; it was just that Uncle Mathew was closer to Jennifer in age than he was to his own fiancée and naturally gravitated towards his contemporary. He enjoyed Jennifer's company; they shared the same taste in music. But by far the biggest problem, Jennifer realized, was that they got each other's sense of humour. Try as she might, she couldn't help laughing at his jokes, the very ones that were lost on her mother.

One evening as she was running past their room, late to meet Alana at the local cinema, Mathew called out, 'Hey Jennifer, that you? Come here. I want to ask you something.'

'What?' She stopped at the threshold of their door. 'I'm late.'

'What d'you call a black man flying a plane?'

'What?' she said, in too much of a hurry to guess.

'A pilot, you racist bastard.'

They both cracked up, laughing really hard. Until Jennifer felt her mother's eyes upon her; they were cold. She knew that look meant trouble. For some inexplicable reason she felt guilty and, since she loved her mother, she, like all the other people who toadied around Sarah Lawrence, pre-empted the inevitable storm that she could see gathering on the horizon and wearily moved out first.

Once again her timing was impeccable. Alana's parents were emigrating to France for their retirement and instead of buying their seventeen-year-old daughter a flat they had given her their houseboat, moored at the World's End in Chelsea. Alana, now a homeowner, had never lived by herself and was desperate for a flatmate. Jennifer, thanking her lucky stars, fitted the bill and seamlessly segued into life on a stationary boat. Reached via a network of gangways that had to be negotiated, their home would gently rock with the swell at high tide, affecting your stomach at first, as did the smells that appeared when the tide went out and left them marooned on the sludge of the riverbed.

Although this unsettled lifestyle did hinder her scholastic efforts somewhat, Jennifer still managed to graduate from the American School. Anticipating that her maybe-father might like to continue paying for her to attend a college in the United States, she had accordingly scraped up the grades required for acceptance to most of them.

She made a plan, and although filled with dread, went to visit him for a weekend in Manhattan. Miss Nablova was away, which was a great relief, off dancing *The Nutcracker* or something. Jennifer didn't know or care and hated ballet now. The betrayed toast to eternal friendship remained isolated as a seminal moment in her memory. Her maybe-father was thrilled to see her, and she, grudgingly, him. He was living in a suite at the Plaza and showed her to her room. The whole set-up reminded her of their last days together at the Regency. They hadn't seen each other for three years and Jennifer, overwhelmed, pretended to be jet-lagged and went to bed, where she lay staring at the ceiling and remembering. She made a special effort to look as pretty as she could for dinner. 'Jenny, you look beautiful,' her longed-for Daddy said as she walked in the suite's drawing room and she felt good for a moment. They went to the Quatre Saisons somewhere off Madison Avenue. It was very grand and delicious, and over dinner he happily fell in with her plan of attending an American-based college. 'Give you a break from Sarah,' he said. They talked it over.

'I like Cal Tech,' she admitted. 'I want to major in anthropology. Human behaviour is infinitely fascinating, don't you think?'

'Yes,' he agreed, 'well worth submerging yourself in.'

Strange, she thought, knowing instinctively he didn't count himself among the spectrum to be studied. Three years of normal life, secure in an apartment of her own, found and paid for by a man she called her father. A man who told her he was proud to do it, as he was proud of her. It made her sad and she didn't know why, but was glad when she left him and went through the departure gate at JFK.

As soon as she landed in England, after dumping her bags at the houseboat, on Blossom's entreaties – 'M'Lady's in an awful state' – she went at once to face her mother and a torrent of abuse. 'You've betrayed me, seeing that scum. After all I've done for you.'

'Please, Sarah,' Jennifer said, exhausted, 'I'm back, aren't I? It was only a weekend.' How, in heaven's name, was she going to tell her about Cal Tech?

'You know I hold you personally responsible for breaking us up in the first place,' Sarah said, not listening to her daughter.

'What?' Jennifer was floored at this new accusation.

'We were fine until your birthday. It gave us a sense of occasion to live up to and when we failed, that's what did it. Before then the Dada and me had never spent a night apart.'

Sarah was being just so ridiculous Jennifer didn't bother to argue. Instead, she formulated her own question. The one she'd been longing to ask for over four years. 'Am I Daddy's daughter or not?' she braved.

'How would I know?' her mother replied.

'What do you mean?' Jennifer gasped, incredulous.

'Oh, come on, Jennifer, you know the facts of life,' her mother said. 'If you're sleeping with two men at the same time, how can you possibly know?'

That was it. Nothing more definite was offered. Sarah, who looked as if she felt she'd done her bit, started to go out of the room. Jennifer sat there stunned. How was she feeling? It was hard to tell. Suicidal? If not, why not? She certainly should be, or at least scarred for life by her mother's callous admission that her very origin was in question. She continued to sit, not moving a muscle yet feeling oddly rational in this most surreal of situations, desperately trying to understand her emotions. Her mother looked back, said nothing and smiled. No, Jennifer realized, she wasn't scarred. In fact, she felt just the opposite. She'd never thought of herself as created by the random act of two people having sex, even though she understood the facts of life. It had simply never occurred to her. The father she knew had accepted her as his own without reservation and, until doubt had ensnared her, Jennifer had reciprocated. Why should all of those years of absolute certainty about her arrival in the world be thrown out and discarded because of the one simple, little fact that her mother had been sleeping with two men nine months before her birth? It was all so easy now, she understood; her father was her father, and that was that. Honesty was the best policy and that's official, she thought, since this had been the first time that her mother had been remotely honest with her. And by speaking the unspeakable truth, Sarah had dispelled the spectre that had haunted Jennifer for years.

She had an inkling as to who the other candidate for fatherhood might be. Blossom had always harped on about a lovely foreign gentleman friend her Ladyship used to know. So much so, that Jennifer had once wondered if it had been in the biblical sense. Not that it made much difference, as this great lover and maybe other father had died long ago. Jennifer could remember Sarah's grief. She was only five years old and it had been the first time she'd seen her mother, looking whiter than paper, carried out on a stretcher, her arms punctured with needles and a tube up her nose.

The hours preceding this incident had disturbed her even more. Having never seen the movie star who was her mother cry for real before, she'd tried to comfort her. But every time Sarah looked at Jennifer, her tears flowed afresh and she'd hold her daughter's face in her hands sobbing, 'Look Blossom, look! Identical.'

'Shall we have a bottle of champagne, darling?' her mother asked gaily, breaking into her thoughts, as she popped her head round the door.

'Why not?' Jennifer replied, standing up. She kissed her mother on the way to the little drinks fridge under the window seat in the drawing room.

Free from subterfuge and recrimination and feeling that a weight had been taken off her shoulders, Jennifer left for college a month later. Surprisingly, she managed to obtain her mother's blessing and accepted a pretty lacy bag filled with lavender from Blossom, who instructed her to put it in her underwear drawer.

And in this singular way, Jennifer managed to negotiate her own transition from adolescence and ease into adulthood, as a relatively well adjusted, predominantly happy human being.

It was not until many years later, standing in the dock of the Old Bailey, that she was convicted of first-degree murder and incarcerated in HMP Durham's high-security wing for life.

New York

It was 1972. Lilly was just sixteen years old, English, privileged and sexy, someone who would now be described as an 'It girl', meaning, she could do and did nothing, but could do, and did it with great charm – an earnest innocent who knew no boundaries and, while certainly brave in one way, a death-defying horsewoman and fearless in the face of mice and snakes, she was at core a country girl who believed all urban myths and lived her Manhattan life in a perpetual state of adventurous terror.

One of life's ubiquitous young drifters, biding her time before the inevitable marriage and children, she was spending a year in New York and living in her godfather Ronnie Gemmel's brownstone on 69th and Lexington, a residence of great opulence. Ronnie was a collector and his house was a trip. Lots of precious objects covered every surface – horizontal and vertical – and soft lights trained delicate, precise pools of illumination on to superlative examples of heavily gilded American empire furniture and paintings from every period. The problem being that if you weren't a work of art you lived in a netherworld. So Lilly always kept a small torch hanging around her neck in case anything required vision.

She had a job of sorts, working for Uncle Ronnie at the 57th Street Gallery, where she'd show up periodically. Her job description was never quite clear. As far as Lilly could see, it was to look pretty for the decrepit art collectors that sometimes dropped in. The 57th was on the corner of 57th Street and Fifth Avenue, twelve blocks from the house, next to Carnegie Hall. Whenever Lilly did deign to put in an appearance at her so-called work, the quickest route was through Central Park, which always looked so inviting from the inside of a checker cab, an oasis of calm in the middle of concrete chaos. She longed to cut through the park, down to the gallery, and had got as far as the entrance a couple of times but never dared step in. She'd watched far too much television not to know that this was the big-bad-Apple, where your personal safety changed, with no warning from city block to city block, and heaven help you if you strayed over into the wrong area. Young kids carried guns and knives. Cops were as likely to shoot as look at you and, most relevant of all for Lilly, Central Park was where rapists lurked, ever ready to pounce, even in broad daylight. It was a vicious circle. The less she dared, the less she dared and the more frightening everything became.

Uncle Ronnie had never been entrusted with a young life before. He took it very seriously and, while being anxious that his charge should have a good time, still tried to make sure that she was safe. He was walking the fine line of acting like a parent without actually being one, and the result was that he coddled Lilly past the point of a joke. She could feel his protection like a shield when he slipped her cab money or his Bloomingdale's charge card and, despite being grateful, felt like one of his art objects trapped in a ring of precision lighting. He didn't even mind her erratic attendance at the gallery, for even though she was adorable and eager to please when around, in truth she was not much use to anyone and was, in fact, a bit of a hindrance. Whenever she did report for duty, Ronnie would pay her a pittance in cash and her grateful father would, in turn, pay Uncle Ronnie a clandestine ransom, via the 57th, purchasing extravagant art pieces; everyone was happy.

Lilly first met Ben Jackson when he'd schlepped his paintings into the 57th. Living downtown he'd travelled up on the subway carrying most of his work rolled up in a black cylindrical container almost as long as he was tall, except for one that depicted a stunted dwarf dressed up as a foreign potentate; it was four foot square and fully stretched on its wooden frame. Arriving two hours late for his appointment, he explained, by way of an apology, that it was all the fault of this unwieldy object, which had made his progress through Manhattan's subterranean networks awkward.

Joey Fatazzna, an old friend of Uncle Ronnie's and a bit of a smoothy in Lilly's eyes, was the owner of Fatazzna's, another more conventional gallery; and it was on Joey's recommendation that Ben had come to the 57th. Consequently Uncle Ronnie scrutinized the art Ben set before him with great consideration. Not that he wouldn't have, had Ben walked in off the street unannounced. That was one of the nice things about Uncle Ronnie. His mind, open to all, was ever ready, whenever possible, to try the untried, but willing as he was, while acknowledging Ben's obvious talent, Uncle Ronnie feared the work was too divergent for a show at the 57th. 'I wouldn't know how to sell them,' he said.

It was true that Ben's paintings were rather peculiar and dark, but so was New York. Lilly felt her godfather had missed the point: Ben painted the world he lived in. He was a figurative artist pure and simple, so surely, Lilly reasoned, you'd sell him as you would the city? She didn't dare say so, not liking to interfere, and Ben took his rejection with fortitude. Lilly empathized and they clicked.

Lilly was nine years younger than Ben and they were as different as chalk and cheese. He, a Coney Island street kid, had grown up on welfare. His father had disappeared when he was born, leaving his mother to raise their baby alone.

Watching his mother's efforts had given Ben the kind of hunger that deprivation sometimes creates, and he fought his way out of the projects by being a workaholic. If it was art Ben made it and made it well; he painted paintings, constructed light sculptures from neon-coloured tubes, made jewellery, took photographs, created music. The only thing he couldn't do was sing.

He lived in a loft – an entire floor on the corner of Bleeker and Lafayette in between Broadway and the Bowery, a lonely part of town that had recently stopped being purely commercial and had yet to become properly residential. The artists who lived near Ben were few and far between, as lofts were still hardly considered viable as living spaces, let alone desirable ones. There were no shops for blocks, Chinatown was near but too specific to be of any daily use. 'I mean, where do all the Chinese get their toilet paper?' he said when showing Lilly around his neighbourhood. Then there was little Italy, which had Mr Ballotti's, the one restaurant frequented by the chic upper East Side crowd, who, if they did come down to eat, still thought themselves adventurous. 'Pathetic,' Ben said as he dismissed them to Lilly, which she liked as it meant she wasn't.

Ben was avant-garde in every way. He ran far ahead of the pack, which impressed Lilly and she loved being with him. They'd alternate their dates. One evening he'd come uptown to see her and the next she'd go downtown, which was always, without exception, more fun. She loved those times. As long as he was by her side for protection, he made everything seem fun, thrilling and most importantly of all, safe.

Lilly, an upmarket drifter, possessed innate confidence, which wasn't surprising as she had her safety net of connections and nebulous wealth to fall back on. Ben, on the other hand, made up for this deficit by being ruthlessly focused and constantly driven to home in on one of his many talents and commercialize it. They were opposites who, once they'd met, were bound to attract.

They never actually discussed the fact but liked the way that they looked similar. It was primarily the bone structure. Both had square faces with wide cheekbones, full mouths and large beguiling eyes and both were blessed with lithe frames that took no exercise to keep in shape. When they were asked, which was often, 'Are you brother and sister?' they sometimes took a quiet pride in answering 'Yes'.

'We were separated at birth by the Atlantic,' Lilly explained to excuse their radically different accents. The idea amused them and made them feel closer. It almost convinced them they belonged in each other's world.

'You're defaulting on your own life, Lilly,' Ben teased, challenging her timidity. 'Choose your own life path, not the one laid out for you,' he said. 'Stop gawping from the sidelines, take the plunge.'

'I'm in New York, aren't I?' she snapped defensively as they moved through the city at night passing from one bizarre situation – which would have tested the social skills of a far more sophisticated person than she – to another. Like when he took her to Miranda's apartment. She was a fellow artist, throwing a dinner party to unveil her nearly healed facelift to her unsuspecting friends. Lilly was fascinated: plastic surgery was a rarely performed novelty, expensive, shameful and certainly never openly discussed. The chance to study the scars up close was a thrill that made Lilly wince. Then there was the transvestite dance competition held in a tiny club on the West Side near the garment district. They went there after a black-tie event at the Metropolitan Museum of Art, and Lilly, resplendent in her ball dress, won the first prize – a bottle of champagne. They grabbed it and ran giggling into the night, afraid they were going to be lynched by a crowd of militant men in frocks. They bought a cup of coffee from the twenty-four-hour café on Broadway and drank it while they walked the streets, discussing whether the two monstrous skyscrapers that were under construction, and already looming over them from several blocks away down in the financial district, would ruin or enhance the delicate skyline of his beloved city. All of these experiences were extraordinary and often terrifying to Lilly; and although she did try to be brave, she had no false veneer of sophistication and was floored as each new event unfolded. Ben called her PLRK, his acronym for Poor Little Rich Kid, which he pronounced 'plaque', intending to goad her into action, but she refused to take the bait and remained impervious to the fact that Ben realized, even revelled in the fact actually, that all these things 'sort of scared her'.

For all the street credibility Lilly pretended to be gleaning from Ben, she never took the bus unless accompanied by him and never even contemplated the subway with or without him. She was an uptown girl who took cabs each time she went downtown, and if it was to see Ben, which it invariably was, she'd be sure to give the driver a large tip to ensure that he would wait cheerfully until she was safely inside the building. She often felt a bit foolish as Ben always appeared immediately, sometimes even before she'd rung the bell if he'd been 'goofing off' as he called his habit of staring out of the window. She'd see him descend feet first through the wire-enforced glass set in the front door of his building. The rackety old freight lift would inch its way down until it finished its journey with a couple of ominous bounces before finally groaning to a standstill at street level. Ben would throw up the double wooden freight gates in a swashbuckling sort of a way, sending the doors gliding surprisingly smoothly and swiftly up, like a big sash cord window, accompanied by the distinctive rubbing sound of pulleys and weights. She loved those clanks and bangs made by the elevator; they were honest noises, in some way intrinsically satisfying to Lilly's ears. Ben would walk through the lobby towards her, pull back the heavy metal door at the entrance, usher her inside and it was then, and only then, after she was safely ensconced in his building, that she would turn to the cab and make a thumbs-up sign to the driver.

Ben would sneer kindly at her cowardice. 'Gonna have to go it alone one day, PLRK,' he'd say, or he'd utter some equally disparaging remark, which Lilly would shrug off as they walked back to the antiquated lift. On the way up she savoured the clanking, snail's-pace ascent of the murky old contraption, because when Ben raised the gates at the top Lilly would always be astonished by the contrasting lightness and space of his stylish modern studio. It got her every time, making that lift a perfect example of what she loved about New York. (She'd always imagined a state-of-the-art modern city; no one had ever prepared her for the old-fashioned mechanics of it all.)

One morning in early May Lilly woke up with a courage that suffused her veins. She'd been in the city nearly two months, and it was a beautiful spring day. The time had come. She jumped down the stairs taking two at a time, and a massive five steps at the bottom, flung open the door and hit the streets. Crossing straight over on to Fifth Avenue, then turning left, she went the ten blocks to 59th where she walked blithely down the steps into Central Park. It was divine. The first thing she saw was the zoo. She stopped by a small group of children who were gazing upwards transfixed, and saw the minute hand of the clock in the tower above the arch strike nine. Life-size, dancing metal bears began to revolve around the clock. Seeing the children's delight, she was charmed and walked on feeling a bit of a fool as she made her way safely down through the park towards the 57th. She could have been doing this every day. Ben was right. Fear had paralysed her, stopped her exploring and enjoying her new life.

Arriving at work, she felt so free and alive she practically hugged Bert, the grumpy old man who operated the lift that took her up to the fourth floor. As soon as she entered she went around and opened all the windows to rid the gallery of the smell of stale smoke and spilt wine from the previous night's opening. Next-door Carnegie Hall's windows were also open and a dress rehearsal was in progress. That was the big plus of

Uncle Ronnie's gallery. If the day was hot, you'd hear music, usually singing, wafting above the city's din. She cleared up the mess, putting glasses and overflowing ashtrays into the little galley kitchen for Lucia, the feisty Colombian cleaning lady, to deal with when she arrived. Then she sat behind the reception desk. A repeated segment of an aria from *The Magic Flute* enchanted her like a mantra and by the time Uncle Ronnie came in she was lost in a reverie.

'Hey, Baby. Looking good,' he said, echoing her smile.

'It's such a beautiful day,' she replied.

'Yea, why not enjoy it. Take off and have a good time,' he said, producing thirty dollars from his pocket and handing them to her. 'We'll be quiet all day; no one buys when it's sunny. I'll be cool alone, but be careful. OK?'

'Marvellous, thank you,' she said, needing no encouragement. She gave the immaculate desk an imaginary dusting and gathered her belongings while considering her options. She was cashed up and could go to a museum or a show, or she could take Ben to lunch. It was possibly too early to ring him, but she tried anyway.

'Fantastic,' Ben answered, wide-awake. 'Come whenever. I'm here working. Maybe we'll do Coney Island. It's a great day for it.'

Thrilled – she'd always wanted to see where Ben grew up – Lilly leapt into a cab, longing to tell him about her park adventure to impress him with her newfound courage, and impatient to bask in his reaction. She was imagining his look of admiration when she realized that it was going to be a ghastly letdown and immediately began to prepare her defence. One small step for Lilly, one giant step for mankind? She puzzled to find a better phrase, something that would really stop Ben in his tracks; the taxi ride took no time.

The cab driver turned on to Houston and did the necessary ride around the block to reach Ben's door further down on Bleeker. Strong sunlight accentuated the ice-blue sky overhead, bleaching out the desolate squalor of the wide street. They drew up outside Ben's where, without premeditation, she placed a five-dollar bill in the little plastic drawer of the dirty, bullet-proof, see-through plastic screen separating her from the driver, and started to get out.

'Thank you. Keep fifty cents please,' she said, scooping up her change and, before she had time to take a breath, let alone change her mind, the cab had sped off and there she was, alone for the first time in the Asphalt Jungle. 'Gosh,' she thought, ignoring the rapidity of her beating heart – which was tough as it was beating pretty hard.

Puffed up with pride she strode towards Ben's door and rang the bell. She pressed her nose to the glass and contorted her face into a horrible grimace to amuse him, remaining there frozen for thirty seconds or so waiting for the lift to groan into life. Nothing. She rang again. Zilch. She started to pound on the door, knowing perfectly well her action was useless. What could have happened?

'Right,' she thought, wondering what her next move should be. A telephone, that's what she needed. But where? That was the burning question. She wanted to cry but kept a grip on herself. Falling apart wasn't going to help the situation.

'Right,' she thought again. Apply logic. Logic told her that there must be a phone box on Broadway. Setting off in a stalwart fashion she wondered what exactly she was looking for. She'd never consciously noticed an American phone box, but she suspected they were not like the red kiosks at home. She scanned the pavements until she reached a blue metal letter box. Surely that should be side by side with a telephone. It was not. Diversionary indignation, a surge of resentment at the city's planning, gave her Dutch courage and she lengthened her stride, until she heard a man's voice.

'Look at them gams.'

She stopped dead in her tracks and looked around. No one. She must keep the fear at bay and keep going, and then she'd reach Broadway, where she could stop one of the cars if necessary. She started off again calmly, with steely determination. She heard the voice again.

'I said look at them damn gams.'

This time it was accompanied by the loud thud of hollow metal being smashed on something.

Why in heaven's name was she wearing a flimsy, second-hand print dress, and such ridiculous high-heeled shoes? Her dress was too short, as well as being pretty see-through, and as usual she was not wearing a bra. 'What an idiot,' she thought. Her shoes, which elongated her already exceptionally fine legs, gave her the allure of a Lolita: someone to be looked after or preyed upon depending on the proclivities of the observer and, though Lilly had not one calculating bone in her body, she'd instinctively known the allure she presented, and while being aware of its provocative danger, had liked the power it had given her. But now she cursed herself. 'If I ever get out of this I'm going to dress like Great Aunt Barbara for the rest of my life,' she swore as she hurried on, taking deliberately measured steps.

As she approached the corner the sun was in her eyes. Whoever was behind her – she dared not turn around to look – was hitting the pavement on either side of her and closing in. She knew whatever he was using must be heavy as she felt the rush of air behind her head with the force of its descent. Each loud thump produced so much adrenalin in her body it was as if she, not the pavement, was the physical recipient of the blows. Then, miracles of miracles, she saw seven figures approaching from around the corner. She squinted against the glare to make out their appearance, and as her eyes adjusted she saw they were a group of large black youths, so uniformly tall they had to be basketball players.

'Help!' she called out to them.

At that single word, they, as one, dropped their bodies a notch down nearer to the ground and fanned out like wolves approaching vulnerable prey. The one coming directly at her, who appeared to be the leader, produced a scary-looking knife, which he held out in front of him at arm's length. It caught the light and glinted horribly, making Lilly feel sick. 'This is ridiculous,' she thought, as they closed in. She was so terrified that she completely lost the plot and felt her body propel her violently forward. Plunging her full weight towards the pointing weapon.

'Thank God I've found you,' she gushed.

'Careful lady,' the giant youth snapped, pulling the blade back, just in time to avoid her rapidly approaching solar plexus. 'You crazy?' he yelped, rattled.

'Scared, I'm scared,' she yelped right back. 'Please, please help me, I can't get into my friend's place. And some loony's following me. I need a phone box. And I need to know how to use one. Do you have any coins? I'll pay you back, I promise.'

Her outburst was greeted by a cacophony of derisive hoots, which culminated with one of the taller young men – to the vast amusement of the others – jostling her.

'Hear that?' he jived. 'The honkey's got a phone in her box – check it out.'

He was shoving her up against the knife carrier who, having been as wrong-footed by Lilly as she had been by him, had gathered together his Sunday manners and hidden his blade.

'You mean a *pay-phone*, lady?' he asked quietly and Lilly nodded. At this point something extraordinary, close to comical, occurred. They all, excluding Lilly, forgot their objectives and became rather embarrassed, looking as if some ghastly, social gaffe had been committed. They were in uncharted waters. No one spoke. Then Lilly felt the former knife-wielder take her elbow and effortlessly propel her around the corner in complete silence and there, not ten feet away, stood a hallowed telephone. She'd been right to suppose it would look different. It wasn't a kiosk or red; a metal covering protected the telephone from the elements but not the person using it. The spell broke and whole gang started jabbering at once. It sounded as if they were arguing, but Lilly could see they weren't. The knife-man handed her the receiver, which, she noted in a detached way, looked tiny cradled in his enormous hand. Her fingers visibly trembled as she dialled Ben's number. A recorded voice told her to deposit twenty-five cents before continuing. Helpless, she turned to her assailant for help. He dug in his pocket and produced a coin, which he deposited in the appropriate aperture.

'Ben, is that you?' she said, as the ringing stopped, but the call had gone through to his answering-service company.

'How may I help you?' the irritating, machine-imitating woman asked.

'Where is he?' Lilly asked as graciously as she could under the circumstances. 'I'm here at his place you see and I don't believe the bell's working. I'm at the telephone on the corner and I'm not sure what to do.'

'Who shall I say called?' the melodious android inquired.

'It's Lilly and I'm in trouble,' she hissed urgently, with an apologetic little half-laugh of acknowledgement directed at the gang.

'I'll see that he gets your message Lilly,' she said, adding, 'have a nice day' in precisely the same singsong tone. And with that fatuous remark the beastly Droidess hung up. Lilly stood for a few seconds in stunned disbelief. She stuffed her hands in her pockets to hide her by now uncontrollable shaking, and nervously fingered her change. Oh yes, change!

'Look, here we are,' she said, producing some coins. 'I forgot I had these. What do I owe you?' she asked the giant knife-man who was standing immediately in front of her.

'A lot more than that, lady,' her ally replied to the amusement of his compadres. 'Where's this asshole live?' he demanded.

'Just around the corner, Bleeker and Lafayette,' she replied, 'but,' she added in a mumble under her breath, 'he's not really an asshole, he's just not in.' Then, for a second time Lilly felt his enormous paw support her elbow, and her body slightly levitated as he escorted her back to Ben's loft. She felt as if she were skimming the pavement and leaned into the curve, gliding around it like a passenger on a motorcycle pillion. It was rather nice, in a way, being on foot but not in charge of your own volition. She looked for the crazed gam-guy, who'd either hidden or gone.

No one spoke until they reached Ben's building, where Lilly was vastly relieved to see Ben waiting outside the door. Apparently the Droid, God bless her, had rung and rung his number until he'd finally heard it in the back.

Even in her distraught state of mind Lilly was delighted to see Ben's expression. His mouth dropped open and his eyes fairly popped out of his head with surprise at the company she was keeping, and the more so the closer to him they came. It grew to outraged shock when the knife-guy let go of Lilly's elbow, lunged forward, grabbed Ben by his lapels, lifted him up and growled, 'Don't let her wander alone down here, man; you never know who she might meet.'

He let go, dropping Ben unceremoniously to the ground like a sack of potatoes. He scrambled to his feet, humiliated, as all the seven youths turned again as one, and sloped off.

'Goodbye,' Lilly called out after them, 'and thank you,' she added to no acknowledgement.

After there was what Ben felt to be a safe distance between him and the thugs, with a lot more effort and less result than knife-boy, he yanked Lilly by her elbow inside his building. When he had made sure the door was safely closed he turned on her. 'What the . . . how the . . .? Who the fuck were they?' he shouted.

'Don't scream at me,' she exploded with the horror, pummelling the floor with her feet and beating the air with her hands. 'That was so . . . so . . . Frightening! And all your fault. Where were you?'

'Sorry PLRK, come on,' he said, losing his initial fury as he saw the extent of her distress.

They rode the lift up together in silence; he desperate to interrogate her, she oblivious of his concern, turning everything over in her mind. Once inside the loft they sank on to the leather couch. After a while Lilly said, 'That big guy who picked you up. He had a knife, you know.'

'Gee PLRK, I'm sorry,' Ben replied. 'What can I say?'

'You always said I should go it alone,' she said.

'Yea, but I was wrong, you must never, do you hear, never . . .'

'Never what?' she interrupted.

'Go it alone from now on. If needs be I'll come and fetch you – wherever.'

'You must be joking; this has been the best day of my entire life,' she said, defiant, and turned to fix him with a gimlet eye, the colour rising in her cheeks.

It took Ben a few beats to process what she'd just said and absorb its implications.

Lilly was radiant, and now that she was safe, she felt exhilarated by her adventures. Ben was seeing a vibrancy in her as never before. The idea of Lilly let loose in Manhattan chilled him to the bone, but he knew what she was feeling. 'Be careful what you wish for,' he thought to himself, remembering his own entreaties for her to break free.

'Welcome to New York City,' he said with a resigned trepidation at the thought of the hazardous days that were sure to follow.

Home

'I want to go home,' Zita Perino says out of the blue.

'We *are* home, Angel,' Cosmo, her life-partner-in-love replies. He's too busy watching the latest footage on the Army of the Heart to give her his full attention.

The inroads the army are making in the offensive on Cirexus are fantastic. The Fusion's embedded reporter is explaining that the shock troop divisions have successfully dealt with the miscreants and brought peace and democracy to Cirexus. 'The beacon of freedom is lit,' he says.

'It didn't need to be,' Zita says, 'they were plodding along just fine.'

'Ssh, Zeets, I'm trying to listen,' Cosmo says. The elite Pure Bloods are being shown as they walk freely among Cirexus breathers wearing no body armour. 'Proof positive,' the reporter is saying, 'of how we're winning the love and devotion of the indigenous Breathers.' The scene switches back to the studio anchorman. 'Within the next five rotations,' he announces, 'the previously enslaved Breathers of Cirexus will be free and, under the protection of the New Fusion, allowed to form their own independent, democratic council.'

'They already had one,' Zita shouts at the screen.

'Zeets,' Cosmo sounds hurt. 'We're helping them.'

'You said Pluraton would be the place of milk and honey,' she says. 'It's not, and I want to go home.' Her voice is sulky.

'Come on, baby,' Cosmo's tone remains placatory, 'you can't. You know that. Earth's gone. We blew it sky high.'

'Cosmo,' Zita comes back quick as a flash. 'I have been reliably informed Earth's just fine.'

'Baby, just think how bad things got. We escaped in the nick of time.'

Zita tries a new tack. 'Why don't we have an assessment? Feign mental and moral deficiency. They won't want us then, will they?'

Cosmo doesn't know what to say and settles for, 'We've had our assessment, honey. They won't believe us.'

'What? We can't develop psychological aberrations?' she asks.

'Not on Pluraton,' he reminds her, 'or do you want to be a Flat Rotator eligible for extinction? Remember,' he says, 'it's more than permissible, if not exactly compulsory.'

Cosmo's at his wit's end with Zita's delusions. Granted her hormones are rioting, but why carry their baby in such an archaic way if she isn't going to enjoy it? No other Earth Breather bothers any more. It's an act of passive aggression, quite apart from being, visually, extremely selfish. Why *choose* a distended belly in this age of absolute physical perfection? Riding the hoverways with Zita, Cosmo witnessed first hand how, when other Breathers catch sight of Zita's condition, they recoil in instinctive disgust before stealing a quick apologetic glance at him and turning away, confused and embarrassed. Cosmo never takes offence. Instead he admits to himself that he'd probably do the same if confronted by such an unexpected reminder of his base Earth antecedents.

'You promised we'd be free to leave if we ever wanted to,' she persists.

'Since when did *you* become a *we*?' He is sharp, precise.

Zita's face falls. 'Oh, I thought –'

'Yes, you thought,' he agrees, 'about lots of things. You always do. But does it ever occur to you to think about what I thought?'

The turn of his voice makes her hot. He sees the colour rush up into her cheeks. Her bottom lip starts to do its thing. She's going to cry. 'I'm going out,' he says, 'to view the cultivations.'

Damn, he used the 'out' word and she notices. He sees a flash of triumph in her eyes. Doubly irritated, he spins around. Before she has time to come back at him he stands and faces the exit portal. It sucks back, letting him pass through, before it re-forms just as fast behind him. Cosmo feels bad. He loves Zita and has done from the moment he first clapped eyes on her, back when they were both children in the year 2027, fourteen years before they emigrated to where there was no 'out'.

Pluraton, the space station where Cosmo and Zita Perino have chosen to make their home, is a prefabricated structure assembled as a supply ship by and for the Citoys of the Order of the New Fusion. Never intended for permanent habitation, it's covered in domed farms based on Earth's Eden Project. Pluraton grows cloned flesh and genetically modified vegetation spliced with blends culled from all the known arable planets. Each individual farm is accessed via large interconnecting tubes. Sealed ante-chambers at each portal keep the risk of a cross-pollinated-superbug infestation down to a minimum. These farms have been flourishing for a while under the ideal conditions simulated by the meteorologists of the New Fusion and provide most of the food that feed the millenarian colonies.

When the gallant struggles of planet Earth became acute it was necessary to enlarge the space station to accommodate the legions of refugees. Plans originally drawn up for penal space colonies, which were rejected by Earth despite its own notoriously low building standards, were approved and implemented by the Order of the New Fusion. Once this floating aberration was deemed finished and habitable, Earth Breathers flooded in, along with Glishers, Numoroos and a smattering of the other Breather species. Twelve years have passed since then, and during this time the aesthetically bereft station of Pluraton has evolved into a sprawling, autonomous junk heap housing more than five hundred thousand Breathers from the ever more worlds that are falling under the Fusion's fold. Located around two and three-quarter light years from Earth, Pluraton is nevertheless close to the centre of the Milky Way's galaxy where the atmosphere is too thin for Breathers.

So 'out' means out beyond the membrane where noxious green and yellow heavy gases hang, occasionally sludging together to form bubble-like explosions that are fun to watch. 'No air equals no out, which equals no win,' Cosmo thinks, 'and that means no going back to Zita until I've given her enough time to begin worrying and forget my beastly anachronism.'

He steps up on to the Sunburst Hoverway, where the cool white lumen strip suspended above his head makes him feel better immediately. A bonus to travelling anywhere on Pluraton is the municipal light therapy that is set by the Order of the New Fusion at least a hundred thousand lux higher than domestic. Headache, eyestrain, irritability or any of the other symptoms, such as an overwhelming desire for hibernation, violent impulses, severe memory loss, all associated with Seasonless Affective Disorder, are considered extremely detrimental to socialization by the New Fusion, and protected against with extra lumen. Dissatisfaction Square, where Breathers gather, usually to demonstrate against some surgical strike on a home planet whose policies are thought to threaten democracy, has the highest lux settings of all. Domestic arrangements are, 'naturally', Zita says, your own affair. You either pay for lumen boosts, make your own light boxes (a relatively simple thing to do) or – and this is what most Breathers do – you pop on to a hoverway to bathe in what hover-riders call 'a bit of cool' if things get too heated on the home front.

The lumen strip rolls, the hoverway synchronizes, all adjusting to the movement of the tunnel. The extreme shift of axis doesn't alarm Cosmo. On the contrary, he finds amusement in the clicks and clacks made by the short-looped, self-levelling system. He likes making up rhymes to fit:

Suppress all your frustrations and inspect the cultivations.

Zeets'll be ecstatic as her 'mones get less erratic.

Comforted by his silliness, he looks up through the protective lucent skin of the colossal circular tunnel he is travelling down. Directly above him, as if on cue, the gaseous shrouds part for a moment to reveal the epic orb of Pluraleas. Pluraton orbits Pluraleas and takes its gravity from the red dwarf as well as a derivative of its name. 'Stars alive, Zeets would love to see this,' Cosmo thinks as he corners off the moving thoroughfare on to the large stationary square platform that denotes the centre of the cultivations. At the station's inception, an inaugural Wollemi Pine had been successfully transplanted into a vast well in the centre of the square. Taking to its new home remarkably well and growing beautifully, the ancient species was now well over nine metres tall. Cosmo leans back on the thick trunk to stare through the pendulous dark green foliage for a moment before the insidious gases swirl back in and obliterate his view. 'That's why we came, to see stuff like that,' he thinks and pats the bubbly dark brown bark of the evolutionary marvel before stepping back on to the hoverway.

Gliding on, he recalls the views from inside the shuttle on their journey out from Earth to Pluraton, when they lay entwined together for ages in the Zita pod, gazing in awe at the star system and all its interstellar wonders. Microscopic dust particles picked out by nebulous light from no visible source created patterns that glittered against transfiguring swathes of plasma. It was in that same pod, on the last week of the eighteen-month flight, that Zita conceived. Cosmo was thrilled when Mula Dias, the fleet's obstetrician, a Breather from an outer galaxy, told them that the presence of a live embryo was detected in Zita's daily medi-scan.

'When would you like it out, dear?' Mula asked, all bright and cheerful.

'I wouldn't,' Zita said.

Cosmo was amazed. There was a long pause and an angry red weal appeared across Mula Dias's face, making her look as if she'd been whipped. Time froze for a beat as the single pupil dilated in her one, very beautiful, eye. Shock. Cosmo knew the signs. He'd seen a lot of it during Earth's final troubles. Doctor Dias hid her condition well.

'My,' she said blithely, taking out her compact and applying the unsightly skin eruption with Renu-u-skin to hide the weal, 'have they zapped up the lumen or am I going through my de-ovular?'

'I think it's the lumen,' Zita said tactfully.

Dr Dias smiled at Zita before weighing in with the facts. 'The thing is, dear,' she said kindly, 'your gestation period will take a full three years. The electromagnetic time spans, you see. You've crossed three on the journey out from Earth and they've altered your body's molecules, slowed down its growth process.'

'Wow,' Cosmo said. 'So it's true. We really will stay younger longer?'

'Yes,' Mula answered. 'Don't you remember when Dr Greensthick bought the obsolete V2 Challenger and renamed it the Youth Ship?'

Cosmo and Zita did remember. It had been a big scandal at the time. Dr Greensthick had enticed rich women from all over Earth into buying his luxury spa trips to slow down the ageing and decay of their bodies. Once on board he'd drugged them and packed them in like sardines with an inadequate oxygen supply. A lot of the women had died, but the urban myth had it that the ones who'd survived returned looking marvellous.

'So you see, Zita dear,' Mula said in response to Zita's obvious dismay, 'what's good for one woman is anathema to another, and it's much better to part with your embryo now. Let it be born in the secure natural environment of a laboratory.'

'But –' Zita began, only to be cut off by the still optimistic Mula.

'You needn't worry about the cost, dear. It's a free service for every Earth émigrée.'

'I know. You're right.' Cosmo was impressed by the gravitas in his partner's small voice. 'But, please, I want to have my baby as my mother had me, however long it takes.'

At the time Cosmo stood by Zita. Now look where his loyalty has got him, he thinks, passing through two vacuum-sealed chambers into the Quinoa farm. Zita still has eleven months to go and I'm not sure I'll be able to endure much more of my beloved's interminable pregnancy.

The crops are struggling. Every spike, no taller than three inches high, displays worryingly small seedheads. In a rainbow array of dramatic purple, green, lavender, orange, wine-red, black, yellow and all are wilting on their magenta stalks. At this rate the whole farm will produce a tenth of what is needed, although the Fusion had implemented five harvests instead of two. Production is down 20 per cent. The soy soil is losing its potency and refusing liquid, which makes it hard for the station to meet its interplanetary obligations. Unrest, unlike the starving seedlings, is beginning to flourish. Cosmo knows. A few rotations back he was sent to work on the lumen grid and there he saw that, according to the application's recent history, the Fusion was boosting the lux levels perilously high. He was surprised no burns were being reported.

Fortunately for Pluraton's farms it was recently discovered that the core materials used in construction on the planet of Cirexus happened to contain the perfect ratio of nutrients and bulk to enrich Pluraton's failing soy soil. Cosmo who, for all the right Breather reasons, was glad that the Fusion were helping in the reconstruction of Cirexus, is now doubly grateful, as his farms stand to benefit. Clearing the detritus of devastated dwellings in the bombed cities of Cirexus may not end up as a purely altruistic service after all and could possibly provide a bonus for Pluraton. Instant karma for promoting freedom and democracy throughout the galaxy is the Fusion's line. Cosmo knows that Zita questions this, but then she would, as she does anything official.

Turbulence makes the entire field ripple as the ship adjusts itself and Cosmo is reminded of his youth on Earth and the magical little two-storey house he was sent to in the year 2027. He was eleven years old and wore a green plastic security bracelet with a barcode on his wrist. Gas-masked travel officials in shell suits scanned it for his destination before herding him towards the appropriate form of conveyance. He never saw his parents again. Zita arrived a few weeks later. At eighteen months younger than Cosmo she was given a yellow security bracelet. Both evacuees were privileged offspring of original Citoys, those who founded the Order of the New Fusion.

The beneficial influence of these statesmen-like Citoys waned quickly against the fundamentalist shift in the many houses of worship and in the leadership of the New Fusion. Faith seeped into the governing order and became increasingly entwined in ways previously unimaginable. When the Fusion proclaimed a policy of 'pre-emptive war' and invaded their first planet in the name of freedom the original Citoys pulled strings and paid fortunes for the chance to allow their precious offspring to grow up in relative safety until Earth's bloody interstellar struggles were resolved and peace restored.

The cottage where Cosmo had been sent had a terracotta roof that mirrored the Sienese earth on which it stood. Camouflaged in the middle of olive groves under a mantle of jasmine and grapevine, it was untouched by the rampant technology overtaking the rest of the planet. Three brick arches supported a balcony that ran the entire length of the upper floor, where he could sit with his feet up on the balustrade and catch any cool breeze, however small. At ground level, the same three arches shaded another welcome spot to linger just outside Cosmo and Zita's deliciously cool room, reclaimed from the livestock that used to winter there. Between the two little beds, a sheet attached to a rope by brass rings could be pulled lengthwise for privacy. Neither Zita nor Cosmo ever bothered.

'I loved that little room,' Cosmo reflects as he punches in the order that will direct Pluraton's nerve centre to extract soy soil from beneath the crops. The samples sucked along subterranean pipes will pass through filters that convey their data back to the nerve centre. As Cosmo waits for the results, he thinks of Bruno and Rosina Perino, his surrogate parents. He misses them and is glad that he has their name. A beep from the workstation tells Cosmo that the soil gradations are completed. He walks over to the retro-styled monitoring board. All the information is there and he does his cursory checks. An unexpected weariness comes over him. The results are even worse than he anticipated, every mineral severely depleted. He's thankful a test shipment of the Cirexus rubble is arriving on the station within the next rotation. Resting his back against the metal wall, he lets himself slide down until he comes to rest on his haunches.

In his mind's eye he can still clearly see the view from that little bedroom window. Its sheer expanse took his breath away: first a patchwork of random fields delineated by small woods or tall cypresses, stretched across the foreground, then a wild holm oak forest, bordered by hills marking what he supposed to be the horizon until, on a clearer day, he saw that further still there were mountains rising out of distant plains that must have gone on for kilometres, culminating in Monte Amiata. Cosmo felt a wave of satisfaction. 'I no longer calculate distances in kilometres but light years no less.'

Feeling marginally better he stands up and passes his finger across a small computer screen set in the centre of a robust, industrial stopcock. The valve opens and Cosmo waits until the dial moves up to show that the humidity level in the dome has risen sufficiently and harshly enough to mimic the plant's natural habitat. He shuts it off with a wave of his hand.

Continuing on, he checks on two more of Pluraton's farms. At the Frux the small trees are also giving a poor showing of their long red, corkscrewed fruit. Cosmo plucks one and breaks off a segment. The paper-thin bitter rind peels back easily and he eats a little. It's dry and tasteless with no hint of the sweet and nutty flavour the fruit will have when ripe. He spits it out and throws the rest away, hoping he hasn't already strained his digestion.

The flesh pastures are refreshing. The cloned calves appear healthy and plump and the lambs gambol on their over-developed legs. 'It is marvellous,' Cosmo thinks, 'that no biological parent has been used to create these foods in over thirty years.' It creeps Zita out, of course, but Cosmo doesn't agree – although it is a shame that all this fresh produce has to be processed down and made unrecognizable before being ingested by Breathers. He understands the hygiene protocol encapsulated in the three Ds – Digestion, Disease and Death – but even so it upsets him.

His work, which Pluraton's nerve centre would have taken care of anyway if he were honest, is complete and he now has time on his hands. Remembering his earlier glimpse of Pluraleas from the hoverway, he decides to drop in on the Observation Club for Intrafusion Hour. 'It'll be glorious this rotation,' he thinks, 'the entire spectrum on show.' Infusing sunsiders is not something Cosmo indulges in often. They make him feel 'off' the next day, but right now he feels different; he doesn't care about tomorrow.

Life in the den with Zita is becoming a nightmare. He feels excluded by her and the longed-for baby. Her two years of physical bonding with it have left him out in the cold. And the mood swings! Cerebrally he understands that they are brought about by the pregnancy but it still hurts. The way she goes on about 'having to return to Earth for the baby'. He doesn't like her inference; it's unfair. As if it is the two of them against him.

After gliding a short distance on the hoverway, he angles himself off at the Observation Club. At the entrance there are Corinthian columns of graded grey steel alloy either side of a central portal. The moment it sucks back to let Cosmo through he knows he's made the right choice. 'Welcome-you-belong' chimes suffuse his consciousness as diminutive Glishers ease near to serve him. He purchases a sealed beaker containing a liquid named the 'chemical of life' from a pretty little mauve thing: 'I'm Gladness and I'll be your Glisher for the duration.'

Gladness undulates wonderfully and transfers her thoughts with great charm. Cosmo is pleased with his choice and proffers his arm. The many-limbed little Glisher hooks his refreshment beaker up to the permanent nutrient catheter in the crook of his arm. Solids cannot travel through the narrow catheter, making it is almost impossible to inject air through at a dangerous rate. With no risk of an embolism, it's safe to get 'squiffy' on the oxygen-enriched blends and lie about watching the Citoy powered heating satellite Old Flamer oscillate across the galactic void.

This ritual is essential to some Breathers, who always visit the club on a certain hour of the rotation to get out of it. That 'out' word again. Who cares? Cosmo thinks as he steps across the threshold and feels himself gently lifted off the floor in the zero-gravity clubroom. By letting his thoughts drift back to Earth he's been indulging in forbidden nostalgia. But surely, he thinks, this defiance must represent free will. A fundamental right held up by the New Fusion. So fundamental that they are engaged in many wars in its defence.

Against the idyllic background of Cosmo's memories, images of Earth's ceaseless feuding loom and intensify. The rest of

Earth versus his pastoral idyll. Babies weaned on violence imprinted on to their absorbent brains via the multiple viewing screens free from the Fusion with every new home. Pulverize something; explode it; pulverize more; explode something bigger, etc. This kind of nonsensical credo had become prevalent. Teenagers, adults, let alone the hapless babies, succumbed to the adrenalin of annihilation. Altogether, Cosmo remembers, they demonstrated the direction that Earth's collective psyche was taking on its blatant progression through the twenty-first century. 'That's why we had to come Zita!'

Cosmo must be talking aloud, maybe even shouting, as his Glisher is swimming like an octopus through the air towards him. At his side in a trice she envelops him in a tactile embrace, rocking him, soothing him, while her spare tentacles adjust the flow of juice to his arm. He really is wasted. His toes feel funny as if they want to escape from his feet. 'Sorry,' he says to his neighbour, a large red-headed Breather of indeterminate age, who nods at him sagely.

'Don't mind me,' the Breather says, looking rather like a giant Quinoa plant to Cosmo's inebriated eyes. 'It's all good. The death of an empire always, but always, involves a lot of nasty thrashing about. Death-throes.'

Cosmo snuggles back down into the softness of the nothing that surrounds him. 'That's right,' he says, 'life became an endless round of explosions and political shenanigans. Every baby step Earth civilization took was wilfully smashed. Zita was there. She should understand.'

'It's all good,' Quinoa boy says. But in Cosmo's opinion it wasn't.

Why didn't Zita get it? They came to Pluraton for a better life. She should be thanking her lucky stars that they escaped the Fusion's draft into the Army of the Heart and had been accepted for residency in the first place. Pluraton is overcrowded. It has stringent immigration laws. Colour charts around disembarkation portals that look as pretty as rainbows are the first of many hurdles faced by the hapless Breather. Too dark a shade of pink, purple, black, green or yellow and you are sifted down a winding corridor that leads you straight back, by a long and devious route, to the rear entrance of the craft you'd just left. Then off you go to who knows where. Light of skin, pale of eye, long of limb and generally low on wit are the bywords for legal entrance to Pluraton.

Except, of course, if you are a trained agriculturist. To have served an apprenticeship on the land is good, but to be descended from generations of farmers is up there with alchemy in this cold computer age of facts. After the Heart's drones began to bomb the rural areas, farmers became scarce. Trucks driven into the cities laden with vegetables were repeatedly mistaken for miscreants and 'taken out'. Zita imagined that it was a tactic aimed at the deliberate starvation of the urban areas, which are so notoriously difficult to control. Cosmo cannot find it in his heart to be that cynical. It doesn't matter who was right, the Italian land quota was not filled, and Cosmo and Zita took the Perinos' name and claimed the lineage of land savants. Many other Breathers were there that day, and all would have given their eye teeth, if they belonged to the species that had some, for the residency holograph permitting their emigration to Pluraton to be burnt on to their retinas. 'But we won, Zita.' He must be speaking aloud again.

'Too true,' Quinoa says, without looking.

'My wife's pregnant. Having it old-fashioned terrestrial-style. Eleven months to go and she wants to go home,' Cosmo replies.

'I'm Sam,' the floating Quinoa youth says. 'Where are you from?'

'Cosmo,' Cosmo replies, identifying himself. 'I'm from Earth.' Sam stays silent and Cosmo feels his heart rate increase.

'Bummer,' Sam says after a while.

'Did you hear what I said? My wife wants to go home.' Cosmo realizes that he's laughing and he's not sure why. His heart rate is getting faster by the second. 'What can I do?' he pleads.

Out of the corner of his eye he sees his Glisher hurrying over.

'I know what you can't do,' says Sam the red-headed sage.

'But she doesn't. She says Earth's still there.' Cosmo is shouting and Gladness folds him in a soothing multi-tentacled embrace. He wants to fight her.

'It's a truth flash,' Sam barks, and turns towards Gladness. 'Careful. Get him to gravity. Pronto.' The Glisher curls her pretty little spare purple limb around Sam's waist, angles down like a swimmer, contracts and pushes off against air. The three of them speed, as one, like a bullet down to the door.

'I'll take him to chill in a bubble,' Sam tells Gladness.

Cosmo overhears a 'Thank you' intended for Sam's brain, followed by the vestige of a strange little melody that gets fainter the further Gladness moves away.

Sam takes, rather than waiting to be allocated, a bubble. He orders an altogether less attractive Glisher than Gladness to settle them into the visco-elastic memory-foam recliners before pushing them out into space. As they come to the end of the life-supply line their bubble bounces to a halt and Cosmo relaxes. Hard not to, in a near free-floating bubble.

'So,' Cosmo says after a good while, 'how do I convince her?'

'She honestly doesn't believe you?'

'No. Maybe I was wrong to let it go on so long, but it makes her feel good. I don't know. It's too late now. She's obsessed.'

'How long before the sprog arrives?' Sam asks.

'Too long.'

'How long?'

'Eleven months.'

Sam whistles and shakes his head. 'You've got to persuade her.'

'Not an option.' Cosmo is resolute.

'This isn't what I signed up for either, you know.'

'What?'

'All this shit.'

'What?' Cosmo repeats. 'You mean you want to go back too?'

'Too right. I'm freaked by the rise of the Fusion's radical policies as well as . . . what's your chick's name?'

'Zita.'

'Nice. Yeah, well Zita's on the money. She's just got to lose the hope. Look, we've already lost our commitment to peace, to economic and social justice. Civil liberties. Breather rights. It's done. Finished. She needs to relax.'

'But she can't, Sam, couldn't even before she was having this baby. She feels responsible. She feels she has to make life better for it and,' he adds slowly, realizing the words to be true as they form in his mouth, 'so do I.'

Sam takes a deep breath. He looks weighed down by invisible woes. 'I like you, Cosmo, I really do, but you've both got to come through this. It's prophecy. It's happened before, it'll happen again. You only have to look.'

'At what?'

'Anything. Take the environment.'

'We make our own,' Cosmo says.

'Come on man, what are you on?'

'Compensate our emissions perfectly,' Cosmo quotes from the Fusion's handbook.

'Yes *in* Pluraton sure, but what about *out*?'

The 'out' word again. Cosmo feels depression settling in on him. 'Let's down the bubble,' he says. 'I need to get back to Zita. She'll be worrying.'

'No,' Sam adopts a firm tone, 'let's talk this through. What do you think is going to happen when we collide with some dumb space weapon? The galaxy's bristling with them, man. Open your eyes.'

Cosmo has no answer.

'Sorry man.' Sam is contrite. 'But you've had a truth flash and they're contagious.'

They both fall silent.

'So you're saying there's no hope. I should tell Zita the Earth's gone and she'd better get used to it.'

'There's no other way. If she's half as bright as you say, she'll have known it from the moment the Fusion seized power and abandoned their interplanetary agreements.'

Cosmo realizes that Sam is right. Zita fought it every step of the way: marched until her feet blistered, visited neighbouring worlds to sign petitions against the lifting of restraints on the proliferation of nuclear, seismic and biological weapons in space, and railed against the diseases introduced by negligence into every new planet conquered by the Fusion empire. While a thirst for the new and sensational was busy consuming their entire generation – and Cosmo had been no exception – Zita remained firm in her convictions.

'We exhausted our quest for cheap thrills and gave our politicians free rein to move on to expensive, more sophisticated and deadly ones. Bombs, force-shields, death-rays. More, more, more.' Cosmo is speaking fast. He's on a roll. He can see it all. 'We unbalanced the globe with our deadly games, caused massive 'quakes, floods and all the shit disasters that go with them.'

'All the while fighting, fighting invisible enemies,' Sam agrees.

'And I'm just meant to say to her, "This is how it is, Zita, get used to it"?'

'She needs to know.'

'I don't believe it,' Cosmo says.

'What?' Sam asks.

'I'm with Zita, Sam. She's got integrity. She knows. She's not stupid.'

'And?'

'Well,' Cosmo says, 'she's sure Earth's still there, and I believe her. I don't know why I didn't before.'

'Astrologists, Nostradamus, the Mayan calendar, it's all been predicted. Ordained, man. Just like now. Study the New Order.'

'I have and I can't accept it any more, Sam. Nor does Zita. Anyway the Mayan calendar finished in two thousand and twelve, and life on Earth didn't.'

'No, but it went through a pretty big fucking change,' Sam says. 'How's your arm feeling?'

'OK. Why?'

'Gladness said she nicked the catheter when she was bringing you to gravity. Shall I check?'

Cosmo extends his arm for Sam to examine.

'Seems OK now,' Sam says. 'Shall I flush it through to be sure?'

'OK.' Cosmo watches as Sam take a phial from his tunic and connects it up to Cosmo's catheter. They float in the sereneness of their bubble waiting for the phial to empty. An enjoyable sensation, to feel the iced liquid move rapidly up through his veins.

'You see, you had a level-seven truth flash, highly infectious and too hard-hitting to suppress. Like I said, Zita's on the money. But nobody can go back, not Zita, not me, not even your blameless baby. Contamination, man. We can't risk it.'

'No room for error, eh?' Cosmo asks.

Sam shakes his head.

'So this is how it feels to extinguish,' Cosmo thinks, but says nothing. He closes his eyes and there is Sam, standing in a burgeoning Quinoa field.

'Cosmo,' Sam calls out across the rippling rainbow display of perfect plants, 'don't fret about the sprog, man. The Fusion will see it right.'

Femme Fatale

This was to be Cranberry's first trip to Mexico and Oaxaca sounded as exotic a place as any to start. Confronted by the small piles of clothes covering the bed, she wondered if she'd got them down to a bare minimum – she so envied people who could pack; it was an artform, one that she'd never mastered. Nearly fifty years old, travelling the world since she was fifteen, and still in a mess when it came to choosing essentials to fill a suitcase. She chuckled over her conversation with John the night before. He'd managed to reach her on her cellphone while she was in the lobby of the Average Hotel, an achingly trendy hot-spot on Sunset Strip in the heart of Hollywood. Above her, suspended in a large perspex container over the front desk, people had been intent on filling in an oversized jigsaw puzzle in a slow-moving tableau that passed for art. Her phone had been playing up.

'Where?' he said again.

'Oaxaca,' she screamed, hearing her voice echo back like a transatlantic call of old.

'Wh . . . What?' he yelled.

'Wha-ha-ka, Mother-fa-ka,' she bellowed, exasperated at his apparent obtuseness.

'Oh, right,' he said, 'have a good time.'

By his tone she could just see his expression of resigned good humour. It made her grin, and people turned to stare, which made her laugh as she continued to walk through the lobby to the bar out by the pool. Thinking of John always softened her mood. He made her feel secure. Before many of her trips, he wandered into their bedroom to inspect the clothes laid out on their bed and inevitably suggested she remove two white T-shirts from the tops' pile. She did so now and sure enough, magically, everything fitted into her carry-on bag. Thank God that the In-House film company was continuing to pay the hotel bill while she went away; she doubted she would have gone otherwise. Looking around, she saw nine weeks of frustration in the expensive clutter that disguised the impersonal hotel room. Nine weeks with loads of cash from In-House and nothing but shopping to relieve the boredom.

She'd been persuaded to come over to Los Angeles when In-House optioned her film script. She was amazed they wanted it, even more that she managed to fight for – and get – final approval on any changes made. And, almost more important, a first go at any rewrites. Bob, her producer at In-House, told her over the phone that there'd be hardly any. 'Just a few minor adjustments here and there,' he assured her, 'a little bit more of your magic, that's all. I'm telling you, baby, it's all but green lit.' After he'd made a few more calls, buttering her up and making her feel clever, he managed to entice her, against her better instincts, into the fabled minefield that is the Hollywood film industry. Cranberry had been excited at the prospect. Three weeks to tinker, as Bob put it, with minor aspects of her story, which weren't quite flowing as they should. In-House sent her a first-class ticket, hired her a rental car and put her up in a junior suite at the Chateau Marmont, a charming, slightly seedy but glamorous hotel that looked like a quasi-French castle. They paid her the writer's guild minimum, a paltry – by Hollywood standards – $35,000, plus $150 cash 'per-diem living expenses', but as her living expenses had already been taken care of, Cranberry saw the wads of dollar bills as glad-money. Yippee, she'd thought as she pocketed them.

It was a Friday afternoon when she'd landed, giving her the weekend to, as Bob suggested, relax and acclimatize. 'Get yourself up for the week ahead.' She did, lying by the pool, ordering treats from the handsome, easy-going waiters who glided by, and spotting stars: Iggy Pop and Burt Reynolds to name but two. Monday morning came around, along with a limo to take her to the studio for the first and only time. Bob had explained in his welcoming Friday-night call that he'd send one so she could learn the route. Jilly, a friendly receptionist with whom Cranberry had shared pleasantries over the phone from England, met her in reception and walked her down a small, dank-looking replica of a New York street in the blazing Los Angeles sun. Turning a corner, they entered a white clapboard antebellum house with green trim, where Jilly introduced her to four other writers.

'Jane, Arkie, Simon and Claire will be working with you,' Jilly said. It was the first Cranberry had heard about collaborating with anyone, but before she had time to remonstrate Jilly had gone, leaving the five of them sitting together in the small room waiting. No one seemed to know for what. Claire, a slender woman with a crewcut, said that over the weekend, without warning, the studio's 'head honcho' had gone, been replaced. 'I guess this new guy's anxious to make his mark. That must be why he's brought us on board.'

'Oh,' Cranberry said.

'I don't know what the project is but I hear it's crap.'

'Oh,' repeated Cranberry, wounded.

Twenty minutes later, Jilly came back through a door, which Cranberry imagined must lead to an intermediary chamber between her and the new head honcho's hallowed ground, to tell them that Mr Ratner had to reschedule. Surely that's a 'don't call us we'll call you', Cranberry thought. The writers appeared to think the same and Claire lost her razor-edged definition as all four filed meekly out of the small office. The door closed behind them and Jilly turned and explained to Cranberry, in the kindest possible tone, that Bob had been fired overnight and her project had, sadly, gone into turnaround. Not good, she added, seeing Cranberry's blank look. Worse was to come. As the days blurred into weeks then months, her script continued to twist and turn in a positive vortex of incomprehensible studio jargon. In-House kept paying for Cranberry's luxurious existence and she stayed on, thinking something was bound to happen soon. It was such a colossal waste of money otherwise. Nothing did and as time dragged on Cranberry understood that she had two choices: to fight and try to achieve some sort of resolution, or to let go and allow things to take their course.

Uncharacteristically, she chose the latter and, resisting the urge to pitch battle against In-House, she decided to go on holiday. Why not? Leave it to the studio suits to sort out. Was she perhaps, finally, growing up? There was a silver lining in the form of the Fourth of July break. Basically no business happened in the USA over the long weekend; it was bigger than Christmas and gave Cranberry the opportunity to visit Mexico for the first time, and see Alice-Ann, her oldest friend. Grateful at the prospect of her imminent escape from La-La land, she fell asleep and dreamed of Zapata, Che Guevara and other handsome revolutionaries.

She was given a rude awakening the next morning, with a call from the front desk telling her that her car had been waiting for fifteen minutes. Damn. Hopeless as ever, she'd forgotten to set the alarm – or hang her breakfast order outside on the door. Nightmare. Luckily it was Sunday, so less traffic and, with the leeway of the extra two hours suggested by the airlines for security checks, she calculated that she had the time to shower quickly, gulp down a cup of tea and still make the plane. Perhaps the growing-up thing had been a bit premature, she thought, muddling into the car. Feeling like a teenager, she checked the zippered compartment of her bag containing passport and tickets for the eightieth time, sheepishly relieved to find them, as ever, right where she'd put them. Relax, she thought, retarded adolescent or not, Mexico here I come: *arriba*, *arriba*, *arriba*.

The first flight was uneventful and gave Cranberry time to enjoy anticipating the days ahead. She hadn't seen Alice-Ann for at least five years, but knew they'd pick up exactly where they'd left off. That was the kind of friendship they'd achieved since they first met, by accident, over thirty years ago at a barbecue on Long Island. Somehow, Cranberry couldn't quite remember how, they discovered that they were sharing the same boyfriend, fiancé in Alice-Ann's case. The upshot was, that after much furious weeping, neither woman blamed the other. Each knew her lover too well. Instead they washed their hands of him, and became the best of friends themselves. Their friendship had proved enduring, even though they were as unlike as chalk is to cheese.

Alice-Ann was svelte and chic, deeply sexy in an ice-maiden sort of way, with luminous, totally natural, blond hair. Always beautifully turned out, she was one of those curious people who repelled dirt; in the slums of Calcutta she would have remained immaculate, and although aged over fifty, she looked to all the world as if she were in her mid- to late thirties. Neurotic, obsessive even, she was set in her ways and profited from an intriguing remoteness, that came, Cranberry imagined, from having to fend for herself since 1959 when, coming up for her fifteenth birthday, she'd given birth to a baby boy out of wedlock.

Unmarried mothers were hardly acknowledged back then. Their illegitimate offspring would sometimes be placed in an orphanage, or face-saving grandmothers would claim that they, not their daughters, were the foundling's parent, relegating the real mother to the position of a sister, with no say in her own baby's upbringing. This type of subterfuge had to be performed if the wayward girl's marriage prospects were to survive.

Alice-Ann raised her son Tom single-handed, doing whatever was necessary, including being a nude model during the sixties for Mr Stone, as Alice-Ann insisted on calling the club-footed multi-millionaire, porn pimp Jerry Stone, publisher of *The Trick*, a gross, prototype glossy magazine, part straight-forward, albeit strong, pornography, part instruction manual on the finer points of utter degradation and sexual humiliation. Its blatant unpleasantness had cachet among the cognoscenti. When women's liberation took hold in the seventies it lost its popularity. In the nineties Jerry Stone reinvented himself as a civil rights activist and preached to the women he said he'd helped to liberate from their antiquated inhibitions. Through all his incarnations Alice-Ann continued, deferentially, to call him Mr Stone, revealing an unexpected trait in her character: that of genuine respect and affection for the sleazebags who, throughout her life, had exploited her. Being so consistent in her loyalty paid off over the years, as it was reciprocated, giving her a most unusual coterie of close friends.

Cranberry, on the other hand, was less feminine and malleable, her appeal more androgynous. Younger than Alice-Ann, she had put on weight since they last met – not a lot, but it would be enough for Alice-Ann, who always spoke her mind. Cranberry anticipated seeing her friend's eyes narrow to appraise her fuller figure. Myopically she'd press her spectacles to her nose the wrong way round (the optician had fitted the lenses inside out years ago) and pinch any excess flesh with the detachment of a surgeon. 'Careful,' was all she'd say, but that one word would be enough to make Cranberry eat every calorie she could lay her hands on to prove she didn't care. It was always the same. Only this time Cranberry decided to pre-empt her friend and announce, up front, that she wanted to go on a detox during her stay, some sort of juice fast. Alice-Ann was bound to know one and being borderline anorexic, would join in, happy at any chance to deny herself.

Landing in Mexico City she looked at her watch; twenty minutes to make her connection to Oaxaca. Where was the gate? She couldn't see any announcement board and, although the airport was packed with people, there was no one to ask. Everyone was queueing in very unEnglish snaky lines outside polling booths dotted all over the concourse. Each queue, flanked by ominous, even-more-unEnglish armed militia, had a hysterical, chaotic air, unnerving Cranberry. Until she remembered it was Sunday, 2 July, 2000. She'd chosen to travel on the day of Mexico's general election. Idiot, fool; how could she have forgotten? Frazzled but thrilled by this extreme immersion into a strange new world, Cranberry managed to find and board her connecting flight with time to spare. Shown to her seat, she buckled up for the last leg of her journey, feeling better than she had for the last couple of months.

The man in the seat next to her reached up to stow his bag in the overhead locker and his passport fell out, open on the photograph page, allowing Cranberry to read his name as she picked it up. 'Excuse me,' she said handing it back, 'you dropped this and I'm sorry but I couldn't help noticing your name. Is it really Jesus?'

'It is,' he smiled, 'pronounced "Hesusse". There are many called Jesus in my country. None I fear are the Messiah.' Jesus was handsome in a Mexican way, with a droopy moustache and the most compellingly soulful, dark blue eyes that caught the light like star sapphires and crinkled up with secret amusement. Between these two features sat a prominent nose. Well. Cranberry knew what that was supposed to mean. Or was it big feet? She couldn't remember. In any case, it didn't matter; she was looking for mental, not physical stimulation. Jesus was a charmer, Oaxacan, a local artist returning from San Diego where he'd been visiting some old college friends.

'Who's going to win the election?' Cranberry asked. 'And are any of them any good?'

'The pre-ruling party guarded their power for seventy years – too much corruption – and no one suspects change,' he answered, in perfectly pronounced English of a different syntax and rhythm, before he went on to give her a crash course on Mexico's political history. She listened enraptured, thinking how she couldn't have asked for a better travelling companion. The longer he talked, the more appealing he became. 'The people of the country – of the earth – they *dare* not look forward for change. Excepting me. For I believe in the power of the people,' he added passionately.

Cranberry caught his fire. 'Hear, hear,' she cried, stabbing her fist in the air revolutionary style, narrowly missing the air hostess, who was coming up the aisle with a tray of complimentary boiled sweets. After apologizing profusely to the flustered woman she turned back to Jesus. 'Do you know Raul, the freedom fighter?' she asked.

'Sargento Raul of Chiapas National Freedom Force,' Jesus corrected her. 'He is a true Mexican.'

'Pretty wild and romantic,' she said.

'Life itself is pretty wild and romantic with the politics they play in my country,' he replied. 'One election, computers crashed during the vote count. *Misterioso*. When they start again – *sopresa, sopresa* – they show a very big, very different result. Carlos Salinas de Gortari succeeded to take the presidency. This same product of fraud Gortari who chingared Mexico.' Jesus used the word 'chingared' a lot; he told Cranberry it was a Mexican slang word for swindled, although she was convinced 'fucked' would have been more accurate and that Jesus was too polite to say so. Her head chock-a-block with the subtleties of chingaring, she was unprepared for the plane's sudden death-defying angle and she gripped Jesus's arm. 'In Mexico,' he said, 'the worst thing that can happen to a human being is to be Indian, with all its burden of humiliation, hunger and misery.' Jesus continued seamlessly, apparently oblivious to the dangers of a plummeting plane, 'In the village of Acteal one Christmas fifteen children and twenty-one women, among many others, were shot or hacked to death with machetes,' he said, diverting her fear with his righteous anger.

'Yes,' she said, 'but violence doesn't excuse violence. It breeds it.'

'Maybe. But Raul, he expects a favourable reaction from the people who give birth to his fight. On their behalf it is just. You can question his method of combat, but never the reason for its inspiration.'

'He's still guilty of terror.'

'The only thing Raul is guilty of is having let down the hem of hope,' Jesus stated with certainty. If the hours of the last flight sped by, this one must have broken the sound barrier, as the plane touched down long before she grew tired of listening.

It was raining when she stepped down on to the steaming tarmac. She looked around at the ring of encompassing mountains.

'The Sierra Madre,' Jesus informed her. 'You see. Oaxaca has nature in its defence.'

She watched as another plane cleared the peaks and dive-bombed down on to the runway. Now she understood Jesus's insouciance at the violence of their approach. It was the only way to fly in, given the region's topography. Alice-Ann had been wise not to warn her, or she'd never have boarded the plane. Out of the rain and inside the terminal, Cranberry cursed the efficiency of her packing. With no bags to wait for, she regretfully had to take her leave of Jesus.

'We meet in the Zocalo, yes,' he stated with certainty.

'The what?' she replied.

'No matter. We will,' he said. 'The pleasure now is for me to wait.'

She laughed at the quaintness of the compliment.

'For me too,' she smiled and said goodbye.

Turning, she immediately spotted Alice-Ann looking every inch the femme fatale. Distinct with her shining blond hair and palest of pale skin, at least a head taller than the throng of brown-faced, black-haired Oaxacans behind the arrival barrier, who jostled her, desperately searching for that first glimpse of a much-missed relative. Cranberry produced her passport at the barrier and was ushered through into Mexico and the waiting arms of her friend.

'Fantastic you got here. Sorry I didn't warn you about the approach; I knew you wouldn't come.'

'Bastard,' Cranberry laughed, hugging her friend. 'You're looking beautiful.' Alice-Ann smiled her acceptance of the compliment; she was as soignée as ever in a spotless white shirt over a pink voile dress. Cranberry felt grubby by comparison.

'Is that all your luggage?' Alice-Ann asked, looking suitably impressed. Cranberry nodded.

'Well done,' she said, navigating a route through the airport. 'Come on, let's hurry, there's a high probability of revolution today.'

Cranberry realized that Alice-Ann wasn't joking, and was alarmed for a second, before remembering that hysteria and exaggeration were her friend's preferred conversational currency. 'Where's Carlos got to?' Alice-Ann said, urgently scanning the parked cars and producing two rolled-up straw hats out of a woven, pink and green plastic basket. Even that looks chic on her, Cranberry noted jealously. 'Here, put this on; the sun's merciless. All the ancient women you see around here are in their teens. Remember that and beware.' Cranberry did as she was told, aware that hats rarely suited her and instinctively knowing this one made her look like an albino *campesino*, while it gave Alice-Ann an Audrey Hepburn allure.

An electric-blue jeep careered towards them and out jumped Carlos, the obligatory hunk. Alice-Ann always managed to have one in tow, if needed. This one, shorter than usual, exuded virility and was the proud owner of the vehicle that would take them into Oaxaca and Alice-Ann's home.

Cranberry absorbed everything. The colours, smells and buzz of another culture were intoxicating. Travelling was good for the soul, she thought. It reminded you of how singularly unimportant you were in the general scheme of things.

The outskirts of Oaxaca had the air of a grim carnival. The faces of political candidates loomed out from hundreds of posters, plastering every last available, and non-available, space.

'Who's that, and that?' Cranberry asked.

Carlos, who clearly adored Alice-Ann, answered her mainly in Spanish, occasionally straining to add an odd English word or two; Alice-Ann translated, 'Cárdenas, Democrat,' she said pointing to one giant face, 'and that one's Francisco Labastida, of the Pre, the dinosaur party in power. Looks like a wanker, doesn't he? The money spent on those posters could feed a small country. Isn't that right, Carlos?'

Carlos spoke for a few minutes, and when he finished Alice-Ann said, 'He says yes.'

'Took a long time to say it,' Cranberry said sceptically.

'OK,' Alice-Ann was piqued by the doubt in her friend's voice, 'you asked for it. He said each one is made not of paper but incredibly thin plastico, and costs between five to ten pesos each. An average day's wage in this country is approximately sixty pesos. Satisfied?'

Interestingly enough with hindsight, they didn't see a poster for Vicente Fox, the third presidential candidate from the PAN party. 'Where's Fox, Carlos?' Alice-Ann asked.

Carlos answered.

'He was there,' Alice-Ann translated, 'displayed on an intersection billboard on the outskirts of town, but he says we were looking the other way.' Which meant that when they eventually arrived on the busy Avenida Juarez and the beautiful colonial building that housed Alice-Ann's apartment, there was a gap in Cranberry's political education. What did Señor Fox look like? As dodgy as the others, she imagined.

Alice-Ann lived bang opposite the governor's residence. No cars were allowed to stop, let alone park, under strict military enforcement, so with the jeep still practically moving, they had to, literally, throw themselves and Cranberry's bag on to the pavement. 'Justifiable precautions,' Carlos said, nodding at the armed guards. 'Revolution is most popular. See you this morning.'

'In the . . . In the morning . . . This . . . is today. Oh never mind.' Alice-Ann kissed him. 'He's taking us to Monte Alban tomorrow,' she said as Carlos drove off, leaving her scrabbling in her pink plastic bag for the latchkey. The congested street was making them gag. Lorries spewed disgusting emissions, and the buses belched a putrid black smoke.

'It's the tragedy of Oaxaca that you run through some of the most beautiful avenues on earth, because the pollution is so bad that if you walked you'd vomit. In a city where there's no industry!' Alice-Ann complained, throwing open the door.

Once inside the noise and fumes disappeared. The house was typical, built around a courtyard, with a fountain in the centre surrounded by pots of cheerful red geraniums. Cranberry unpacked, freshened up, and they hit the streets.

Alice-Ann took her on a tour of the city. You could walk everywhere in Oaxaca, she told Cranberry. Nearer the centre, a few of the wider avenues had been pedestrianized, which was a wonderful relief. Cranberry was surprised by the grandeur of the architecture; Alice-Ann, in turn, was proud of the beautiful colonial city she had chosen to call home. She raced Cranberry around the sights at breakneck speed due to the imminent revolution. Realizing this dread was dear to her friend's heart, Cranberry obligingly joined in her paranoia. At any rate it gave their sightseeing added zest.

The Church of Santa Domingo was impressive. 'But it's too baroque for me,' Cranberry said.

'Me too,' Alice-Ann agreed and took her on to the museum, a converted monastery crammed with pre-Hispanic treasures. 'They date from 500 A.D., can you imagine?' Alice-Ann said. 'Found in a tomb at Monte Alban, where Carlos is taking us tomorrow.'

Cranberry could hardly believe that the sculpted gold, silver and turquoise and their contemporary designs could be that old, but she had no similar problem with the human remains found alongside them. 'You must be exhausted. Let's go to the Zocalo and have a drink,' Alice-Ann suggested.

The Zocalo, Cranberry thought; maybe she'd see Jesus.

'I am. Wiped out,' she agreed. 'A man on my plane said he'd meet me there.'

'When? Who was he?' Alice-Ann asked, animated at the prospect of intrigue.

'Jesus. An artist.'

'What nationality?'

'Mexican, from Oaxaca.'

'A local artist named Jesus?' Alice-Ann sounded puzzled.

'That's right,' Cranberry confirmed.

'He can't be any good,' she said, stopping to give some change to an old Indian lady huddled up in a doorway. 'I've never heard of him, and I know all the artists worth knowing in Oaxaca.' On seeing Cranberry's expression she added, 'I think.'

The Zocalo was a beautiful tree-filled square, mercifully free of traffic and surrounded by arcades. A Moorish-looking building stood in the centre, into which you could descend and go to the lavatory or buy a single cigarette. They purchased two as a special reunion treat, since both were perpetually in the act of giving up nicotine, and went to sit at a table belonging to one of the various cafés that sheltered beneath the arcades. Little children crowded around trying to sell them gum, woven bracelets, lighters and other gee-gaws. Alice-Ann brought some candy, unwrapped it and put it in the little merchants' mouths; each piece produced a small, shy smile of thanks. A mariachi band played giant guitars at the next-door table. Alice-Ann paid them to come over and serenade Cranberry as they ate quesadillas and drank Corona beers with a shot of chilli sauce in the bottom of the glass and the juice of half a freshly squeezed lime.

'Refreshing, eh?' Alice-Ann asked.

'Life's blood,' Cranberry confirmed, thinking that the mariachi players reminded her of London's pearly kings and queens. Instead of flat caps they had on sombreros and their suits were tighter, more fitted, but just as flashy, sequined and embroidered.

Alice-Ann calmed down and as they caught up on the missing years, Cranberry became mesmerized by the leisurely pace of the town's people as they promenaded gently by. Toddlers to geriatrics stopped at tables, kissed friends or relatives, moved on to the next table, exchanged pleasantries with others. The enjoyment of each meeting fascinated her. Evidently just daily routine to them, it struck her as remarkable. America, just a hop skip and a jump away geographically, was light years away in the appreciation of what life had on offer for free.

Night had begun to fall by the time they moved on. Cranberry nursed a tiny regret, having kept a fruitless eye out for Jesus all evening, which she soon forgot as they turned down an unlit cobbled street, where Alice-Ann ducked under some low arches into the darkness of an apparently ruined building. Cranberry's big-city survival instincts kicked in and she was reluctant to follow, until yanked, by Alice-Ann, through to the other side. She found herself in a grassy courtyard lit by a flickering light coming out of a long stone building on the left. Once a stable or barn, it had been transformed into a cinema. Through its three open doorways they could see rows of people seated on plastic chairs.

'Francisco Toledo,' Alice-Ann whispered, 'a very famous Mexican artist from Oaxaca, donated the building to the city, to show free art movies to the people. I hope you get to see Toledo while you're here; he's ravishing.' She spotted some vacant chairs and they snuck in and sat down. Bertolucci's *1900* was playing on the taut white sheet stretched along the back wall. They were just in time to catch the endless pig disembowelment scene. Not up for it, they left as quietly as they could to walk back to Avenida Juarez and bed.

Taking the same route, Alice-Ann stopped by the homeless Indian to whom she'd given money earlier. Huddling up next to each other they yabbered in Spanish, leaving Cranberry to look on bemused. '*Adios querida*, *adios*,' Alice-Ann said and tucked a small bill into the woman's hand before standing up to join Cranberry. Both smiled and nodded to the lady then walked on. Alice-Ann turned back to wave one last time as they approached the corner. 'Poor Juanita, she shares a room with her daughter, who's a prostitute, I think.'

'Really?'

'Well, I'm not certain, but she can only go back after 3 a.m., then has to be out by eleven and I can't think of any other reason for that.'

Cranberry tried to think of one until they turned the corner and the streets suddenly turned into a seething mass of people. There were loud explosions in every direction.

Alice-Ann gripped Cranberry's arm. 'Move,' she hissed, 'the fucking revolution has started.'

'Walk with a purpose,' Cranberry's voice was like steel as she took the lead and forged ahead.

'What if they break into the house and ransack all my lovely frocks?' Alice-Ann joked, calling her own bluff as the image made her feel more hysterical by the second.

A cowboy-hatted *campesino* grabbed Alice-Ann. She screamed as he kissed her full on the lips. 'Viva El Presidente Fox,' he cried. Phew. Unimaginable relief.

No one was hostile. Everyone was singing and dancing and not, as they'd imagined, stampeding and screaming for blood.

The 'bombs' were firecrackers let off in celebration and hope now that the government had been democratically overthrown for the first time in seventy years. Music started to play from somewhere and the two friends, infected with the optimism of the moment, were propelled with the crowd back into the Zocalo, where a great cheer arose at the appearance of a man in a balaclava and combat uniform, armed with a machine gun, being carried on the shoulders of others.

'It's Raul, how fantastic,' Alice-Ann gulped as the formidable figure came nearer. The crowd let him through, revealing his entourage, who all wore an approximation of his uniform. 'They're his bodyguards – called the Silver Coyotes,' she said, referring to the similarly clad men who triumphantly bore the freedom fighter aloft. People chanted his name. Cranberry and Alice-Ann joined in, so when Raul passed they were in full cry and followed him dancing and drinking their way around the square. Placed, by the Coyotes, on to a platform that hadn't been there before, he began to speak to the crowd. 'People of Oaxaca, our form of armed struggle is just and true,' his voice carried over the distance without effort; 'If we had not raised our rifles for the Chiapas poor, the government would never have concerned itself with the Indians and *campesinos* of our land.'

'He's speaking in English,' Cranberry said.

Alice-Ann nodded and pointed to the numerous news cameras and film crews that had set up around the base of the stage. 'They're all in the country because of the election. Clever bugger, showing himself now.'

Raul's address ignited the crowd all over again, until he urged them to be quiet. 'My friends, tomorrow we meet to march. Rest well. We need to be strong. Change is a good thing, and we have it; Fox has almost 50 per cent of the votes. Good or bad man is of no matter. We are at a new dawn.' The eyes behind the ski mask found Cranberry's for a fleeting moment and crinkled into what she thought looked like a hidden smile.

'It's Jesus,' Cranberry gasped.

'What?' Alice-Ann replied.

'Raul is Jesus,' she said urgently, forgetting to use the Mexican pronunciation. At that moment she saw him turn to one of his 'Coyotes', point towards her and call out, 'Bring the *extranjeras*.'

The crowd fell back and before Cranberry grasped what was happening they were marched from the square by four of the Silver Coyotes and bundled into the back of the last of two waiting jeeps. Cranberry looked at Alice-Ann; was this kidnap? It was surreal but not unexpected. To Cranberry it belonged on the same plane as those highly sought-after backstage passes for the rock concerts she had loved in her youth, which would fall into her lap without effort – something to do with attracting the essence of the moment, as a magnet does metal filings. And let's face it, Cranberry thought, being abducted and squished up in the back of a jeep with a bunch of revolutionaries is undeniably the essence of today. She was excited, unlike Alice-Ann, who looked deathly scared as the driver swept them off to who knew where.

The jeep travelled on through the night, leaving the city and entering a village, where the driver drew up outside a large church. No one moved until Raul had safety left the leading vehicle and was out of sight. Only then did the Coyotes firmly escort the women inside. After locking the massive doors they dispersed like moon dust into the recesses of darkness, leaving Cranberry and Alice-Ann to stand alone, dimly lit with candles, in the aisle of an impressively embellished church. The Coyotes re-emerged from the pews on the right carrying small flash-lights on elastic bandanas which they pulled on over their balaclavas and turned on, like miners ready to descend the shaft of some coalface. The small, randomly aimed beams of light only added to the unreal quality of the situation. Cranberry could see that the interior of the church was intensely baroque, but with more of a local Indian influence than Santa Domingo. The walls were decorated with gold, its ubiquity relieved only by a silver altar rail. What is it with the Catholic Church, Cranberry wondered; its ostentatious display of wealth was often at such odds with the local poverty of the people. She didn't get it.

Raul stepped out from the shadows behind the altar; a warm pool of light from the candelabra either side bathed him in a heroic glow. 'Why have you brought us here?' Cranberry braved, squaring up to him. She heard the Coyotes gathering behind her, and Alice-Ann tugged at her hand. 'What right have you?' she continued unabashed. 'Are we hostages . . . to what? I'm English, you know, there will be a big stink if anything happens to me.'

His eyes twinkled behind the balaclava. 'Forgive me, I thought you know I mean to be harmless. We are here to hide me. Not you or your beauteous friend.'

Cranberry was stung; of course she'd known Jesus meant them no harm, but had only just realized that it was Alice-Ann, rather than herself, who had inspired their abduction. Like any other red-blooded man the world over he'd fallen for her friend. She was crushed.

'No, forgive me,' she replied. Then, 'It is you, isn't it?'

'Madame?'

'Jesus.'

'My name is Raul, I was born of my spiritual father Subcomandante Marcos, of the Zapatista National Liberation Army, over six years ago in the Lancandon jungle, just as he was years before.' Raul spoke softly, enunciating well. 'Since then I have lived, eaten, drunk and fought alongside the indigenous people of Chiapas.'

'Of course,' she said. 'Sorry. I'm glad to meet you.'

'In the Zocalo,' he reminded her, his eyes sparkling in the candlelight.

'What is this place?' Alice-Ann interjected. Having recovered somewhat, she had walked over to the left of the altar and was standing in front of one of the painted statues that nestled in alcoves along the walls. 'Cranberry, come and look at this.'

Cranberry crossed over the dais to Alice-Ann and found her staring at a most extraordinary plaster figure. She looked around and saw worse. The whole church was full of life-size depictions of saints, presumably, each more horribly disfigured than the last. One had his head split through by an axe. Garish red blood spilled from the dagger that pierced the heart of another. The figure nearest them cradled his own severed head in one arm. All were grotesque and although Cranberry took them in her stride, as just one more quirk in an already seriously quirky evening, she still turned to give Raul a querulous look.

His eyes radiated enjoyment at her unasked question. 'We are in the Chapel of the Martyrs,' he chuckled. 'A safe place. Not many come to visit here when night falls.' He exploded into a hearty laugh that echoed around the arches and made the women relax and smile at the logic of his explanation. 'The reason I bring you here, *señoritas*, is to ask you to come to the communities. See and listen to the people. Perhaps you will not find the absolute truth, but it is certain that you will discover where the lie is. We need outside eyes to tell the world.'

'What?' Cranberry asked, shocked at the sudden serious tone in his voice.

'I am not trying to kidnap you, madame, even though some of your acquaintances are most certainly going to say this,' he said, evenly eyeing Alice-Ann's suspicious countenance. 'I am only inviting you to join the work for peace. That is why I am telling you something very simple and urgent: Acteal must not happen again. And, in order for it not to be repeated, it is necessary to recognize the rights of the Indian peoples and to stop the war of extermination. Does that seem like a slogan? Believe me, madame, it is not. It is something more imperative: it is a duty.'

Raul was so persuasive that Cranberry stole a look at Alice-Ann. How was her friend reacting? Definitely not even beginning to waver.

'Where and when are you going?' Cranberry asked.

'Tomorrow as the dawn breaks, I, with my Silver Coyotes, will return into the mountains to gather our strength and numbers.' Small rays of light from the torches on the foreheads of his *compadres* shone on his face as he spoke. 'We then march on Mexico City. First passing through the Zocalo at around 5.30 a.m. Now I am too busy and sadly must send you back. My perpetual hope throughout the night is to see you at dawn. Wear good shoes for long walking.'

'Oh God,' Cranberry said, her stomach a knot of indecision. Then remembering where she was, added 'Sorry', and curtseyed to the crucified Christ above the altar. Painted blood dripped from his crown of thorns; she crossed herself for good measure. 'I'll try to come,' she promised Raul. Then turned to beseech Alice-Ann, 'How about it Al? You in?'

Alice-Ann remained implacable.

'If not,' Raul dropped his voice and came closer. 'Please, please,' he whispered directly in her ear, 'send in a parcel sealed with gum and paste, a German fuck doll. Address it to me: Sargento Insurgente Raul, Playa de Trigo Headquarters, mountains of the Mexican Southeast Chiapas, Mexico.' Raul took her hand and pressed it to his heart. 'Women for me are hard to find, you understand? Now I fear I shall think of you.' Moving away, he stopped whispering and spoke to them both. 'Finally, to increase your confusion, we have a motto here, "Against Reactionary Bad Taste, Revolutionary Elegance". How about that? Isn't our perversity obvious? Farewell, my friends. I hope to see you in the morning – unless you wish to come now.'

The invitation, vibrant in the air for a few moments, dissolved to nothing as Raul moved back into the shadows. Behind them a Silver Coyote opened the great ecclesiastical doors and stepped to one side. They were free. Alice-Ann reached out and took Cranberry's hand and they started to walk tentatively, one with regret, the other scepticism, down the aisle between the pews, away from the glittering gold and disfigured martyrs. Stepping out of the church into the crisp night air, Cranberry felt a spell had broken.

The Coyotes were gathered outside, around the same jeep that had brought them, only this time the *extranjeras* were allowed to choose their seats and were given only the driver for company. Cranberry sat in the front, safe from Alice-Ann's sharp eyes. Filled with a triumphant inner glow, she couldn't stop smiling. Weird as Raul's proposition had been, for once it was she and not Alice-Ann who'd been the lure, the reason for their inclusion in the inner revolutionary sanctum. The trip back was made in silence. Neither they, nor the Coyote, showed any desire to talk. Cranberry ran and reran Raul's bizarre request in her head, trying to imagine what else he could have meant to say. Nothing she came up with sounded like anything even remotely approaching 'German fuck doll', and anyway his eyes had confirmed what she already knew; she was being offered the adventure and romance of a lifetime. She felt an alter ego coming on. A bandit-queen. What a diary that would make, immersed in a revolution untainted by personal realities.

The driver stopped a fair distance away from Alice-Ann's home to minimize the risk of any encounter between the Silver Coyote and one of the governor's guards. As soon as they were safely inside, Cranberry and Alice-Ann collapsed, and discussed the proposal she'd received. Cranberry admitted to her friend that she yearned to go.

'Are you insane?' Alice-Ann cried. 'We're lucky to be out with our lives and you're thinking of going back.'

'Aren't you tempted?' Cranberry asked. 'He's Raul, for Christ's sake. Could that be more interesting? And I was even taken with him when he was plain old Jesus, remember.'

'How d'you know he's Raul, eh?' Alice-Ann snapped. 'How d'you know he not some serial-killing, raping wannabe in a balaclava?'

'Oh come on. You don't seriously believe that, do you?'

'No, I don't – but you never know. And even if he is Raul it's too dangerous. You don't know Mexico; they'd shoot as soon as look at him, and you'd be in the way.'

That night Cranberry didn't sleep a wink, thinking of John and the happiness they had at home, of Hollywood and the tortured progress of her beastly script. Then she thought of Raul and adventure and couldn't decide which path to take, for one surely obliterated the other. At around 4 a.m. she left her bed and went to the dirty laundry basket where she'd hidden her computer to log-on and retrieve her e-mail. Maybe there'd be a sign via cyberspace. And there it was. Subject: GREEN LIGHT. Opening it, her worst fears were confirmed. The e-mail was from her agent. It read: 'Congratulations Cranberry, we're on. Alexander Payne has agreed. He would like to work on rewrite with you. I've set up a meeting the afternoon of your return. Hope you're having a good one, Bx.'

There it was in black and white. The sign. Alexander Payne was her favourite director. Bugger, bugger, bugger. She returned to bed and stayed awake. As light filtered into the room she got up and went to sit on the balcony at the back of the building. It looked out over the roofs of Oaxaca towards the Zocalo; she saw only passion slipping irretrievably by.

Cranberry and Alice-Ann didn't, after all, go to Monte Alban, or anywhere else after that evening. They made little sorties to the Zocalo for a drink, or La Red, a local fish restaurant, to feed themselves. They still had a good time, but a spark had gone. Cranberry was going through a fantasy heartbreak, almost the worst kind, she felt; for after all, you have no right to it. Alice-Ann was sympathetic but resolute. In her opinion Cranberry had made the right choice.

Two days later Carlos and Alice-Ann drove Cranberry to the airport. She knew she was heading for the worst bout of culture shock, even worse than after her six-month stint in China. Also, she was deeply depressed by the certain knowledge that she had finally achieved her goal and grown up.

Back in Los Angeles, she went to Mr Stone's sex emporium on Hollywood. There, with a discount arranged by Alice-Ann, she purchased a top-of-the-range German fuck doll, which she mailed to:

Sargento Insurgente Raul,
Somewhere in the southeast mountains of Chiapas
Mexico

Months later she saw him in a programme on television for the BBC. A young woman with a good figure and Asian eyes in a black balaclava stood next to him throughout the interview. 'I suppose that means my gift's obsolete,' she thought ruefully, smiling as she climbed the stairs into the bedroom where John lay fast asleep.

Acknowledgements

My thanks go to Gerard Noel and Andreas Campomar of Timewell Press for looking after me so beautifully, to Jimmy Rip for forcing me to write the first story, to Maud Demi, Scylla Higham, Judy Geeson, Scott Zimmerman, Anjelica Huston, Polly Siegal, Robert Kovacic, Philip Prowse and Sabrina Guinness for their constant encouragement, to Nick Reading for reading them out aloud for me and giving me an excellent line, to my editor Marsha Rowe for her endless patience and help. Last, but by no means least, many thanks to Erica Silverman.